DEATH SILENCES EVERYONE

DEATH SILENCES EVERYONE

BILL SHEEHY

ROBERT HALE

First published in 2017 by
Robert Hale, an imprint of
The Crowood Press Ltd,
Ramsbury, Marlborough
Wiltshire SN8 2HR

www. crowood.com

British Library Cataloguing-in-Publication Data
A catalogue record for this book is available from the British
Library.

ISBN 978 0 7198 2439 5

Typeset by Chapter One Book Production, Knebworth

Printed and bound in India by Replika Press Pvt Ltd

Chapter 1

THEY GOT THE name the old fashioned way: torture.

Busting into Freddie's bedroom in the early hours was the first thing. Half awake, Fat Louise didn't have time to see who they were before Freddie was simply wrapped up in one of the blankets and hustled out of the house. There were two men, that's all she knew.

Louise hadn't always been called Fat and Freddie was careful not to use the word in her presence. But she was fat. As a young girl living over in the little mill town of Samoa, just outside Eureka, California, she'd been skinny with bony knees and elbows. Once out of high school, Louise had gone to work checking at the new Safeway supermarket down in Eureka. Ten years later, she came back home, looking like she'd swallowed a whole handful of watermelon seeds. Some said she got fired from Safeway for not bothering to pay for the candy bars she was always munching. Sitting around the house all day didn't help her waistline so she went looking for work. That was how she hooked up with Freddie. He liked his women hefty.

Freddie had left high school a couple years before Louise. He didn't bother to graduate, just left. Why sit in a hot classroom, he wondered, listening to some pinhead teacher who took home a little more than minimum wage when there was money to be made up in the forests. That's what Freddie was going to do; grow dope.

Fat Louise was happy to clean and cook for the man. Shoot fire, she thought, he could afford it, being self-employed as he was. It wasn't but a few days before she moved in. For a while, life was good and both were happy as bugs in a rug. Until those men took Freddie.

When Fat Louise thought about it, there wasn't anything she could do except go back to bed. Looking bleary eyed at the beaten up alarm clock, she saw there were still a lot of hours of dark left. Hours best used for sleeping.

Freddie didn't get any more sleep.

Still wrapped in the musty smelling blanket, he was thrown on the floor in the back of a car. Someone held him there by putting their feet on his back. The blanket had been on the bed for as long as Freddie could remember but before, he had never noticed how stale it smelled. Wherever he was being taken was far enough away; he had lots of time to get used to the smell.

Even when he was pulled out of the back of the car he couldn't see anything. Rough hands ripped the blanket off and then someone grabbed him from the back by his upper arms. The moldy blanket smell was replaced by fresh air. Air carrying the bite of pine trees with it. Before he could react, his wrists and ankles had been bound with some kind of sticky tape. Duct tape probably, he thought. Damn, everybody's got a use for duct tape.

'OK, Freddie. I'm only gonna ask it once. Where's the money?'

Freddie's eyes hadn't had time to adjust to the night's darkness but nothing was wrong with his hearing. He heard the voice and thought it was somehow familiar. He also noticed he hadn't really been asked a question. Fuck, this wasn't going to be good.

'No, man,' he said, trying not to stammer. 'I don't know nothing about no money. What money are you talking about?'

It wasn't a night with a moon. Everything was in shadows from the trees. What faint light there was coming from the stars wasn't enough to see by. He couldn't make out who he was talking to. There were two of them, just big blobs in the darkness. Before he could squint his eyes a little, trying to see who had him, one of them slapped him hard enough to make his ears ring.

'Nope,' the almost familiar voice said. 'Guess you need some work done on your ears. Now you just go right ahead and yell all you want. Ain't nobody close enough to hear.'

He knew what they wanted but he couldn't give it to them. Freddie held on to the thought, letting it shape like big black letters on the white board of his mind. It was all he had. Suddenly he was lifted up and dumped face down on the ground, his breath knocked out of him. For a brief time, he lost track of things. Instantly, things changed when someone sat on his back and grabbed a handful of hair, pulling his head back. Fingers grabbed his ear and … he shrieked as pain exploded, filling his head.

From someone standing over him, through the fog of pain, he heard the hard voice. 'Now, you've lost one ear lobe. Should help your hearing some, don't you think? You want to, go ahead and tell us. Where's the money?'

Moaning as the sharp pain slowly changed to a dull pounding throb, Freddie tried to shake his head. 'I don't know what the hell you're talking about,' he screamed.

'Aw, hell.' Again someone took a handful of hair and lifted his head.

'No …' was as far as Freddie got before his other ear lobe was snipped off. He could actually hear the gristle being cut before pain took its place.

'Damn it, Cully, be careful. He's squirting blood all over the place. Those are new shoes he just ruined.'

Cully dropped Freddie's head into the dirt.

'Come on, Freddie, tell us where you put the money. You gotta give us something to take back. Do we gotta go back and talk to the fat hunk of lard you been pokin'?'

Freddie couldn't catch his breath; all he could do was moan.

'Oh, shit.' The voice sounded disappointed. 'OK. Let's get serious. Hold him.'

This time Freddie felt a heaviness pulling at his ear a heartbeat before the tsunami of pain struck. They'd sliced his ear off.

'Gawd, who'd ever guess there was so much blood in his ear.'

'C'mon, Freddie. Don't make it so hard. Just tell us where you're hiding the money.'

Crying and slobbering, Freddie shook his head, spreading more blood around as he tried to catch his breath, tried to answer.

'Damn it,' the hard voice said, 'now he bled all over my pants. Sit him up.'

A hand grabbed his neck, half lifting him and dragging him across the ground before propping him up with his back against something. A log or something hard.

'I don't know anything about any money,' Freddie finally got the words out, whimpering. 'Oh, God. Believe me, I don't know…'

His head was rocked back with another slap.

'But someone does. You better tell us. Who knows about it?'

The words came out almost lost in a whine. 'Foley. I don't know. He might know.'

'Who the hell is he talking about? Hit him again,' the other man, Cully, said.

'No. Wait a minute. I know who he's talking about,' the familiar voice said. 'He's lying.'

Freddie wanted to duck his head and cry but the pain wouldn't let him move.

The bright flare of a lighter blinded him and before he could focus enough to see anything, a cigarette was lit and except for the glow, darkness returned.

The two men stood looking at what they'd done.

'Hey, you know what?' the smoker said. Freddie wanted to deny knowing anything but he could only moan.

'C'mon, look at it,' the one said. 'We've cut off his ear lobes. Hell, you even sliced off an ear. He's bleeding like a stuck hog. Now with all the pain he's feeling, he still says he don't know about the $40,000. Maybe he doesn't. But he gave us a name. That much pain and he's suddenly gonna stop lying to us? I don't think so. Not old numb nuts Freddie.'

'Ah, fuck. OK, so what do we do?'

The glow flared as the smoker inhaled. 'Well, not much we can do, I guess. Freddie, you still got one ear to use so you better listen. Forget this. Don't go causing any trouble, you hear?'

Cully laughed. 'You're funny.'

The smoker grunted. 'Yeah, I'm a real comic. C'mon, let's get the fuck outa here.'

Freddie tried to lift his head but the movement brought back the sharp pain on one side, cutting through the dull pounding on the other. Dimly he heard car doors slam and the engine start.

Then silence.

He was alone.

He was alive.

Chapter 2

IT WAS A few minutes after nine in the morning when Brad Foley pushed through the door into the offices of Discreet Inquiries, Inc. He was late but knew Gorman would make him wait anyway. A simple part of the way the man operated; always make them wait. Foley figured the old fart thought it added to his importance, making people sit outside until he was good and ready to meet with them.

Catching the eye of the grandmotherly type sitting behind the desk, he nodded and sat down in one of the worn overstuffed chairs. He didn't look at the pile of magazines on the low table. They were all at least six months old and the movie stars shown smiling on the covers had gone through marriages and divorces since the cover photos were shot. It was better to sit and study the young woman talking to Leonie Weems.

Someone had told him Ms Weems had been sitting at the same desk since the first day Francis Gorman opened up the business. That would make it more than twenty years. Christ, Foley mentally shook his head, a lot had certainly changed in his life in the last twenty years. Even ten back when he was happy as a pig in clover. Back then he'd been certain life was damn good and could only get better. Wow, had he been wrong.

With all those thoughts running through his mind, he hadn't taken his eyes off the young woman standing in front of the older woman's desk, reading some kind of document.

From where he sat, Foley had a clear view. Bending over as she was, he couldn't tell how tall she'd be but from the back, he guessed she had to be on the short side. He couldn't see her face either and couldn't tell much about her but what he saw he liked. Long, soft looking brown hair hung down hid her profile but her face wasn't the part of her he was studying.

Leaning over, her skirt, a smooth tan cotton, ended a few inches above her knees. The pair of nylon-clad legs looked smooth and firm. From where he sat he could see how her blouse, looking like a starched white man's dress shirt, hung down a little in front. From this he made a mental bet with himself; he bet she had perky little breasts.

There was no reason for him to think those kind of thoughts. it was just what he would order if he had his way. Foley liked perky breasts. Bigger, more rounded breasts, too. Even having been celibate for the past, oh God, how long, he still liked to look ... to dream. The fact was, he didn't want to think about the last time he'd been close to a woman's body. Anyway, checking out the young woman's body was, he thought, like looking at fine art ... he didn't want to have it, just appreciate it. In any case, it was a normal reaction for a man, wasn't it?

Busy as he was, he didn't notice Gorman's office door open.

'Hey, Brad,' Gorman called, a big welcoming grin on his face.

If there was one attribute stereotypical of the old fashioned man standing in the open door, it was the distinct lack of a sense of humor. Francis Gorman was blessed with not having a single funny bone in his body. The big smile worried Foley.

Gorman was one of those older men who took great pride in his appearance. Foley doubted the man owned a pair of Levis or sneakers. Always in a suit, always in style. Today his suit was quality, cut to measure and looking like something out of the 1960s. The three-button blazer was in dark brown with a deep navy pinstripe, his matching pleated pants ended with an inch cuff riding gently on the smooth toes of his highly shined dress shoes. The jacket's dark color made his white shirt almost sparkle, setting off the red striped rep tie and gold tie-tack. The man was a fashion statement.

'Come on in, will you, please?'

The bon vivant-type friendliness bothered Foley, too. Gorman was a shark. He had run one of the city's more profitable private investigation companies for a long time and his success wasn't built on being a nice guy. Hell, from what Foley had been told, Gorman was almost a San Francisco institution and he believed it. Just look at where the man's office was.

The office of Discreet Inquiries, Inc. took up most of the top floor of a two-storey brick building at 354 Fillmore Street. The ground floor was a popular eating establishment, the Westside East Restaurant and Bar. San

Francisco seemed to have more than its share of strangely named places. If you were to ask a local where the Westside East was, they'd tell you it's in Cow Hollow, smack dab in the middle of the financial district. Brad didn't know how this section of town got its name and didn't care.

Actually, it wasn't a case of Foley not caring much for Gorman, it was more like he didn't entirely trust the older man. There was no reason for it; the man had treated Foley fair, being quite free with the bonuses when something went DII's way. Maybe it was because the old man was almost never this nice. Obviously this time he wanted something.

'I'm glad you could come in this morning, Brad. There's a little job I'd like to pass your way. Please, sit down and let me explain. Would you like a cup of coffee?' he asked, taking the tall-backed leather chair behind his massive desk.

Coffee? Again, too nice. Foley couldn't remember the old man offering him coffee before. The "little job" must be something else. Foley shook his head.

'No, thanks. What exactly have you got for me? What little job?'

Usually when given a job, Leonie Weems would simply hand Brad a folder. Gorman rarely talked to his 'gofer'. He'd been hired on a part-time basis to do all the company's grunt work. Foley never thought the boss was ignoring him, there just hadn't been any reason for them to meet. He'd felt it was merely the nature of the situation and ignored it.

Unlike all the other employees of DII, with the exception of Ms Weems, Foley wasn't licensed. He'd been hired to take care of the jobs the rest of the investigators didn't want to spend time on. Things like process serving, repossessing vehicles, making deliveries for the office and even filling in as a bodyguard. And anything else not calling for a licensed investigator. Foley was the company's gofer. Well paid, mind you, but still just the go-to man.

'Look,' said Gorman after hesitating for a long moment, 'this is something I can't hand out to any of the others. To be clear, I have to tell you it's something I'd rather the company not get involved with. Unless it becomes strictly necessary, you understand. But...' He stopped and looked up.

In the months since going to work for DII, Brad Foley couldn't remember the old man acting this tentative. This worried him a little. He liked working for the company; it had a transient quality he found very suitable.

11

He wanted to keep this job, as impermanent as it was. Serving court documents to defendants or sometimes following someone as part of a divorce action paid pretty well. Anyway, when he finally decided to go get a real job, he wanted it to be on his terms. He didn't like the idea of getting fired, even if this type of employment had no kind of stability factored into it.

Once before, Foley had been fired from a job he liked. When he had been kicked out of the Humboldt County Sheriff's office, he'd simply drifted south toward San Francisco.

'To tell the truth, it's just a favor for a friend,' said Gorman in an angry sounding rush. 'I honestly don't think there's anything to be done but I feel obligated. It's not something I can hand off to just anyone and, well, damn it, I don't know what else I can do.'

Francis Gorman came from the old school. This was the first time Brad had ever heard him cuss. Fact is, this was the first time he'd ever seen the older man unsettled.

'OK, what is it?'

'What I'd like is for you to take a week or so off. Sign out as being on vacation.'

'Vacation?' Brad shook his head. 'Except for the couple days a week I'm in here, I'm always on vacation.' He hesitated and then got it. 'You really mean it, by not having your little job connected with the office.'

'Yes, that's it. But only if it's possible. This type of thing isn't something we'd handle anyway, normally. But the way I see it, you take the job on your own, work on it for a while. Come back in, say a week or ten days and everybody will be satisfied. When finished, make your report saying you've done all you feel can be done and there isn't any other avenue to explore. I can then share your report with my friend before shredding it.'

'A favor for a friend, you said. What kind of favor?'

Gorman handed Brad the slip of paper he'd been holding.

'Henry Steiner is the man's name. Go talk to him. He'll tell you all about it. He knows I can't officially send one of my operatives but I told him I'd be sending him someone with a police background. Keep track of your expenses and when you get back, I'll add a bonus.'

'You're not telling me what this is about, are you?'

Gorman's shoulders slumped and he went back to studying his hands.

'It's Henry's daughter. She's been murdered.'

Chapter 3

'MURDER?' SAID FOLEY. 'Murder is a police matter, not something for me to get involved with.'

'I know, I know,' said the older man, almost wringing his hands, 'but Henry and I go way back. I can't simply turn him away. It happened three weeks ago and until last Monday, she was a Jane Doe. The police have simply written it off as unsolvable, or whatever they call it. He's just asking if we can dig a little deeper.'

Foley sat quietly for a long minute. 'And you want me to do what, exactly? Is this the Henry Steiner who rumor has it owns half of San Francisco? The old pioneering family Steiner?'

Gorman's shoulders remained slumped. He nodded without looking up.

'Yes, he's the one.'

'And the police aren't busting a gut to find out who killed this man's daughter? Something doesn't sound right to me.'

'Henry can explain it all to you better than I can. I understand your hesitation, and it's not what you agreed to when taking the job here. But I'm asking you; please, talk to the man and spend some time on it.'

Gorman wasn't saying it but Foley felt he could read between the lines. Take a look, make Daddy feel something was being done. Write a report and DII could wash its hands of it. Everybody is happy.

'Well, I don't know,' murmured Foley slowly, 'this is likely to end up getting some attention from the police department. They won't like someone, especially a civilian, digging around one of their open unsolved.'

'The thought crossed my mind,' said Gorman, looking up with hope showing in his tired gray eyes, 'to make it more satisfactory, and for a number of other reasons, I've decided to send along one of our new operatives to assist you.'

Picking up the phone, he touched a button. 'Leonie, will you send Gretchen in, please?'

The old woman must have been ready because Gorman hadn't even replaced the phone when his office door opened. Foley felt his mouth drop when the young woman in the short skirt came in, turning to close the door behind her.

'Now wait a minute …' he started to say, but was cut off by Gorman.

'Brad Foley, this is the newest member of our staff, Gretchen Bongiorno. Gretchen will work with you on this, uh, business.'

Gretchen Bongiorno was too young, was Foley's first reaction. Not wanting to stare, he quickly looked away, turning to look squint-eyed at the man behind the desk.

It was the same woman he'd studied out in the outer office but now he could see her face. She couldn't be even eighteen. Too damn young to be crossing the street by herself. He had to admit, though, he was glad he'd worn his best and newest pair of Dockers, a Madras shirt with a light blue woven tie and loafers, the pair he'd spent time putting a shine on. Damn, he said to himself, you'd think I was back in high school, hoping to impress the cheerleaders.

Shaking his head, Foley spoke low and clear. 'She's a child.'

'I am not a child,' said the girl, still standing by the door. Foley thought she even sounded like a petulant child. 'I have a university degree in criminal law, have more than 2,000 hours as an internal investigator for the State Insurance Fraud Division and hold a license issued by the State of California as a Private Investigator. On the other hand, you, Mr Foley, have a degree in police science, earned nearly twenty years ago, more than fifteen years with the Humboldt County Sheriff's Department and don't have a state PI license.'

Foley sat speechless, stunned by the sudden attack. When he finally found his voice, he didn't know what to say.

'Uh, look, I didn't mean, I mean, uh, don't take it so personally. I mean, well, hell's fire, you're too young, is what I mean.'

'Brad,' said Gorman, holding up a hand to stop the girl from whatever she was going to say, 'Ms Bongiorno is old enough and as she pointed out, she has a California license. Now if you're to carry this little piece of work off then you'll have to talk with people and as was pointed out, sooner or later the police will hear of it. Having a licensed investigator at your side might make them a little more understanding.'

He still didn't like it. 'Yeah, maybe so, but for Christ's sake, this isn't the way to break in a new investigator. Not something like a murder. Even if you don't really expect much, it isn't the same as serving a subpoena or taking photos to get proof of adultery of some woman screwing the chauffeur.'

'Brad,' said Gorman softly but with enough seriousness in his voice to let Foley know he'd lost the argument, 'Ms Bongiorno will work with you on this and nothing more needs to be said.' The older man smiled before going on and Foley knew he was being soft-soaped. 'Look, she's new to the business but she has to begin somewhere and where better than with someone like you? I mean, you've got the street smarts she'll need to succeed. Take her under your wing, so to speak, and mentor her.'

Mentor her? Foley gave up. More like mother her. For a week, or maybe ten days? Yeah, well, what could go wrong?

Chapter 4

'I'M NOT AS young as I look, you know.'

Going down the stairs when they reached the street, Foley had not opened the street door for his new partner but had barreled right through and continued on. He stopped at the edge of the sidewalk, trying to decide which way to turn; where to go. This was something he was going to have to think about.

'Look,' said the girl standing next to him, 'this wasn't my idea. I don't like being saddled with an oldie any better than you're enjoying having me here. Let's make the best of what it is, though. C'mon, I'll buy you a cup of coffee and we can get to know one another.'

'I don't want to get to know you,' snarled Foley, speaking without thinking.

'OK, let's just stand here and watch some of San Francisco's finest people go by. I don't mind.'

He didn't know what to say so he kept quiet. Finally realizing how foolish he was being, he nodded.

'All right, then. There's a Starbucks down at the corner.'

She fell in beside him, matching him stride for stride.

Waiting for the coffee to be served, Foley studied the girl sitting opposite. He had to admit, up close she did look a little older than he had first thought. Along with all the other little signs of his advancing years, judging the age of young people was getting harder and harder for him. Gawd, he thought, if I had to work behind the bar I'd be afraid to serve anyone not gray haired and wrinkled. He couldn't decide how old she was.

'Does it matter?' she asked as if reading his mind.

'You said you've got a degree in law. How come you're working for a PI firm and not becoming a lawyer?'

'Oh but I am. You see, working here is part of the plan. I'll work as an investigator for two years and then go back to school. With my background with Discreet Inquiries and my bachelor's degree, I'll be able to get the school I want. Plus in those two years, I'll be banking tuition money.'

Foley hated to admit it but her plan sounded better than any he had for himself.

'My turn,' she said and then waited for the waitress to put their coffees on the table. 'Why did you leave the sheriff's department?'

'How'd you know about my background?'

'Ms. Weems told me. I asked about you after Mr. Gorman told me I'd be working with you. She told me all about you.'

'I'll bet she did. But not about my leaving the department?' He thought about it and then shook his head. 'It isn't important.'

'No, but if I'm going to be your partner on this, then I have to know your weak spots.'

'We'll do this little job and then you can go on to doing your PI stuff and I'll go back to doing whatever it is I do. There's no need for you to know anything more about me.'

'OK, OK, don't get huffy.'

Foley couldn't help himself, he liked the way she backed down without seeming to back down. Watching her sip her latte, he almost smiled; he liked the way she licked the foam from her upper lip, too.

Damn it, he scolded himself, stop looking at her. She's young enough to be your daughter.

'OK then, why are you only working part time for Mr. Gorman? You're not old enough to retire, are you?'

'Won't give up, huh? Yeah, I'm almost retired. Working for DII part time gives me something to do and he does pay me quite well. I've got a little money coming in so I'm not hurting financially. Anyway, I enjoy the work, dealing with the kind of people I do and getting around like I do.' He stopped a moment after putting his cup down. 'Except something like this so-called little job he gave me.' Glancing up, he frowned. 'Gave us.'

'What is it, exactly? All I know is that someone was killed and the police have put the case on a back burner. Mr. Gorman said you'd fill me in. So, fill me in.'

'Has to do with a murdered girl. But to tell you the truth, I don't know much more than you do. Gorman said little, wanting the dead girl's father to explain. I figure we'd talk with the man then see if we could get whatever we could from the police.'

'Think they'll share much with us?'

'Not likely. But let's see what the girl's father can tell us. We might get enough there not to need bothering any officer of the law.'

Looking at her, he pursed his lips before going on. 'Understand, we're not expected to find out much.' He stopped at her frown. 'It's like this. Gorman's friend asked for someone to look into his daughter's death. Gorman couldn't say no but he knows there's not much we can do. We're to spend a few days, talk to a few people, write up a very detailed report and in a week or so, turn it in.'

'This doesn't sound like something a friend would do, just make it look like the murder was being taken seriously.'

'We are, in effect, private citizens. Yeah,' he held up a hand to stop her from cutting in, 'even with your license. When it comes to police business, and murder, if nothing else is police business, we're only citizens. When private citizens try to do the work of the police, it's called vigilantism. Now, such activities were acceptable in San Francisco way back in the mid 1800s or so but not now. So we do as much as we can, as citizens, and go home. It's police stuff. The kind of work they get the big bucks for. You have a problem with that?'

'Nooo,' she drew the word out, obviously thinking about it. 'I guess not. But at least let's give it the best we can. After all, we're representing Discreet Inquiries, Incorporated.'

No way, he said to himself, is this going to work out. Especially when the cops find out we're getting involved with something beyond our level. But a week or so in the company of an attractive young girl, uh, woman, and getting paid for it? How good is that?

Chapter 5

GETTING AN APPOINTMENT with Henry Steiner was easier than Foley thought it'd be. Gorman had called ahead.

Foley wasn't surprised; Steiner, of course, lived on Steiner Street.

'Those are beautiful, aren't they?' Gretchen said, her awestruck tone sounding like any hayseed tourist.

They had taken a taxi up into Steiner's neighborhood and while Foley paid the fare, his new partner stood, taking in the row of restored Victorian houses.

'They are known as the Six Sisters, you know,' Gretchen said, 'and are famous. The houses and the park across the street there have been used in a lot of movies.'

'Uh huh. That's what the City really is; an over-crowded movie set. C'mon, let's go talk with the bereaved man.'

'You know, I would have bet money on it. It's obvious you're not the kind of man who could see beauty when it's right in front of him. And I'd have won.'

'Don't bet your money foolishly, remember, you're saving for college.'

'Which one is it? Oh, I can hardly wait to see what the interior looks like.'

'It's the end one, number 720. And don't forget, he's just lost his daughter and we're here to work.'

Henry Steiner wasn't a man to be pushed into anything. Foley thought he looked a little younger than his boss but after listening to the man a bit, he decided it was that Gorman had lived a harder life than his friend. Right from the get-go Steiner took control of the conversation. It was doubtful anybody had ever got away with being ahead of the man. After all, as he quickly pointed out, he was one of the few fourth generation

19

San Francisco natives one would ever meet.

'This house,' he explained, 'was built in the 1890s by a popular developer of the day, Matthew Kavanaugh. My great-great-great grandfather, for whom the street was named, bought it before it was even finished. Kavanaugh lived for a time in the first house beyond these six houses.'

After introducing themselves, Foley had wanted to get the interview rolling but hesitated just a little, wanting to gauge the man's feelings about losing his daughter. His hesitation was enough. Steiner waved the two toward a rich brocade covered couch and smiled.

'I do hope you didn't have any trouble finding my home. Some people do, you know, even though it is among the most famous homes in the City. The park out there,' he lifted his chin to point, 'is very popular and these homes have appeared in countless postcards, movies and TV shows. I'd like to have a dollar for every snapshot taken of these houses by tourists over the years.'

He chuckled softly but with signs of great pride while, Foley thought, trying to sound dismissive of it all. Obviously he didn't feel depressed over his daughter's death. Clearing his throat, he decided this was a good time to bring up the reason for their visit.

He didn't have a chance.

'The first Steiner was a great friend of another pioneer, Charles Gough. Old Charles delivered milk by horseback through the streets. Grandfather Leopold Steiner delivered water. Charles Gough had the job of laying out many of the city's streets and naming them. He used his own name for one and Octavia Street named for his sister. Oh, yes, the Gough and Steiner families go back a long way in San Francisco history. Yes, indeed.'

Foley didn't hesitate. 'Mr. Steiner, we're here to discuss the death of your daughter.'

'Ah, yes. I know. However, I wanted to explain why I'm not the grief stricken man one would expect. The same error in judgment is more than likely why the city's police department is doing as little as they are about finding her murderer.

'You see, my daughter was an only child. My pride and joy. Her mother passed when Anne Marie was just reaching puberty. Things would have been different if Mona had lived but one cannot cheat death. Neither Anne Marie nor I ever got over her death. It affected our daughter more, though. At one stage I took Anne Marie to a child psychiatrist. She went once but wouldn't go back for a follow up visit. The psychiatrist, who came highly recommended, explained how the death couldn't have come at a worse time for our daughter. She never fully recovered from the loss.'

Foley didn't want to interrupt and glanced quickly at Gretchen when he heard her take a breath; he frowned and shook his head quickly, stopping her from speaking. They didn't have long to wait for Steiner to break the silence.

'Well, to shorten things a little, it was in school she first started getting involved with drugs. A very good private school. The most highly rated school in the City. But by the time I discovered it, it was too late. I suggested counseling, but Anne Marie only laughed. From that time on we grew farther and farther apart. I even planned a European trip, hoping if I could get her away from the influences she was under, she could be saved. She wouldn't go. As a last resort I contacted an expert on the problem. My, uh, our family doctor recommended the man. He talked of using something called Tough Love. Have either of you heard of this?'

Foley had but shook his head. Gretchen, taking Foley's lead, did the same.

Tough Love. Foley didn't frown but mentally agreed with the idea. True, he'd had no experience with kids but from what he'd seen over the years as a cop, too often teenagers were self-destructing. Especially it seemed, teenage girls. Raising a daughter would be difficult enough; what with the drugs, sex and rock and roll which appeared to be the basis for people of that age, it could be tough. Steiner apparently had faced a losing proposition. It looked as if Gorman was right, thinking there wouldn't be much that could be done with this. There didn't appear to be much he and Gretchen could do except write a report and make it look good.

Looking down at his fingers, he stopped talking. But the man wasn't finished with his explanation.

'Well, I followed the man's instructions; took away Anne Marie's car, stopped her allowance and canceled her credit cards. She fought back. The result was what turned out to be our last battle.'

For another long moment Steiner sat, staring at his hands folded in his lap.

'In one way I believe the argument was memorable. It was the first time in months she had bothered to speak to me. And it was the last time.

She packed up a suitcase and left the house that night. This house I'm so proud of.'

Gretchen frowned. 'What gives you the idea this dead woman is your long lost daughter? I understood the police have her down as a Jane Doe.'

'Yes. But you see, Anne Marie had been fingerprinted once and when the report came back, Chief Sands got it first and called me. He wanted to know how I wanted to handle it.'

'Why would she have been fingerprinted?' Foley asked.

'Oh, it was when she was still in school. Anne Marie and a few of her friends had been caught shoplifting in the Nordstrom's downtown. She had given our family attorney's office a call and they contacted me. It was at the beginning of the Tough Love program and I thought it'd be a good idea if she was shown how criminals were treated. Chief Sands was in agreement and she was photographed, fingerprinted and given a tour of the jail. The one located there in the Hall of Justice building. I thought it might scare her into changing her outlook. It didn't.'

Steiner hadn't looked up as he explained but went on, his words coming almost as a whisper.

'A few weeks later she disappeared.'

'And you went searching for her?'

'Oh, yes. First the police did what they could but lost track of her. I then hired Francis to find her but she wasn't to be found. The last sighting we had was of her taking a bus south, getting off at the East 7th Street station in Los Angeles. She apparently bought a ticket for Long Beach but didn't take the bus beyond the 7th Street station. There was no sign of her from that point on. Until three weeks ago. When her fingerprints identified her was when Chief Sands called me. He brought a photo of her and ... I formally identified her.'

'I don't understand,' said Gretchen, finally overlooking Foley's frown. 'You and your family are, well, important people in this city. If the police knew she was your daughter, why didn't they go beyond listing her as a Jane Doe?'

'That was my error coming back to sit on my shoulder. You see, when she left, I first asked the Chief of Police for help. Chief Sands was able to trace her to the bus depot. When he came here to tell me where they lost contact with her, I reminded him of the Tough Love program. At the time, I thought it best to not go further on an official level. All I asked Francis to do was to find out where she went from there, not to try to bring her back or even contact her. Let her discover how big the world can be without a safety net such as she'd grown up with. Past a certain point, Francis wasn't able to discover where she'd gone or what she was doing. Then when the police finally identified her body, Chief Sands came and told me she'd been stabbed. Nobody had seen anything. Nothing was found at the scene and there was nothing for the police to do except treat it as a drug or prostitution deal gone wrong.'

The last sentence came out slow and painful.

'Drugs and prostitution?' Foley asked quietly. 'You think your daughter was involved with drugs and prostitution?'

'No, not really. Least, I hope she wasn't. According to the police report, she was drug free and had apparently been for some time. If this was my Anne Marie, well, at least it's good to know she had somehow gotten off drugs.'

'But the police still didn't take the case any farther.'

'I ... I asked them not to. Don't you see,' he asked beseechingly, 'as far as I was concerned, she had died long before. When she ran off to wherever she went, to whatever she went to, she had turned her back on her heritage, on what the Steiner name had come to stand for.'

Once again he dropped his gaze to his hands.

'At first I couldn't let the Steiner name become headline news. I asked the police to let it go, treat it as any other such unsolved murder.' Lifting his head, he glared at Foley. 'Do you know how many girls die in this city each year? Mostly prostitutes or with some involvement in the drug trade. And most of them are never solved. The police are unable to bring anyone to trial in the majority of cases. Why couldn't this be another?'

'But you called Mr. Gorman?' Gretchen asked, not understanding.

'Yes. A few days later. It sat there, riding me, not letting me sleep. My daughter, our daughter, killed. Murdered. I couldn't go back to the police and say I'd changed my mind. You have to understand. When one has a name like Crockett or Stanford or, yes, even Steiner, one carries the pride and tradition of San Francisco. With such a legacy comes responsibility.'

Foley wasn't having any of it.

'But?' he asked harshly.

'I did the only thing I could think of; I called Francis to ask what I should do. He suggested he look into it.'

Gretchen and Foley looked at each other. Foley was frowning.

'I don't suppose you have a recent photo of your daughter, do you?'

The older man shook his head.

'No. She was a thin girl, like a model, when she left home. She had always been slightly built. Her mother was too, you know. Mona had beautiful long hair, thick and luxurious right up until she died. The chemotherapy destroyed her hair and did little to stop the cancer. It killed her. Our daughter looked a lot like her. Other than the photo Chief Sands showed me – well, it wasn't a good photo. She had changed so much. There is much I don't know about after she left. That is what I'd like to know now.'

Gretchen frowned. 'When we start asking questions, your friend, the Chief of Police, isn't going to like it. Right now the murder has likely been filed away as being unsolved. The police have far too much to do to keep such crimes on the front burner. The information they have, however, is the only starting place we have. How do you see us getting around that?'

'I talked to Chief Sands right after Francis said he'd see what he could do. The Chief will give you everything they have. He doesn't like it, but … oh, I've really messed things up, haven't I?'

'Yes,' said Foley, getting to his feet, 'I'd have to agree, you have. But you do have a lovely home to live in, on a very lovely street with a very memorable name.'

Finding out what really happened would be difficult. Even with help from the police, Foley couldn't see where they could go. Too late the father had decided he wanted to know more. Well, Foley thought, tough stuff. What were the chances of them finding anything? Glancing at his new partner, he grimaced; she had a determined look in her eye. Oh god, what had he gotten himself in for?

Chapter 6

GRETCHEN USED HER cell to call for a cab. While they waited, they walked over to look at the park. Standing on the lush grass, Foley watched a man throwing an orange colored Frisbee to a dog. The big animal, a German Shepherd, jumped, ran and cavorted but didn't miss making the catch.

'I think you were unnecessarily hard on Mr. Steiner,' said Gretchen. 'He's an old man and he just lost his only daughter and is feeling bad about it. You could at least have cut him some slack.'

'Yeah, he lost his little girl but he still has his one-of-a-kind house on a special street right here in what a lot of people think is a special city. Now from what I heard your poor old man say, he's more interested in keeping his good name out of the gutter so the tourists will go on taking pictures of his house than he is about who stabbed his daughter or why.'

'Is this,' she asked coldly, 'what I have to look forward to if I stay working as an investigator? Growing hard and cynical and unforgiving in my old age?'

Foley was saved from having to answer by the arrival of the taxi.

Most travel around town he did by either one of the cable cars, a Muni bus or walking. San Francisco is known far and wide as being a so-called 'walkable city'. When out of the City, he drove his old Chevy Monte Carlo. When in town, he parked it in a garage, a perk paid for by DII. Taking cabs wasn't high on the man's list of fun things to do.

'Hall of Justice on Bryant Street,' he said to the cabbie.

Foley thought the fares cab companies charged, which were set by a taxi commission, were excessive. But the fare wasn't the thing upsetting him and turning him off using cabs. It was a little item on the fare list most people missed until they found themselves sitting in a cab, hemmed in by traffic and then charged almost half a dollar for each minute they were sitting there not going anywhere. He saw the practice as being highway robbery. To add insult to it all, the taxi companies expected you to tip the cabbie another twenty per cent. Outrageous.

Gretchen was quiet for a while, watching out of the side window. Foley didn't think it would last and it didn't.

'A while ago,' said the young woman quietly, 'you were talking about simply asking a few questions, writing up a report and going on to other things. Are you still working on that plan?'

'Why not? What's changed? Look, if the police call it an unsolved, who are we to argue?'

'Don't you think he deserves better? Yes, he may be a bit batty about who he is and where he lives, but he has lost his only daughter. Doesn't such a loss count for something?'

He didn't answer, but sat frowning out of the other side window. Women, he groused to himself, knowing he'd be in big trouble if he didn't stay silent.

Chief Sands wasn't available but one of his assistants, a man named Carl Lynch, was.

'Ms. Bongiorno, Mr. Foley, Chief Sands told me what you would be after,' said Lynch after closely inspecting their identification. Gretchen had her PI license ready but all Brad had was his driver's license. Lynch didn't seem to think anything about it, studied both before handing them back. 'I'm not entirely clear of what this is about but one doesn't argue with the Chief. Do either of you know him?'

'No,' answered Gretchen, turning on her smile which Foley thought made her look even younger than she was. When Lynch had returned their ID, Foley had glanced at her license and caught her age. Hard to believe she was twenty-five.

'Well,' when nothing else was offered, 'as I said, Chief Sands directed me to copy the entire folder on the death of one Jane Doe, DOB: unknown, cause of death, several stab wounds to the chest. Is there anything else we can do for you?'

'Yes.' It was Foley's turn. 'Could you put us in touch with the first officers to find the body?'

'Of course.' Quickly looking at a sheet in the folder, he smiled. 'It was Pan and Mazzucco, two uniforms on the night shift that week. They

26

called it in at, let me see, shortly after ten on the evening of May twelfth, a Tuesday. Those two are now on days and you'll likely find them out on the street. Can I call and have them meet you someplace?'

Gretchen nodded, smiling sweetly at the man. 'We would appreciate it. How about the coffee shop I noticed just down the street?'

'Ah, the Caffe Roma. Every cop in the place is familiar with it. OK, I'll give them a call. Say half an hour? They'll be getting off shift about then.'

Foley had found it best to have a list of questions ready to ask when interviewing someone, especially when the someone was a cop. What questions could they come up with in thirty minutes? Where had the body been found? The file would have the 'where', 'when' and 'how' facts. Did she have alcohol in her system? Again, the file.

About the best he could come up with was to discover how the body had been dressed. And what, Brad Foley asked himself, would knowing the color of her dress tell them? Not much. The fact is, he thought, the file would give them enough information for a report. What else was there to do about it? Nothing.

His new partner came up with other ideas, though. Well, of course she did.

The two cops found Gretchen and Foley without any trouble. Brad thought they were probably the only two in the place not part of the police force. The two officers had come directly from their patrol car and were still in uniform.

Daniel Pan was the youngest of the pair and Foley thought at least one of his parents was Chinese; the officer's face was smooth, wrinkle-free. Pan ignored Foley, greeting Gretchen with a big smile, holding her hand a little too long Brad thought.

The other officer was in many ways the opposite; his big blocky body made bigger by the armored vest worn under his uniform shirt. And needing a shave. From a distance, his bullet-shaped head looked to be hairless. Up close, Foley saw the fine close-cut white bristles of hair growing in a fringe just above his ears.

'The Chief's office told us to stop and talk to you,' the bigger man said, his voice coming from somewhere deep in his chest. 'I'm Vincent Mazzucco and my partner, Daniel Pan.'

Foley nodded. 'The hand Officer Pan is holding belongs to Gretchen

Bongiorno and I'm Brad Foley. Pull up a couple chairs, why don't you.'

Foley watched as Mazzucco tore the tops off three sugar packets and emptied the sweetener into his cup. Sipping his own, he thought the coffee was better than over at Starbucks.

'OK, what can we do for you?' asked Pan, not touching the coffee the waitress had placed in front of him. 'We were told to give you everything we had on the latest Jane Doe.'

Gretchen frowned. 'Latest Jane Doe? You say that as if it's a weekly occurrence.'

'Naw, not weekly,' said Mazzucco, 'but often enough to make us crazy. Drug deaths, mostly. The drug scene isn't as in your face as it was a couple years ago but there's a lot of it out there. Lots of drugs mean lots of money. Big money seems to breed violence. They come here from all over, no families and their only friends are other druggies. And those aren't what you, or I'd call, real friends. Nobody knows who they are or where they come from. They die and we call them John or Jane Doe. Kinda tradition, I suppose.'

'The one we want to know about,' said Gretchen, 'was stabbed, her body found three weeks ago or so. Young, say in her mid to late twenties, said to have had long hair, a brunette. We're told you two found her body.'

'Yeah, I know which one you're talking about. We got a phone call about a woman lying in an alley down in the Tenderloin, just off Market Street. A tough neighborhood. Turned out to be a young woman about the age you're saying, hard to say exactly. She was well dressed, the labels were from one of the better shops and someone said her handbag cost $150 at least. It was empty, by the way, no money or credit cards. Nothing except a couple bits of paper and a switchblade with a six-inch blade. Illegal under California law, but available on almost any street corner. It wasn't the knife used on her, though. She'd been stabbed by a longer blade, longer and wider. Stabbed at least half a dozen times. Under all the blood and dirt from the alley was a quite attractive woman.'

Pan had not been saying anything but now piped up.

'I'm curious,' he asked, looking directly at Gretchen, 'What's your interest in this? How come we get orders from Justice to come around and talk to you about one of our unsolveds?'

Gretchen flashed a smile. 'We've been asked by the girl's father to find out what we can. As a favor, you understand, not as a private investigation.

Apparently she'd left home a couple years ago. Had gotten into drugs, quit school and disappeared. Your Chief identified her and made the notification. Seems the Chief and the father are old friends. He knows his daughter was murdered but doesn't know anything else. That suited him for a while but now he'd like to know more. Anyway, we're hoping to find something to tell him. Something to make it a little easier for him. You understand? We're definitely not trying to get in your way.'

'Ha, go for it,' Mazzucco barked, 'I like it when someone comes along to take the load off our shoulders. Look, no matter what the reason, the facts are there for all to read. If you know what to look for and believe me, we've had enough experience, we know.'

Pan chuckled. Foley had noticed how the slender officer continued his study of Gretchen. Maybe he had seen her short skirt and legs after all.

'OK,' said Foley, 'what facts are you talking about?'

He knew what the officer was saying. It was the same thing when he'd worn a deputy sheriff's badge. In almost every situation there would be little bits of information, little things not really important. Stuff that would take longer to explain why it was in the report that it would take to write it in. So, whatever it was would be left out.

'Think about it,' said Pan, speaking to Gretchen, 'she's a stunner, long legs and short skirt. Her hair was styled and except for being smeared, her makeup was professional quality. No drugs in her system, but the scars were there in places you'd never normally get to see. At one time she'd been a druggie. I'd say she had gone through a rehab program at some point. OK, so she's down there in one of the highest crime areas of the City, violent crimes and lots of robberies. I ask myself why was she down there, looking like she did. And until you guys come calling, nobody's yelled their wife or daughter is missing. In my book the only answer reads high priced hooker.'

'Was your conclusion part of your report?'

'Naw. I did mention it to Lynch, though. Man, face it. Prostitution and drug dealing, two of the most usual occupations in the alleys south of Market Street. I think it's a no-brainer.'

Foley nodded. 'Dead by stabbing and nothing at the scene to point the way?'

'Uh huh.' Mazzucco smiled coldly. 'Dead in an alley, bled out over a couple hours before we got there. No credit cards or cash in her purse.

No identifying marks or tats. Definitely the kind of crime the gang in the investigative bureau are interested in. With the case load those Johnnies carry, it'd sit in someone's basket for a while then get filed. Unless you hotshots come up with something.'

The burly officer finished his coffee and stood up, dropping a business card on the table.

'And there you go. You think of anything else, give me a call. Never know what you'll find, if you've got the time to go digging.'

'Where would you suggest we dig next?' asked Gretchen. She had listened to the bigger man, keeping her eyes focused on his square stubble darkened jaw. Apparently she hadn't noticed the attention Pan had been giving her. Or simply had ignored it.

Mazzucco locked eyes with her, thinking about something. Foley wanted to laugh. The big cop knew, or thought he knew, something. Something he hadn't shared with anyone else.

'OK. Here it is,' he said, leaning with both hands on the back of the chair he'd been sitting in. 'I've been working the Tenderloin down below Market Street for more years than I care to remember. Too big, too dumb and too crude to get invited anywhere else. So five, six years ago, before Danny here and I partnered up, I get the word on the street there's a new guy in town. A tall, white drink of water pimping a string of young girls and calling himself King Cock. A bunch of bullshit, I thought, until one of the street girls turned up all beaten and bruised. She wouldn't tell me who did the trick on her but street talk was she'd been paying off this King Cock guy. I busted him a week or so later. With him at the time were a couple young cuties. I was taken by one of them, a young beauty queen in the making. Oh, how I remember her. Not only because she kept me awake nights for the next three weeks but because she said her name was Steiner. You know, like the street up in the ritzy part of town? Anyway, when I saw the dead girl down in that alley I thought at first I knew who it was. A lot older but, well, these girls age fast. Anyway, if I was you guys, I'd go looking for King Cock.'

Chapter 7

O N THE STREET again, Foley suggested they call it quits for the day.
'You have to remember,' he smiled at his new partner, 'I'm a lot older than you and I get tired quicker. Plus, while you're a real card carrying PI, I'm just a part-time gofer. So here's what I propose. You go back to the office and write up our day's labor. Set up a log for the expenses so we get some of it back. I'll go home, putter around in my wheelchair, get all rested up for tomorrow.'

'And what then, go looking for this King Cock? Yuck! How would someone get a nickname like King Cock?'

Foley smiled inwardly, not wanting to share the first thing he thought of. Once again, the young woman was ahead of him. Maybe she could read minds.

'Don't try to tell me it's self-promotion. That old bugaboo of black men having longer sexual apparatus than whites has been discounted. Taking a nickname like this one sounds childish. I can't believe there are whiteys running around bragging about their endowment.'

'I wouldn't know anything about it,' said Foley, trying not to laugh. 'But if this dude is in the pimp business, it might very well be that he's counting on the importance of good marketing.'

'I'll feel funny putting that in the report. It might embarrass Ms. Weems. Or even Mr. Gorman.'

Foley chuckled, shaking his head. 'My bet is not much could embarrass either of those two. But if it makes you feel uncomfortable then don't mention it. And about any report we make on this, remember, Gorman wants it off the record. So nobody except old man Steiner will see it. It's just a favor for a friend. But when you write up an unofficial record to show the old man what we've accomplished, you can just mention the good officers of the law did give us a possible lead which we'll follow up. Now, go write your non-report while I find my way home.'

Pursing her lips a little, she turned and with a little finger flutter of a wave, headed down the street toward the DII second floor office. Foley watched as she strutted through the afternoon crowd. Gretchen was his partner and one didn't diddle with one's partner. That was a set in stone rule. There was, he told himself, something else to consider. Gorman's "little job" was only supposed to take a week or so and then they'd no longer be partners, would they? No, and what are rules for anyway; to break. Uh huh. We'll see.

Getting his old Chevy out of the parking garage, Foley wound his way through the going-home traffic and across the Golden Gate Bridge. Working in the City could be a pain in the butt but take city traffic out of the equation and it wasn't so bad. One of the perks he'd been given by Gorman was the parking slot in one of the city's many multi-storeyed parking garages. Life was really pretty good. Considering.

The drive home was, most times, pleasant. The twenty minutes or so it took to get to Stinson Beach gave him time to unwind from whatever he'd been doing all day. Anyway, he didn't go into the City every day, only two or three days a week. Working for DII wasn't hard, the pay was good and the job, he told himself, would do until the time came to get serious and find a real job. When that happened, he wanted the leaving to be on his terms. He didn't like getting fired, even if it was a kind of deal with no stability about it.

Once before, Brad Foley had been fired from a job he liked. When he had been kicked out of the sheriff's office he'd simply drifted south, no destination in mind. No goals. Taking a wrong turn one late afternoon, he'd ended up in Stinson Beach.

Stinson Beach, off any main highway, is a small, quiet coastal town. A village more than a town. He looked it over and thought it might be a good place to stay for a while. At least until he found something worthwhile to do with himself. Money wasn't a real problem. He'd invested his share from the sale of the vineyard in Microsoft stock. Each month, a check from the interest paid on the computer stock was deposited in his bank account.

Renting a small house on the beach side of Calle Del Arroyo, he settled in. Until he went to work for DII, his days were simple. Mornings he'd get up and, weather permitting, have his bowl of Wheaties on the back porch overlooking the Pacific Ocean. The highlight of most of those days had been a long walk along the beach in the afternoon and then to bed early.

He was still thinking about his new partner, a big smile plastered on his face, when he turned off the Shoreline Highway and onto Calle Del Arroyo. A lock up garage didn't come with the place so parking in the street meant making sure the Chevy was locked up tight. He'd never had any problems but better to be safe than sorry, was his motto.

They were on the little porch waiting for him. Thinking about Gretchen's legs and still smiling, he hadn't paid any attention to the big black van parked on the street. Those thoughts vanished from Brad's mind as he looked up to find a familiar face staring down at him. Shock at recognizing someone from long ago had barely registered when he was grabbed from the back by someone wrapping his arms around his chest. He fought it until the man came off the porch and drove his fist into Brad's unprotected stomach.

The attack stopped after the one punch and Brad was released. Trying to inhale, he bent over, his arms clutching his middle. Gasping as he attempted to breathe, he was grabbed again by the second man and held up.

Slowly, almost with a rhythm, Brad's head was slapped first one way and then the other. Finally the slapping stopped. As his eyes focused, Foley found himself eyeball-to-eyeball with his attacker. Trying to make his world settle down, he shook his head side to side, almost as if he was still being hit. The heavily breathing man staring at him waited patiently. Grimacing, he grabbed a handful of Brad's hair and brought his face even closer. His words sounded as if coming from a big steel barrel, the echoing sound cutting through his throbbing head like thunder through a mud filter.

'We've been hearing some bad things about you,' said the big man, his words starting to come clear, becoming hard and clipped. 'There's some cash money missing and your name's been given up.'

On top of struggling to get oxygen into his lungs, Brad labored to understand what he was being told.

'Hell, I didn't believe it but what the fuck am I gonna tell the boss? Should I say the little squealer said you took the money and I let you go?

Shit, he'd be all over me like heat in the desert. No, sir, you ain't worth my getting in trouble over. So, here's what we're gonna do. You and your lame-brain buddy left the north coast. He's gone somewhere. If we have to we'll find him. But right now we know where you are. If I don't hear your name anymore, you're good. Look at this like it's a warning. Don't fuck with us anymore. Don't even let me see you ever again, you hear?'

Brad wanted to agree but couldn't. The man's words were still coming with an echo. He could barely hear them over the roaring in his head. With both hands holding his stomach, he was defenseless and wanted to promise anything but he couldn't move.

'C'mon, Cully. He's got the idea. Let's get the hell outa here.'

'I wanna make sure.'

'All right, but make it quick, it's a long drive back home. The kid's gonna want to know what we found.'

Whoever was holding Foley up let him go. Suddenly the slapping at his head started again, one blow after another. When Brad tried to raise his arms in protection, one of them drove a fist into Brad's stomach again. Brad reacted by folding over and puking the remains of whatever was in his stomach all over a pair of shoes.

'Damn you!' someone growled and slammed a fist into the side of Brad's head.

Only partially conscious, Brad found himself lying on the sidewalk, flat on his back. Faintly, as if it were miles away, he heard the man's voice. 'This is only a warning. You better hope we find who took the money. And hope it don't lead back to you. Just forget anything you think you may know about what happens north of here. You understand?'

Unable to move, Brad couldn't even nod his total agreement. All he could do was watch as a circle of black slowly closed off his vision, leaving only a dot of light before even the dot too winked out.

Brad was unconscious and didn't feel someone kick his thigh or hear the curse. He wasn't aware the van, with a quick little squeal of tires, raced off. For a long time, he wasn't aware of anything.

Chapter 8

For some reason, as he woke out of the fog, someone was spraying him with the garden hose. The spray wasn't hard, they must have been holding their thumb over the nozzle.

A massive, dull, throbbing pain jabbed through his middle, forcing a groan from deep inside. He curled up in a ball, grasping his stomach. Slowly, becoming fully aware, he realized it was raining. Nobody was anywhere near him spraying him with water. The realization almost caused him to groan again.

He hurt. Oh, lordy did he hurt. Slowly, he let one eyelid ease open, so slowly the muscles moved as if they were really just relaxing. His eyeball was the only part of his body that didn't hurt. Not moving anything else, he tried to make out where he was. The rain, no more than a thin drizzle, the kind so typical of the coast for this time of year, caused chills to prickle his skin. Even under his jacket, which wasn't buttoned, he felt the muscles of his chest tighten in a cramp.

As his vision cleared, he found himself staring at the weathered timber railings of his porch. At first the railings were hazy and indistinct, as if he was looking through a thick fog. When he first moved in, he'd thought about putting a coat of paint on the railing. It had been on his list of things to do but he hadn't got around to it. It was unlikely he ever would.

Sooner or later he would have to move. Later, he decided. The memory of getting beaten up came flooding back. He hoped there was nothing busted inside all the pain.

Anton. One of the men had been the big muscle-bound stooge-cum-personal aide who worked for Hubert Ralston. What had he said? Something about money gone missing. Well, those guys were known drug dealers so the money would be drug money. Hubert Ralston was believed to be one of the bigger dope growers in the northern part of the state. It'd been that way when he was a deputy sheriff and it was unlikely anything had changed. Payback for this beating, he thought, feeling a new pain on his upper thigh, was going to be extra sweet.

But first he had to get out of the rain. He had to get moving.

Unsteady on his feet, bent over like a hundred-year-old man, he stumbled toward the porch. His walk up the sidewalk was a slow-step shamble. Luck was with him. His keys were still in a pants pocket. Leaning against the door frame, he unlocked the door and almost fell inside when it swung open. Finally, with the door closed and locked, he just stood, water dripping onto the faded threadbare carpet. Thinking how good sitting in a tub of hot bath water would be, he made his way across the bedroom, stripping off his clothes as he went. Naked, he fell across the bed, forgetting all thoughts of hot water.

It was still early when he woke up. Pain shot through his body when he turned over. Lying still, he tried to drop back into the pain-free cushion of sleep. A full bladder changed his mind. Getting up, he slowly and stiffly made his way into the little bathroom. He was thankful there was no blood in his urine. Taking his time, he filled the claw-foot tub with hot water.

Sitting with the water lapping at the very tub rim and as hot as he could stand caused more pain. A healing pain, he thought. Anton and his friend had done a remarkable job. They didn't break the skin anywhere. It didn't do to think about what was happening underneath the new now-colorful covering, though. A handful of aspirin tablets, a large whiskey and the full-to-overflowing tub helped. Thinking of ways to get even helped, too.

By the time the water started cooling, Foley had been able to relax a bit and the pain from the beating had even faded somewhat. The colorful artwork now decorating most of his upper body hadn't lessened and would certainly grow more mottled, even the interior ache felt more manageable. Until he tried to stand up. Moving brought it all back, in waves of pulsating hurt. Toweling himself off as much as he could without moving more than his arms, he stumbled off to the bedroom. Throwing back the blankets and bedspread proved one part of his body wasn't damaged, his arms worked as painlessly as the blades on a windmill.

Lying flat on his back, he willed his body to relax. Not expecting to get any sleep, he drifted off, waking when the telephone started ringing.

'Ah, hell,' he mumbled, turning over. Let it ring. Whoever it was would call back. Or they wouldn't.

The morning sun, spilling through an opening in the curtains, burned through his closed eyelids. The phone continued to ring.

'Go away,' he called weakly.

But they didn't. Finally, he slowly rolled over and pulled himself up. Shuffling into the front room, he grabbed his cell phone from the top of the table. Blindly he touched one of the icons, trusting he'd hit the right one.

'You better have a damn good reason for calling this early,' he snarled.

'Early? Shit, man, it's nearly nine o'clock. Hey, is that you, Mr. Foley?'

Brad didn't recognize the voice. 'Yeah, it's me. Who the hell are you?'

'Look, I been trying to get you. Calling and calling. Hey, you probably don't remember me at all, but there's something I gotta tell you. I'm sorry, man, but I probably fucked you over good. I didn't mean to, but, man, I had to.'

'What are you talking about? Who is this?'

'Name's Freddie. Freddie Isham. You remember? Way back, a long time ago when you was a cop up outa Eureka. You and your partner picked me up one night and was gonna take me in. I was drunk as a skunk. We struck a deal. I gave you a chop shop and you turned me out. Remember?'

Brad was shaking his head, then stopped. Wait a minute. Yeah, Freddie. He vaguely remembered a Freddie. Back while he was still wearing the deputy sheriff's brown uniform. Yeah, he'd met Freddie. It was when he and his partner, Steve, were out on patrol. The drunk they picked up started talking and told them all about a chop shop. Freddie had been his name, Brad remembered. He hadn't known it but as things turned out, picking the man up that night had been the very beginning of his life spiraling out of control.

Chapter 9

'OK,' HE SAID, 'it's coming back to me. Long beard, kinda scruffy looking. Yeah, I remember. Now, what's this you're sorry about?' Brad's legs started shaking. Fatigue. Slowly using the wall for support, he let his body slide down until he was sitting on the floor with his back to the wall. The wood flooring was cold on his bare butt and felt good.

'Well, man. I got myself in a kinda fix and they was beating on me pretty good. I had to give them something and the only thing I could think of was your name. I mean, shit, everyone knew the last thing you'd be into was drugs.'

'Who was giving you a beating?'

'A couple fellas. Never mind who. They took me outa my bed all wrapped up in a blanket. I never did see who they was. I think I heard one of them before. One of them called the other one Cully. Man, I think it was that damn fool Anton and his buddy Cully.'

Yeah, Brad thought. That's who it was all right. Anton and Cully. And they beat on Freddie?

'So,' he asked, 'why were they beating you?'

'Well, I been working for these people and some money went missing. Naturally they blamed me. When I couldn't tell them anything, they kinda hurt me until I could. And the only name I could think of was yours. So I did it … I gave them your name. Shit, man, you're safe as gold, ain't you? But then I got to thinking and, well, figured I'd better let you know. I'm truly sorry, man, but it was the only thing I could think of to do.'

'Yeah. So you told them my name and they quit beating on you?'

'Well, no. Not then. They hurt me some and then decided it was enough and took off. Now this happened a couple weeks ago and I ain't heard

38

anything more about it, but they're still looking for the missing money so it ain't been forgot.'

Anton had said something about money, hadn't he?

'Uh, Freddie,' Brad mumbled, 'listen, thanks for the phone call and all but it's a little late. Your friends, Anton and Cully, paid me a visit last night. Beat the crap out of me. It still hurts and slowed me down getting to the phone.'

'Ah, shit. Man, I'm real sorry.'

'What kind of work have you been doing?'

'Oh, you know,' he said, now sounding vague, 'a little of this and a little of that. Just making wages, you know?'

Yeah, Brad thought. Drug money missing and they go after Freddie. If Anton is there, the Ralstons are behind it. There had been little love lost between the county sheriff's department and old man Ralston. Keeping his fool of a son out of prison took all the old fart's time and influence. Trying to catch young Hubert had almost become a hobby for the deputies.

'Hey, Freddie, look, don't let it bother you. I think they'll leave me alone now. If I were you, though, I'd be looking for some other line of work.'

'Well, yeah, I been thinking about it. Look man, I gotta go. I just wanted to tell you, you know? I'm sorry I gave you up. But, well, hell …' After a short silence he hung up.

For a few minutes, Brad sat holding the phone, enjoying the coolness of the floor. Moving slowly and carefully, he made his way back to the bedroom and lay out on the bed, flat on his back. Thinking about what he'd been told, he fell asleep.

Waking up a couple of hours later, he found himself just as he was when he climbed in: flat on his back. Testing for pain by weakly moving each body part, he gently ran a hand over his stomach. It was tender and, looking down, saw a large black and purple bruise. The most pounding of the aches was coming from the fist-sized multi-colored bruise on his upper thigh. One of them must have kicked him after he was knocked unconscious. He couldn't remember getting that bruise. Of course, he couldn't remember most of the others, either. Damn them. Double damn whoever had sent them.

On his feet and able to pull on clothes, he was pleasantly surprised to find while still stiff, moving didn't cause any undue stress. Maybe he'd live to play dumb another day. A growling stomach meant at least part of the inner workings was unharmed.

The near emptiness of his refrigerator meant his stomach would have to be satisfied with a breakfast of a two-egg omelet, topped with a little grated cheese, the bits left over after cutting away the mold. And orange juice followed by cups of coffee.

Finished with breakfast, he decided he'd better call the office. He and Gretchen hadn't set a time to meet but he was sure as hell late. With his body covered with such colorful damage, he didn't think he'd be doing much today. Just take things easy. Maybe take another hot bath later in the afternoon. It was a sit around and catch up on his reading kind of day. A good idea, at least until he talked to his new partner.

'Don't tell me, you're still in bed,' she started in, sounding full up with sarcasm. 'Is this the way our working relationship is going to go? You sleep in while I chase down the scumbags?'

'No. Look.' Foley hoped he didn't sound as weak as he felt. 'Uh, something came up last night and, well, I'm not feeling so good this morning.'

'Your complaint falls under the heading of who cares. C'mon, get your butt in gear. We've got an appointment with a fellow named King Cock in about an hour.'

'You found him?'

'Don't think I'm just a pretty face, do you? Get hustling, partner.' The scorn was thick as San Francisco fog on a winter's day. Her tone was as cold, too.

'OK, OK. An hour. Where are we meeting him?'

'Meet me at the Starbucks where we had coffee yesterday. In forty-five minutes and damn it, don't be late or I'll go without you.'

Foley almost laughed as he punched the hang-up icon. He could almost believe she would go one-on-one with a big, black San Francisco pimp. And probably come out the winner, too. No, wait a minute. The cops said he was a whitey. Oh, well. Still probably a dangerous guy.

He hurried to get dressed, leaving his coffee growing cold on the counter.

Chapter 10

TRAFFIC WAS LIGHT going across the bridge and Foley had plenty of time to meet Gretchen. After parking and locking the old Chevy, he took his time walking to Starbucks. The physical movement seemed to ease his pain a little. Maybe a tall, double-shot black something, one of the stronger blends of coffee would be enough to make him feel human again.

Getting dressed, he had honestly tried to hurry but had to give it up. Putting on his shirt was OK. It was when he had to bend over to pick up a dropped shoe that everything came to a halt. Bending at the waist brought back twinges of the pain from the night before. Pulling on his socks was another trial. He was glad he was wearing slip-on loafers; he'd never be able to tie shoe laces.

His Chevy had seen a lot of miles and the springs in the driver's seat had taken on the shape of a man's butt. Settling behind the wheel, he felt more comfortable than when sitting in one of his kitchen chairs. All the way into the City, he toyed with the idea of telling his partner he wanted to put off everything until tomorrow. Or the next day. By the time he walked into Starbucks, he was actually feeling pretty good. Except for his thigh. He decided he could ignore it.

Any points he might have earned being a few minutes early went unborn. Gretchen was already sitting at one of the small tables. A young man Foley recognized as being another of DII's investigators was sitting across from her. The pair looked like two high school students, heads close together, planning the overthrow of the world.

'Morning all,' said Foley, trying for cheerful but not feeling a bit of it. 'I'll get a cup of coffee and join you.'

Waiting his turn to order, he tried to remember the guy's name. Some time ago, when he'd just started with Gorman, he had worked with the man on a case. Foley frowned, trying to remember. All he could come up with was it had been something about recovering a painting stolen from one of the many local galleries. Hell, he almost snorted aloud, he could recall the name of the gallery but the PI's name was gone. First sign of old age, he supposed.

Gretchen was sitting by herself when he came back to the table.

'Good morning, partner,' Foley said, again hoping a bright attitude might make her overlook how careful he was in bending to sit down.

'You're late.' It was the first time he'd heard her snarl.

'Sorry, but, well, I had some trouble last night. Tell me, how'd you manage to track down Tricky Dick?'

'His nickname is King Cock, not Tricky Dick. Tricky Dick was the name the newspapers gave Richard Nixon when he was president. How come you're moving so slow?'

'Got into a little scuffle and came out the other guy.'

'What do you mean, the other guy?'

'As in "You should see the other guy."'

'Uh huh. Cute. How is it Carl doesn't like you? He almost burst out laughing when he saw who I have for a partner on this job. He said something about watching you don't take advantage of my inexperience. What did he mean?'

Carl Dallas. Uh huh, it all came back.

'Oh, nothing much. We met when we were both new hires and were working together, a lot like you and I are now. I helped him return a painting another guy had walked out of a gallery with. The Gough Street Gallery. The thief had taken it to prove the gallery's security needed upgrading. He sold such systems. The guy hadn't thought things through very well, though, and couldn't figure out how to return it without getting arrested. Dallas thought if he just walked in with it, the gallery owner would be happy and everything would be all right. I had other ideas which he didn't approve of. Gorman gave it to me to handle.'

'And that made Carl angry?'

'Well, there was a little more to it. My plan was to call the gallery's insurance company and work through them. Discreet Inquiries ended up with the standard reward the insurance companies like to offer, I think it was ten per cent of the painting's value. I got a bonus and an "atta boy" and Carl got told he should watch and learn. It didn't endear me to him, I guess.'

'No, it certainly didn't.'

'OK, so how'd you go about finding this pimp we want to talk to?'

Gretchen chuckled. 'I'd say it was a simple case of watch and learn.'

Foley gave up. His attempts at cheerfulness and positive attitude clearly hadn't worked. Not reacting to her jibe, he sat and waited.

'OK,' she said, watching as Foley sipped his coffee, 'let's go over it. When I was writing up the report yesterday, Mr. Gorman came by and asked about what we'd found so far. When I told him about what the big police officer had told us, he smiled and picked up the phone. I don't know who he called but he asked about a pimp named King Cock. After waiting a couple of minutes, he wrote down an address and a phone number. I called the number and we have an appointment in exactly ten minutes.'

'What street corner are we headed for?'

'No corner, a real office address. On the fourth floor of the Kroll Building on Union Street.'

'Fourth floor? On Union? Hell's fire, you're talking the high rent quarter. Up in the middle of the financial district. How in the hell does a pimp afford working out of some place like that?'

'I don't know, but if you'll hurry up and finish your coffee, we can go ask him.'

They were in luck; the address wasn't far from the coffee shop. Being young and not in any major pain, Gretchen set a rather fast pace, one Foley didn't find comfortable. The blow he'd taken to his right thigh hurt with each step but he'd be damned if he'd complain or ask her to slow down.

Neither said anything while riding up in the tiny elevator. Foley leaned against the wall, resting.

'Later, you'll have to tell me about last night's fun and games,' murmured his partner as the doors opened and they stepped out into a tastefully decorated hallway. 'Which way?' she asked.

Foley glanced at the door numbers. 'Room 412, so it'd be this way.'

The corridor was well lit and carpeted in a light maroon runner with a foot or so of waxed hardwood showing on either side. Framed landscapes, prints but stylish and obviously quality, had been hung at intervals along both walls. Office doors along the way were of some dark wavy grained wood. Silence hung in the air like an unseen blanket. Foley was impressed.

He let Gretchen knock on the door to 412 and opened it up for her when someone inside called out. The office was not what he'd expected. Instead of girls sitting around on sofas, drinking coffee and leafing through magazines, tall upright shelving lined the walls. A long, wide desk took up most of the center of the room and a man, mostly hidden behind an oversized monitor, looked up long enough to wave them to the only other furniture, two chrome metal chairs, both with light gray colored padding. Foley thought they were probably Office Depot stacking chairs.

'Good morning,' the man said, standing up to reach a hand across the desk, taking, Foley thought, too long to study Gretchen. 'I'm Rex Cochrane and you must be the woman who called last night. I understand you would like to ask me some questions?'

This man was not the typical pimp Foley had expected. In the first place he was white, a man with the kind of tan one would only get from spending time on the ski slopes. Brad guessed his age would be about thirty or so. He was six feet tall or close to it. His slender build and military-style posture – straight back, shoulders square, flat belly – made him appear even taller. Clean shaven, a deep dimple centered his strong chin which, added to his warm smile, made him almost handsome. Recently, and from the looks of it, Foley would have bet earlier the same morning, he had had a hair cut. Unlike the Brad Foleys of the world, this man obviously paid a couple hundred dollars for a good styling. His dress shirt was the brightest of whites and it had a soft look about it, the kind only seen on the highest quality of foreign menswear. Probably cotton from India or Italy. Foley wondered if his shoes were custom-made Italian. Pimps were known to dress flamboyantly but he'd never heard of one dressing with this much class. Maybe there had been a mistake and Gorman had sent his partner to a financial adviser.

'I'm Brad Foley,' he said, 'and my partner, Gretchen Bongiorno. And yes, we are looking into something and we were given the name of someone who could possibly help us.'

Cochrane laughed. 'I'll bet the name you heard was King Cock. Am I right?'

'Uh, yes. Yes it was.'

The man chuckled. 'Now that is interesting,' he said, sitting with his butt on the corner of his desk. 'My name came up and I might know something that would help you? May I enquire as to where you heard my name and exactly what information you're seeking?'

'Well, the way it works is we ask the questions,' said Gretchen, studying the man closely.

Foley had decided to take a wait-and-see attitude, mainly because he wasn't sure this was the man they wanted to talk with. His young partner didn't want to wait.

'Because of the confidentiality nature of things,' she explained quietly, 'we can't really tell you where we got your name and contact number. We are looking into the death of a young woman and in our search, your name was mentioned.'

The man smiled. 'Uh huh. I'll bet you heard my name from one of the uniforms over at the Hall of Justice. Those boys never forget. Never ever. OK, I give up. You've got the right man. Rex Cochrane. On the basketball court in high school I was nicknamed 'Cock' Cochrane. When I decided to go into business for myself I used King instead of Rex and thought I was clever. Boy, was I wrong.'

'The business you went into, was it prostitution?' Foley asked, still trying to figure this man out.

'You got it. I figured if a bunch of not-too-smart black men could make money with the help of a half dozen girls, I, a whitey with a degree in business, should be able to make more. I was wrong there, too.'

'So you got out of the 'business' and into, what, exactly?'

'Oh, no. No, I'm still in it. Only I've taken a different approach. The time I was arrested, it was when one of my girls got beaten up. I didn't do it, another pimp did. A guy people called Fishbone Frank. He was a bad ass pimp and was attempting to take over what he called my stable. When I saw what he'd done to the girl, I can't remember her name, I got out of the trade. At least the street side of it.'

Waving a hand around, he smiled and explained. 'Computers are the way to go. There isn't much you can't do with these machines and the internet. I'm no longer a white pimp, I'm now a webmaster. This is a much better way; the money is as good and if you take into account the pay-offs I don't have to make to the legal establishment, better. And I get to work in classy surroundings.'

'We were wondering,' said Foley. 'This office is the high end of things.'

'And I pay for it, too. These offices, two rooms, just under a thousand square feet of space, even a bay window looking out over the street, bonded clean-up service once a week, a great address and it only costs me $1200 a month. Hell, I've got a couple hundred grand in computer servers sitting on these shelves. This is no street corner business. No, sir.'

'And you're still in the business of making money off of women?' asked Gretchen.

Foley almost smiled. It never failed. He had yet to meet a woman who wasn't positive women involved with prostitution, pole dancing or even stripping for private parties wasn't a case of women being taken advantage of. Why couldn't they ever understand some, if not most, women were in it for the money?

'Yep, you could say it was so but you'd be wrong,' said 'Cock' Cochrane, beginning to sound like a lecturer. 'In my business I don't sell a girl's favors. All I do is make it easier, safer and almost legal for them to do business. Look, it's like this, I'm a webmaster, I sell girls' web pages. If you have to put a name on it, call it e-prostitution.'

Neither Foley nor Gretchen joined his laugh.

Seeing the two weren't having it, Cochrane turned serious. Walking around, he sat in the big comfortable-looking chair behind the desk. 'OK. Look, you've heard of Amazon.com, haven't you? Of course you have, everyone has. OK, Amazon is a company selling to people all over the world. On their websites you can buy almost anything you want. Amazon doesn't produce the products, books, for example. But on the Amazon website, you can find all kinds of books. Nice hard cover expensive books. And it's where people go who want to buy nice, expensive books. Well, this is the same thing. The internet is expanding the high end of the prostitution market. The nice, safe and expensive end of the service.'

Leaning back in his chair, he smiled. 'Someone described internet marketing as being able to present an impression of quality. Clicking through a series of websites is a lot more 'classy', more acceptable than cruising up and down the side streets off Market or thumbing through the adult services ads in one of the free newspapers. And here's the kicker, men will pay a premium for the impressive "specialness."'

Gretchen had to question what he was saying. 'Are you saying the women pay you to advertise their services on the internet?'

'No. They pay me to host their websites. Oh, and if they want, for a fee I'll create high quality sites for them.'

It was clear she wasn't getting it.

He held his hands out, palms up. 'Look, let me use Veronica as an example. She pays me $100 a month to list her site. She says she got more than 250 phone calls the first month it was up and running. Using email, she was able to pick and choose, dumping the 'looky-loos' and those who for one reason or another she didn't think were safe and suitable. From those who made the cut, she ended up with a dozen clients, some of whom became regulars. OK, it was a couple years ago when I was setting up and my site, www.SF-eye-candy.com wasn't very well known yet. She's still with me. Each year she pays an extra $1,000 for me to maintain her site, one I originally created she calls educatedescort.com. She also has listings on an LA web site called worldwide-escorts.com. From these, she figures she gets about 700 internet visitors a day. I'm told she charges $4,000 a day with a two-day minimum. Will travel anywhere the client wishes. She recently spent a week in the Bahamas and another time flew to Fiji to be with a client. The client pays for all airfares, first class of course, nothing less than a five-star hotel and the best restaurants the city of his choice has to offer. If what she tells me is true, she makes about three quarters of a million a year, all tax free.'

'And what cut of the money do you get?' asked Gretchen sarcastically.

'None of it. My income is from hosting the websites, maintaining them, adding them to my site if the girls want and advertising my sites. I have to tell you, my income is in the six-figure range. I have more than 250 clients. And I do pay taxes on my income. Cyber-prostitution is safe; the girls can vet their clients by Googling them. To make it better, it's legal. At least no law enforcement agency has found a way to get around the distance related to the internet. And there's plenty of proof it's quite lucrative.'

He smiled at Gretchen. 'Honey, it's clear you don't approve but look at it this way. I'm an advertising agency. I'm paid for placing ads. This is all I do. I maintain sites for approximately 250 women, mostly those living here in the Bay Area but a growing number who live elsewhere. A few are in Las Vegas and even a couple up north, in Seattle. Another feature of using the internet.'

'OK, so if this is so clean and wonderful,' said Gretchen nastily, not giving up, 'then why, when we started asking questions about a murdered girl, a known prostitute, did your name come up?'

King Cock didn't have an answer.

Chapter 11

COCHRANE'S SMILE INSTANTLY disappeared and he held up both hands. 'Now wait just a minute. I don't know anything about any murdered girl. I run a legitimate business. Maybe I shouldn't be talking to you anymore.'

'Whoa,' said Foley, 'let's not get excited. Nobody is saying you know anything about the murder. What we were told was once upon a time, back when you were working the streets, you might have known a certain young girl. This would go back, five or six years. We're told she was on the streets for a little while and then disappeared down in LA.'

'Hell, girls like you're describing were dime a dozen back then, and probably still are. I worked the street for such a short time, no more than five or six months at most. Seeing what happens to girls was too much to take. Funny thing, when I told my girls I was quitting and why, not a one of them understood. Every one of them hooked up with another pimp. It's like they wanted to get beat up as well as fucked over. Excuse the language. I still get angry when I think of what's happening down there. But as far as remembering one girl five years ago, you gotta be kidding. Five years is more than a lifetime for a heavy druggie, especially one working the streets.'

Gretchen shook her head. 'Think back. She would have been quite lovely, at least that's how one person remembers her. We're told she used the name Ann or Anne Marie Steiner.'

'Hey, most all these girls start out being lovely. But lovely doesn't last long. In the beginning, though, they don't seem to see what's going to happen to them. And names, something like Ann is not normal. Usually they pick some kind of cutesy name like Amber or Lolita. Something they think men will find alluring, I guess,' he said, his weak smile indicating

49

how impossible it was.

Something the man said caught Foley's attention.

'If you don't remember this girl, how'd you know she was into drugs?'

'What? I didn't. Drugs and prostitution usually go together. No, I don't remember anyone like the one you're asking about.'

'But you just said girls on the street, especially heavy druggies, don't last long. Let's stop bullshitting. Tell us about the Steiner girl.'

Cochrane's expression faded, his cheeks slowly sagged as his smile died away. 'Look, I don't know anything about it. Her death, I mean. Yeah, I know Anne Marie. She came to me two years ago, looking like a million dollars. No drugs, just long legs and a clear complexion. Stunning. She said she'd been working as an escort down in Los Angeles but wanted to come back here. I set her up with a site. Very tastefully done. A professional photo shoot, brief description of the services and fees. The pictures of her on the site are pretty but fully clothed. Her text is well-written and laced with humor. She became one of my success stories.'

'This Veronica you told us about?' Gretchen asked, her tone still cutting.

'No, she's another one doing well. But I don't know anything about what you say happened to Anne Marie.'

'When's the last time you had any contact with her?'

'Last month. She wanted to update the information on her site. Said she was becoming too busy so rather than cut back, she thought it was a good time to raise her fees.'

'Did she come in to see you? How was she?' asked Gretchen.

'No, I didn't see her. I haven't seen her since she came in the first time. It's rare I ever see any of the girls. Everything is done by email. They tell me what they want, download the photos and when they're satisfied, they direct deposit my fees.'

This seemed to be the end of Gretchen's questions. She sat back and glanced at her partner. Foley sat quiet for a moment and then thought about coming from another direction.

'Do your customers know each other? I guess, more to the point, do you know if she was friendly with anyone? Anyone we could talk to about her?'

'Well, I wouldn't know. I mean, there's a lot of confidentiality involved with this business. The whole point of what I do is keeping my customers safe and anonymous except through their web pages.'

Foley liked the man's answer. He hadn't been able to see where their search could go from here but now he did.

'OK,' he said, glancing over at Gretchen, 'I can understand how it works. Gretch, I'd say the next step is to get a search warrant.' Looking sideways across the desk at Cochrane, he smiled. 'Of course, it'll mean bringing experts and tearing apart every one of these servers. We don't know exactly what we're looking for so we'll have to look at everything. I can just imagine what kind of fun a crew of nerdy computer freaks will have going through all the 250 sites.'

He almost laughed to see the look on King Cock's face. 'Ah, man. I can't have that. Give me a break, huh? This is my business, my life's work.'

Gretchen liked it and stepped right in. 'Your choice. Give us a name or we'll be back and take a real in depth look at "your life's work."'

'Shit, you're as bad as he is. OK, OK. Emma is the only name I've got. I think her last name's Longenbough, or something. She doesn't use it on her website. Annie sent her to me a year or so ago. I think they've even teamed up a few times when a client wanted two ladies for an event.'

'An event,' said Gretchen, letting her tone speak volumes. 'OK, how do we get a hold of this friend, Emma?'

King Cock turned to his monitor and after hitting a few strokes on a keyboard, scribbled something on a slip of paper which he handed across to Foley.

'Now this is enough, all right? It's all I got on her. Damn it. Try not to let her know how you got her name and address, OK?'

Gretchen smiled. 'Oh, we'll try, all right. Count on it.'

'I wouldn't like it,' Foley said, standing up and heading for the heavy wooden door, 'if you were to let this Emma know we're coming. Remember, if this doesn't help us out, we'll be back. With a crew of young horny nerds and a court order.'

'No sweat, man. I don't ever want to see you again.'

Chapter 12

THE ADDRESS COCHRANE had given them was an apartment on O'Farrell Street.

'O'Farrell,' Foley snarled when he saw the address. 'Almost back where we were yesterday at Steiner's place. C'mon, it's only a half dozen blocks or so. We can walk it.'

'You sure you can make it? You're still moving like you hurt.'

'Yeah, it does. Sitting around listening to some creep tell us how smart and successful he is didn't help, either.'

'Does his success make you jealous? It certainly didn't help your attitude.'

'Naw, sitting in an office punching a keyboard isn't my style. But talk about attitudes, you didn't give old Tricky Dicky an inch.'

'You should talk. Did he really think we could get a search warrant?' She chuckled. 'Your threat of bringing in a crew of horny nerds scared him a lot.'

'Hell yes, he believed me. People watch too much TV. They're used to hearing someone say the words search warrant and seeing a few minutes later the police breaking down doors. We know it doesn't happen, well, not often. And we also know there's no way in hell we could get a court order. But he didn't.'

'What would you have done if he had laughed in your face?'

'Probably smacked him around a little.' Foley smiled to show he really didn't mean it. 'But you weren't hiding your anger at all. I think it bothered him more than anything I said. What was that all about?'

'I don't like men who take advantage of women.'

'Ha. If this Veronica he told us about is making half what he said, the question is who is taking advantage of who?'

'Whom.'

'I give up. C'mon, let's walk.'

'And look for a place for lunch. I'm still a growing girl, you know.'

The hike from Cochrane's high end office across town to the apartment on O'Farrell was a little more than a couple of blocks; it was more like ten blocks. Foley wasn't about to call it off, though. Being a man, he groused silently, even though feeling the dull pain in the muscle of his right thigh. He knew the girl walking beside him was smiling to herself.

They finally stopped at a little pizza place on the corner of Larkin and O'Farrell.

'Emma's building will be down in this block,' said Foley, looking up at the street sign. 'Let's get a bite before we go cause her trouble.'

'Why should we be making trouble for her? All we want is information.' She glanced down the street and then looked back at her partner before following him inside. 'What exactly are we asking her anyway? If she knew anything about her friend getting killed, wouldn't she tell the police?'

'Probably. But then again, probably not. I'd think girls in the escort business would want to keep out of sight. Especially go unnoticed by any cop. No. I'm after a little more information about our Steiner girl. Anyway, I'm curious. I'd like to know more about how the girls handle this e-prostitution thing.'

'Are you thinking about getting a computer and starting your own business?' she laughed, taking a bite of the pepperoni slice she'd ordered.

'Not unless you want go in as my partner,' he said, throwing up his hands to ward off her reaction before quickly going on. 'Just kidding, just kidding. No, but I do think something in the safety features of the way this cyber stuff is done could be helpful. Look, I don't want to cause anyone grief, especially a working girl. All Gorman wanted us to do was ask a few questions, write a couple reports and make it look like we did everything we could. We'll take our time with this. After we finish talking to Emma, we can go back to the office and try to figure out where we're going tomorrow. Right now I can't see there's much more we can do, though. So let's take it easy, stretch it out and then call it quits.'

'Umm, maybe. But I still think prostitution is prostitution and it's wrong.'

'But we're not here to change the world. All we're after is to ask questions about a girl who was killed. Stabbed. This is not about how she made her living, it's how she died. Eat up and let's get this over with.'

Chapter 13

O'FARRELL STREET IS technically still in the part of San Francisco known as the Tenderloin, but on the 'good' side of Market Street. A classier section with nicer hotels, restaurants and apartment buildings. It is home to many artists, writers and worker bees employed in the nearby financial district. Emma's address was a three storey red brick building typical for the area. Looking at the mail boxes, they could see there were six apartments, two to a floor. Resident parking was in the basement. It wasn't exactly low-rent, but not what Foley expected for someone with a tax free, half a million dollar annual income.

He nodded to his partner to press the button for the intercom.

'She'll be more likely to welcome a call from another woman than from a man, don't you think?'

Gretchen grimaced, muttered, 'Sexist,' and touched the button.

The young woman wasn't happy when she opened her second floor apartment door as far as the security chain would allow.

'You're not who I expected. Who are you and what do you want?'

Foley hadn't heard what Gretchen had muttered into the intercom and knew better to say anything now.

'It's about Anne Marie,' said Gretchen, holding up her DII identity card, the one with the official looking embossed Bureau of Security and Investigative Service shield prominently displayed. Brad Foley's DII identity card was just a business card with his name on it. Not very impressive.

'What about Annie?'

'Let's not stand here in the hallway. We don't think this is something your neighbors need to know about, do you?'

The comment got her.

'OK, let me unhook the chain,' she said and closed the door.

Emma was another young beauty. Short black hair so evenly colored it had to come out of a bottle, a pixie face and thin, but shapely body. Foley thought if she dressed in bobby socks, flat heeled black shoes, a short plaid skirt and white blouse she could get into the movies on a child's fare. Probably a good marketing ploy for someone with clients who liked young girls.

'OK,' she said, standing just inside, unmoving with her fists planted on her narrow hips, 'say your piece. And it'd better be good.'

Foley thought he'd been quiet long enough. 'How long has it been since you talked with Anne Marie Steiner?'

'Annie? A couple weeks or so. Why? What's this all about?'

'Anne Marie Steiner's body was found by the police,' he said quickly, hoping to shock her into saying something, 'in an alley down near Sixth and Market. She had been stabbed and left to bleed to death.'

'Annie's dead?' The news staggered her. All of a sudden she wavered and would have collapsed if Gretchen hadn't taken her arm.

Directing her toward a couch, Gretchen gently lowered her down and knelt beside her, with an arm around the grieving woman's shoulders.

Foley watched. From the flowing tears and her posture, sitting all bent with her head held by her hands, he believed she hadn't known.

'You didn't have to be so abrupt,' snarled Gretchen, giving him a glaring look strong enough to have singed his eyebrows.

The crying and hugging went on for a few more minutes, giving Foley an opportunity to look around.

Emma may be making a lot of money but she wasn't spending much on her living quarters. The couch was part of a three-piece sectional that could have been picked up in a second-hand shop. The cover was some kind of flower pattern, so faded it was hard to tell what the original colors had been. The carpet covering the floors was the nicest part. Probably, he figured, came with the place.

In the little kitchen just off the living room, a small chrome table, its Formica top scratched and spotted by cigarette burns, had two matching chairs. It was a two bedroom apartment, a battered dresser and queen sized bed was in one. A Dell laptop computer sitting on a card table and a single office chair was all the furniture in the other. He didn't go into the bathroom. Looking around, he saw a couple of boxes of books but didn't see a single ashtray.

'Who did it?' asked the girl, wiping away her tears.

Gretchen answered, her voice soft and gentle. 'We don't know. For a few days, the police weren't sure of her identity and for a while she was listed as Jane Doe. Even after finding out her name, they simply figured the murder as a mugging or a drug or prostitution death. We were hired by her father to discover what we could. We've been able to piece together a little information but not enough to be satisfied.'

'Are you working with the police?'

'No. Well, kind of. You see her father doesn't want ... oh, never mind. The police have put her death down as a drug and prostitute killing. That means they won't do anything else but will keep the file open in case something comes up in the future.'

'So you're doing their job for them? What was the badge you showed me?'

'We work for Discreet Inquiries, Incorporated. A private investigation firm.'

Emma sat looking toward one of the two curtained windows in the room.

'How did you find me? Who told you about me being her friend?'

'I'm afraid it's confidential. But we're the only ones who have followed anything this far. I don't think the police department know about you or cares.'

'Will you have to tell them?'

'No. Whatever you can tell us, if it helps lead to the name of the person who killed her, we'll do everything we can to keep your name out of it.'

Emma snorted. 'I didn't even know she was dead. Anyway, the people I know who know her, well, the only ones are a few of our clients. You do know what we do, don't you?'

'Yes,' said Foley, having settled onto the other end of the sectional. 'We know about the websites the two of you use. We were hoping you could tell us who some of her clients were. It'd be wonderful if you knew who she was with just before she was killed.'

'I don't know who that could be. The only time I met any of her regulars was when the client requested two girls. It didn't happen often. It's too expensive. Our fees plus dinner, the hotel room, transportation and other costs could easily run into twenty grand.'

'Twenty thousand?' Gretchen gasped at the idea.

'Sure. We'd get $4,000 a night each, two night minimum, then the air fare, hotel and everything else, yeah, $20,000 at least. And it could even be more. We each got a couple hundred dollar tip. "Traveling money," the man called it.'

'What air fares?' asked Foley.

'He had us fly up to Seattle. First class round trip. On Alaska Airlines.'

Foley shook his head. 'I'm in the wrong business.' A comment both women overlooked.

'What kind of men can afford to pay such a big amount for a couple nights' fun and games?' asked Gretchen. Foley wanted to ask her if she was starting to change her mind about going into the business but thought he'd better not.

'Rich ones,' explained the young woman. 'Or powerful ones. You know, like politicians or, back before all the dot.coms went broke, a lot of those guys. One time, the person who got my name from my website and emailed me was a woman, the executive assistant of what she called her "dot.com baby". She wanted to know my bra size, my height and weight and the color of my hair. It was like she was ordering her boss a new hard drive or something. Some of those young computer geeks had tons of money but no social skills. A big hard-on but didn't know how to talk to a girl. It was great while it lasted.'

'So they'd call up and away you'd go?'

'No. It's all email to start. Gives me the opportunity to check them out, or check out their company. It's the best part of the websites. Once I accept the client, we discuss prices and such things as travel. When we've reached an agreement, the man simply makes a direct deposit to my account and I'd go to the hotel he had made reservations in. If it was a long distance, say Las Vegas or Dallas, then there would be a plane ticket waiting for me at the airport.'

Foley was frowning. 'In our business, every so often we're hired to gather evidence for divorce proceedings. What you're saying is you know a lot about some powerful men, men with wives. Doesn't anyone ever get nervous about the possibility?'

'Do you mean blackmail? No. I mean, yeah, I suppose it could happen, but why would a girl do it? Think about it, we're paid a lot of money, so why would we want to piss off one of our regulars? The world isn't so big, you know. Once a girl got a reputation for something like blackmail, she'd have to get out of the business. It's like, if we don't maintain our health, it's the end of the road. None of us want to go back to waitressing or hair styling. Not after making the big bucks doing what we do.'

'So,' said Gretchen, 'you can't think of anyone who might have some information about the Steiner girl?'

The question brought Emma back to her grief. 'No,' she said, her head dropping again until her chin touched her chest. 'She and I were friends, but not close friends. You know what I mean? We worked together because we looked good together. She's more stylish and I'm more little girlish. Doing it together seemed to make some men excited. But otherwise we didn't see much of each other.'

'There's something bothering me,' said Foley, 'you made a lot of money but looking at your apartment, you don't spend much on yourself, do you?'

She laughed. 'No. I like this apartment because it's close to the San Francisco State University Art School and the Art Institute of California. What money I don't put in my savings account I use to pay for tuition and supplies. I've got two more years and I'll have my Master's degree and I won't need to do this anymore.'

'What'll you do then, paint?'

'Paint and teach. I come from a small town in Montana and that's where I want to go back to. A small town with a good school.'

'And no more first class flights to Las Vegas or Seattle?'

'Yeah, and no more men with lots of money and small minds.'

The two left Emma after giving her more assurances they wouldn't make her address public.

'Believe it or not,' she said as they went out the door, 'I have the reputation around here of being just what I am, a student at one of the art schools. God, I wouldn't want anyone to know how I'm paying for things.'

Foley left the building, sure they had followed this as far as was possible. Gorman's little job was proving to be smaller than ever. Old man Steiner would just have to accept the obvious; his daughter had gotten into deep water with no life preserver. It'd be hard to stretch this out to even a week.

Chapter 14

Back on the street, they decided to head for the nearest coffee shop to talk over what to do next. The corner café Brad and Gretchen found offered only perked coffee. They could tell by the smell. Coffee brewed in the morning and kept warm in the pot until the last cup was poured gave the little place a strong ambience.

'Boy, you really know how to treat a girl,' muttered Gretchen as they settled in one of the booths lining the wall, 'pizza for lunch followed by burnt coffee.'

'It's not burnt, just nicely aged.'

After giving the frazzled looking waitress their order, they sat, each waiting for the other to start.

'OK, what have we learned so far we can consider to be useful?' asked Gretchen, just as the woman brought their coffee, smelling strong in thick white porcelain mugs.

'Not much, I'd say.' Foley liked his coffee black and watched as his partner poured milk in hers, after tearing a package of sugar open and dumping it in. 'Old man Steiner's name isn't involved so he can relax in his historic mansion. The police aren't coming up with any leads so it's unlikely their case will go anywhere. And other than learning more than we probably wanted to know about computer prostitution, we haven't done much better.'

'So, oh great mentor, what do we do now?'

'What? Where did that come from?'

'Wasn't it what Mr. Gorman said? I should go along with you and learn from the expert?'

'Hogwash. He just wanted to see what kind of reports you could write.' Gretchen blew to cool the steaming brew. 'What reports are you …

now wait a minute. You're not leaving me to write up a report on what we did today. No, sir. I got stuck with yesterday's, if you recall. It's your turn.'

'OK, so what do I report? Bring it to an end or do you have some idea of what we can do next?'

'You're the expert. You tell me.'

Foley shook his head. 'Damn, Gorman wanted this to take a week or so. Which means we'll have to fake it for another four days at least. Let's think about it overnight. I'll come up with something.'

'And meantime, you'll go back to the office and see what kind of report you can drum up on today's hard work. Right?'

'Sure, as long as you're paying for the coffee.'

Gretchen left Foley at the coffee shop, saying something about doing a little shopping before heading home. Taking his time, he finished a second cup before waving down a cab. Except for the throbbing in his upper thigh, the rest of his body was almost pain free. Even though the thought of walking the long way back to DII's offices wasn't considered for a moment.

Later, driving across the bridge toward home, he racked his brain trying to come up with ideas of what to do next. As it turned out, the decision was made for him.

Chapter 15

Adirty mud streaked 4WD Ford Ranger was sitting on the street in front of Foley's house, right where he usually parked. Stopping his Chevy behind the SUV, Foley sat for moment and thought about it. Somehow it looked familiar.

'Christ on a crutch,' he muttered, finally getting out of his car and starting up the walk, 'all these beasts look the same.'

Glancing up at the porch and thinking about last night's welcoming committee, he came to an abrupt halt. There was someone sitting in the old rocker waiting for him.

'What the hell?' he snarled, wishing he had a baseball bat before calling out. 'C'mon, sucker. It won't be so easy this time.'

The man slowly got up and stepped over to stand next to the railing.

'Now is this any way to greet a friend?'

'Who ...' he said and stopped. He recognized the voice. And the way the man was standing. 'Steve?'

'Uh huh. Your long gone buddy done come back. Well, you gonna just stand there or come on up and unlock the door? I could sure use a cup of coffee. Or a beer.'

'Yeah,' said Foley slowly, 'why not? C'mon.' Foley moved past the man without looking at him and unlocked the door.

The day Steve Tichenor and Brad Foley had turned in their badges, sidearms and the keys to the patrol car they'd been using, one had driven south, the other disappearing north. At least Foley had figured it'd be where Steve would go. He wasn't the kind of man who could take to big city living. Turning on the lights in his little kitchen, Brad smiled to himself at the thought of the man who used to be his partner living in San Francisco. Without a doubt, he would take one look at the buildings, the crowded sidewalks and the traffic and turn his rig around.

Since the first day they were sworn in with the sheriff's department, they'd been partners. They'd know each other a lot longer than that. Which was why it was only natural, when Steve was caught growing high grade marijuana, the plants intermixed with the grape vines on the ten acre vineyard they jointly owned, Brad was naturally painted with the same brush. Steve had sworn it had all been his idea and in fact, Brad hadn't even been aware of it and said so, over and over. To anyone who'd listen. But no one heard him. To the outside world, they were partners in everything.

They had gone together to buy the vineyard, seeing it as an investment. Brad had liked the idea of owning his own business and having a vineyard was a good start. The previous owners, a couple of brothers, had been arrested for stealing cars. They had used the long shed on the property once used for the production of wine grapes to repaint the stolen vehicles. With a new color, the cars were sold to a guy who put them in shipping containers. Where the cars, and not a few pickups, were shipped to and from there was anyone's guess. Countries in the Middle East were a likely home to the end buyers.

When the property went on the market to pay the brothers' legal fees, Steve and Brad pooled their savings and made the down payment on the ten acres.

No formal charges were made when Steve, and later Brad, was brought in. The sheriff, recognizing their years of service and the high arrest records they had run up, decided not to take the matter to the district attorney. But along with their badges and the patrol car, their careers in the field of law enforcement were over.

'What the hell brought you to my front door, Steve?' Brad asked as he poured two mugs of coffee and put out the sugar bowl.

'Well, I've got a little job to do and need some help doing it. Naturally you're the first person I thought of.'

Those words, "little job," did everybody use them?

'What kind of "little job" have you got yourself involved with that you need my help? Fact is, what the hell have you been up to since we split up?'

'Oh, for a while, just a little of this and that. Nothing to brag about. A couple years ago, I did some work for a California State Senator. I've been on his payroll ever since.'

'You, working for a politician? What doing, taking him hunting or fishing?'

If anything, Steve Tichenor had been born in the wrong century. He would have been the perfect partner for Daniel Boone. There wasn't a square foot of forest land in northern California he hadn't hunted over at one time or another, or a creek, river, pond or lake he hadn't fished.

'Nope,' said Steve. 'Other things. Well, I did do some hiking and hunting right after leaving Eureka. Mostly over in the Shasta National Forest. But I got all the photos of deer, bear and mountain lion a guy would want. All the wildlife magazines wanted anyway.'

Steve and Brad had been hunting partners, going out the first of every deer season. Until one year Steve decided to leave his rifle at home and take his camera. From then on the Nikon was what he hunted with.

'Nowadays I'm reasonably well paid, working for Senator, ummm, Senator Froggybottom.'

Foley remembered his quiet chuckle.

'There's no reason for me to tell you exactly who's paying my bills. Froggybottom is as good a name as any. If I told you his real name and you called his office, nobody would know what you were talking about. What he's got me doing are the things he or any of his staff can't be seen doing.'

'Illegal things?'

'No. Well, not usually. Mostly it's stuff that could be politically damaging.'

'Give me an example.'

Tichenor sipped his coffee, frowning. 'Hmm. OK, but this is just between you and me, all right?'

Foley nodded.

'A couple years ago, there was a story about a big rice grower over in the Colusa area. It turned out Mr. Rice Farmer was involved with an operation involving undocumented migrant laborers. The problem was a lot of the cash Mr. Rice Farmer was making he spent through a dummy political action committee to buy people down in the state capitol. Turns out he was a big contributor to the Governor. It was just before the mid-term election campaign kicked into high gear and if the story had broken, you'd have a lot of different names in the state legislature today. Senator Froggybottom contacted me and I was able to work things out

63

so a lot of the pollies' names never came up. The senator was happy and the Governor was happy. I got paid a bundle. Old Froggybottom became the Gov's best friend and Mr. Rice Farmer went to jail. This is the kind of thing I do for the good senator.'

Foley, staring into his empty cup, nodded. 'Well, I suppose I'm doing about the same thing, only for a private investigator's office down in the City. It's only a part time position. I'm not even listed as a member of the organization. Really, I'm just a glorified gofer. I figured with my background of getting fired from the sheriff's department, I'd never get past a background check so didn't worry about getting a license.' Looking up, he asked how his former partner had gotten around the no license problem.

'Simple case of the power of a state senator. But I'm not licensed, either, other than a driver's license and a concealed firearm permit. My income tax return states I'm a freelance photographer. Don't need a license for freelancing.'

'So, all this time you've been up in the northern part of the state?'

'Yeah. I don't think I'd be happy anywhere else. And you've been down there in Frisco?'

'Uh huh. I like the deal I've got. Work a couple days a week, don't bother going in when I don't feel like it and the old man pays me for when I do.' It was Foley's turn to chuckle. 'A few of the things I've done are, as you say, things he or any of his staff can't be seen doing. Mostly though, they're just the small stuff the licensed agents don't want to be bothered with.'

'But not illegal things.'

'No. I have to admit some of them skate pretty close to the law, though.'

Over second cups, the two men sat silently.

'And here you are,' said Foley finally, 'saying it's been too long since we've gotten together and by the way, I could use your help.' Steve nodded. 'My help doing what exactly?'

'You know the forests up in Humboldt County almost as well as I do. There's going to be a push to eradicate the dope farms up there. The culture of marijuana growing is still illegal, you know. And as you're also aware, it's too big an area for me to map it all. I thought you might be the person to call to help.'

Foley had to smile. 'You want me to help you map out the illegal dope growing places? The two of us? The pair who got canned for growing the stuff ourselves? You're kidding. This has got to be the biggest joke of the year, right?'

'No. The senator's Chief of Staff, a guy named Raymond Green, and Sheriff Millard had a talk. Everything relating to our little episode has been erased. It's gone. You want a PI license? File for it and it's yours. No black marks on your history. None.'

'OK, why are they using men to map out the grows? Times, as they say, are changing. Medical marijuana is legal most parts of the state and I'll bet it won't be long before recreational use is made legal, too. Anyway, I thought heat seeking or infrared thermal imaging equipment was used by the drug cops in their high-priced helicopters.'

Steve chuckled again. 'Yeah. The voters are sure to approve to make recreational use legal in the state, even if the federal laws say different. And there are some high tech searching methods being used. There's one story going around about how the Department of Environmental Administration and the US Forest Service went together to buy a couple pilotless camera-equipped aircraft. Drones. The idea was the drones could fly over a suspected area taking pictures and pinpoint fields before sending their agents in. And according to the press reports, they're quite successful. Huge plantations have been found with tons of plants ripped up and burned. But things are mostly different up in the forests. Smart people space their plants out, not in any pattern, keeping them under trees or in natural piles of brush. Having knowledge of how it's done is where I come in. On top of it all, the illegal aspect is choice for the politicians. Those people who have to prove their worth to the voters like the idea of being photographed next to a bunch of uniformed cops burning a huge pile of the evil weed. No, the thing to keep in mind is I've been given enough money to hire half a dozen or so men to go hiking in the forest. We'll be carrying GPS receivers. What we'll be looking for are the big grows hidden in the trees. The major plantations.'

'And then the choppers will drop the agents and make the arrests.'

'Yeah, I guess. What Senator Froggybottom wants is for everyone to know how hard he's been working on getting this done right.'

'Hmm. Well, partner, I don't know. As noted, I'm out of the lawman business. Thank you. Anyway, I'm right in the middle of something I can't easily put aside. Not for another week or so. And even then, I don't know.'

He hesitated then looked up. 'Say, do you remember way back in the day a guy named Freddie something or another? Remember? We ran into him on what could have been a drunk walking charge. Big guy, bushy beard covering half his face. Bring back any memories?'

'Uh huh,' said Steve after a moment. 'I do remember the guy. Yeah, we picked him up on a drunk charge and then let him go. As I recall, he gave us some information we could move on and we let him go before making a good arrest. Yeah. What about him?'

'Oh, nothing much. I was just thinking about him. And a couple other jokers we used to run into. All suspected involved with growing dope. And here you are asking me to go back up into country where these kinds of things happen. Man, I don't need such excitement. I'm very comfortable here in the city.'

Tichneor lowered his head, thinking. 'Look,' he said after a long minute, 'nobody knows the back country like you and me. So, we take it nice and easy, just a couple guys backpacking in the wilderness. Take a long look at the topo maps and it cuts down on the probable sites. Man, it'll be just like old times, you and me.'

'Yeah, you, me and whoever is out there protecting the big man's grow.'

Steve wasn't listening. 'And don't forget the sweetener, there's a big payday for the trip.'

Now it was Foley who suddenly had another thought. Something he'd just said about the big man's grow. The Ralstons. Maybe there was a way to pay back Anton for the beating.

Foley smiled, thinking there just might be something in this for him after all.

'What's your time frame on this plan?' he asked. 'Now remember, I'm not entirely sold on the idea. I still think there's a couple things about it I'm not comfortable with. Anyway, is it a waste of time? To be honest, anything we do won't actually eliminate anything, will it? You know as well as I do, dope growing has been the biggest unofficial agricultural money-maker for northern California and southern Oregon for decades. Since the early 1970s at least.'

'Yeah,' said Steve, wanting everything to be clear, 'but what does it matter? I mean, really. And if you'll remember, we did our little bit after being sworn in as Deputy Dawgs. But getting rid of dope growers isn't what this is all about. This, old son, is politics. Pure and simple. There's a big Statewide election coming, don't forget. Half the senate is up, just as the Governor.

Being part of a well organized and productive drug eradication effort is a sure fire way to get back in office.'

'OK, but again I have to point out; I'm out of the lawman business.'

'I heard you. What was it you've got yourself involved in, something for another week or ten days? No problem. We can work with your job, whatever it is. Here,' he said, laying a business card on the table, 'this has my home phone and cell numbers on it. If I'm not in, leave a message and I'll get back to you. Man, it'd be great, just you and me, partners again.'

Foley laughed at the thought. 'It is a little ironic, when you think of it.'

He chuckled more to himself. If things could be done right, the irony might be used to bring to an end Hubert Ralston and his two bully friends. Ah, the sweet smell of revenge. He'd have to give some serious thought about whether to give old Steverino a call or not.

Later, after Steve drove his mud streaked SUV down the street, Brad sat for a time out on the porch in the rocking chair, chuckling to himself, sipping a small single malt.

When the two men had been deputies up in Humboldt County was when they found a reason to dislike the Ralston family, especially the son. Yes, Brad remembered, H. Fredrick Ralston. The grandson of a pioneering lumber family, and the son, Hubert Ralston, a grand son of a bitch. Where Steve had grown a few pot plants in the shade of the grape vines, Hubert Ralston was producing hundreds of pounds of high-grade dope from back in the Ralston-owned forests. Unlike Brad and Steve, who got caught and fired, when the state police helicopter armed with infrared sensors turned up the Ralston grow, the son didn't get fired. He didn't even get a black mark against his name. The power of money worked every time.

Chapter 16

WHEN HE PUSHED through the office door the next morning, he wasn't a bit surprised to find Gretchen already there, standing beside Leonie Weem's desk, the two laughing at something. Seeing him, Mrs. Weems instantly got serious and picked up the phone and notified her boss. Gorman didn't keep them waiting and Mrs. Weems even got out from behind her desk to open the old man's office door.

'Come in, come in.' Once again, Gorman was happier than Foley thought was natural. 'I was hoping to hear how things are going today. Tell me, have you some good news I can pass on to Henry?'

Brad Foley waited a beat to see if his partner would answer. She didn't.

'No,' he said finally. 'Fact is, what news we have is what we want to talk to you about. We're not sure what more we can do with this to make your friend happy.'

'Umm, well, pull up a chair and bring me up to date.'

Starting from when they met with Steiner, they told their boss everything, ending with their talk with Emma.

'The bottom line,' Foley said, lifting his hands to show how empty they were, 'is we don't have any more places to go. We've talked to everyone we could turn up and, well, we've about run out of anything that even looks like it might lead someplace.'

Gorman turned in his desk chair to stare out of the big window overlooking the street below, pursing his lips in thought.

After a long moment of contemplation, he swung back to face the pair. 'It appears the only possible link between the dead girl and her client is the fellow operating her website. Cyber-prostitution. Whoever heard of such a thing? Well, are you sure he told you everything he knows pertaining to the Steiner girl?'

Foley nodded. 'Yeah. There really wasn't very much. His connection is only through the websites. The way he has it set up, he has no contact with his customers or their customers. The only ones familiar with them are the girls themselves. From what he told us, Anne Marie and Emma only worked with each other once or twice.'

'How about the man he said beat up on one of his girls?' Gretchen asked. 'You know, back when he had a few of them working the streets. Didn't he say one of his girls at the time was Steiner's daughter? What about the man who Cochrane claimed beat up on one of them?'

'Oh, yeah,' said Foley, 'a weird name, uh, Cochrane said it was a bad street pimp called Fishbone Frank. Gawd, where do they get these names?'

Gorman sat with his arms flat on his desk, his fingers laced.

'Fishbone Frank,' he said, frowning, thinking. 'I seem to recall someone named Fishbone Frank. Yes. I think his real name was Frank Fishborne. Uh huh. He was around town, oh, some time ago. Let me make a call.'

Picking up his phone, without looking up a number, he dialed.

'Tolly Mane, please,' he said after a minute. 'Tell him it's Frannie Gorman.'

Foley and Gretchen looked quickly at each other before turning back to see if Gorman had caught them. Frannie Gorman?

'Hey there, Tolly. Sorry to bother you. Know you're a very busy man. But I'm looking for news on a guy I remember used to work for you. Name of Fishbone Frank.'

Gorman sat, staring unseeing at the far wall. 'No,' he said into the phone, then smiled. 'Nothing to worry you, Tolly. No. The name came up in something a couple of my people are looking into.' Pause. 'No, it has nothing to do with you or your businesses. Seems this Fishbone was charged with beating on one of his girls half a dozen years ago or so. Well, the girl turned up dead recently.' Another pause. 'Well, I don't see how they would. What we're really looking into is another matter entirely. Something the dead girl is only remotely connected with.' Gorman nodded slowly in agreement to something he was hearing. 'Yeah, I thought so. Fishborne. I thought so. And you say he's dead?' Glancing quickly at Foley, he smiled coldly and went on talking into the phone. 'No, I don't think I heard anything about it. And to be honest, Tolly, I don't want to know any more. Sounds more like something for you and your priest to worry about.' The old man nodded. 'Well, you know what they say, confession is good for the soul.' Nodding again, his smile grew. 'OK, and I thank you. Yeah, we'll have to get together. Soon. Meanwhile, stay outa trouble.'

Hanging up, he swung the chair around to face Foley and Gretchen.

'OK. It's like this. Tolly Mane runs things. All kinds of things. Over the years, he's been involved with most of the drugs, girls and loan sharking going on around the Bay Area. Tolly and I go way back. Hell, we grew up together down around the Navy shipyards at Hunter's Point. This goes way back. You know, right after the end of the war. Man, those were the days. It's mostly a black neighborhood now. Back then it was Italian. But nothing's really changed. About a quarter of all the murders in the City last year happened down there.'

Foley thought he sounded nostalgic.

'Anyway, Tolly says this Fishborne had a string of girls working south of Market Street until he disappeared. Nobody knows where he went and nobody cares. The man had a bad reputation for damaging his girls. Tolly says he liked it too much. This happened four, five years ago. Now, I can only guess, but knowing Tolly as I do, I'd say he saw Fishborne as a detriment to the business. Wouldn't surprise me if Fishbone didn't become fish food.'

Gretchen scowled. 'Ugh. Is this the kind of people you have to deal with?'

'Get used to it.' Gorman chuckled. 'We're in the business of people who do bad things to other people. Doesn't mean the Sunday church-going group. At least not often. No, our business is dealing with the other ones, those who bend and at times break the law. Now, as far as Fishborne goes, I'd say he's out of the frame for the Steiner girl, wouldn't you?'

The news really didn't help. Only left more questions hanging than answers. Foley had the feeling they were losing the race.

Foley had to nod. 'So, now where do we go?'

Gorman pursed his lips, frowned and shook his head. 'Well, I'd say you two have gone as far as you can go. It sounds as if you've done everything you can do. It'll just have to be enough for Henry. OK, write up what you've found, and, uh, maybe clean it up a little. Something I can take to him. Anything more will have to be left up to the police—'

He was interrupted by the soft buzz of his desk phone.

'Yes?' he mumbled. 'Oh, OK, send him in.' Glancing at the two sitting across the desk, he smiled. 'We've got company. This may not be finished after all.'

'Ah, Chief Sands,' Gorman greeted the newcomer, moving out from behind the desk and holding out a hand. 'How good of you to drop by. I don't believe you've met two of my better staff members, Gretchen Bongiorno and Brad Foley. Ms. Bongiorno, Brad, this is the Chief of Police, Arnold Sands. Please, please, pull up a chair and tell us what we can do for San Francisco's finest cop.'

'Thanks,' said the man. Sands was about the same age as Gorman, the wrinkles on his face and hanging jowls a good indicator. Short, Foley thought, he probably topped out at about five and a half feet. Well dressed, just as with Gorman, Sands's suit was the cut-to-measure kind. A light weight wool, by the looks of it. There was no badge or other indication of the man's profession showing.

'Look, Frannie, this isn't a social call. I'm here to ask you, and your best people,' he glanced sideways at Gretchen and Foley, 'for a favor. It'd be best if you were to stay away from the Steiner thing. It's about to grow into something important, at least to the wrong people down at City Hall.'

Gorman settled himself in his chair. 'What is City Hall's interest in an unnamed dead girl known to be a street worker?'

'Ah, well,' said the police chief, grimacing. 'you have to remember, this is an election year. And as it turns out, our dear mayor and his partner, the president of the Board of Supervisors, are both up for re-election. And both are looking for something positive to lay claim to. Looking to be strong on crime is a sure-fire way to get the voters to think they're the cat's PJ's. When it's reported not one but two prostitutes are found murdered, it allows the powers that be to point the finger at local organized crime.'

'Wait a minute, Arnie,' Gorman held up a hand, 'are you saying there's been another girl killed?'

'Uh huh. Exactly. This is what has changed since the last time we talked. And what brings me here now.' Glancing over at Gretchen and Foley again, he nodded. 'If you two were to get caught sticking your nose in now and maybe getting either in the way of or in front of the investigative bureau, it'd look especially bad. Mr. Mayor and Ms Board President can't have it. They cannot allow anything or anyone to make the bureau appear incompetent. Can't have our fearless leaders appear to the public as if they aren't in complete control, can we? No. So I'm here to tell you to go look at something else. Preferably somewhere else.'

Gorman smiled and nodded his agreement. 'You can count on us, Arnie. Now, what's this about a second woman being killed? Does she have a name?'

'Yes. She's been identified as one Sophie Grant. Is the name familiar to either of you?' he asked, still looking at the two investigators. Foley slowly shook his head and glanced at Gretchen to see she was doing the same.

'Well.' The Chief of Police nodded. 'I didn't think we'd be so lucky.'

Gorman decided not to give anyone time to go on with this line of thought. 'What can you tell us about this latest murder?' he asked, carefully not looking at either of his two employees.

'Nothing much to tell. Strikingly beautiful. Slender and, well, every man's dream of a body. That body was found about midnight last night, up in the trees on the little hill in the back of Lafayette Park. It was spotted half hidden in the brush by two lovers looking for a place to spread their blanket. They had a cell and called 911. No knife was found but the medical examiner says the wounds are the same as with the Steiner woman, some kind of big bladed knife. Very sharp. My people door-knocked the neighborhood this morning but nobody saw anything or paid any attention to non-residents' cars parked along there. No more than usual anyway. The park appears to be a favorite place for couples to, well, couple. We get a call every so often from the neighbors complaining.'

'How did you identify her so quickly?' Gorman asked. 'If she was found about midnight, what, about nine, no, more like ten hours ago. Pretty fast for a fingerprint check.'

'Well, as I said, the mayor's office is pushing this one. But it wasn't from her prints. No. It was her boobs.'

Gretchen reacted. 'Her, uh, breasts?'

'Yeah. She had had breast enhancements. A couple of the stab wounds cut through one breast. When the medical examiner noticed it, he made sure the first thing the pathologist did when he got her on the table was to remove the damaged implant. By law, each silicone breast implant must carry an imprinted serial number. First thing I did this morning was make a few phone calls. That's how we got her name so quick.'

'And you think it was the same guy as the killer of the Steiner girl?' asked Foley, hoping to keep him talking.

'Yeah. Multiple knife wounds to the chest. The medical examiner took one look and said it was likely the knife was the same one. At least, from a preliminary inspection, the wounds were nearly identical in size and shape of blade found in the first woman's body. We'll know more in a few hours. The mayor is really watching this one.'

'OK, Arnie,' said Gorman, smiling and looking satisfied. 'Thanks for the information and you can relax. We'll stay out of your way.'

'I appreciate it. Having crimes like these to investigate will take enough of our effort. We certainly don't want to have a lot of unnecessary pressure coming from higher up.'

Shaking hands all around, the police chief went out, closing the door behind him.

'So what do we do now, Mr. Gorman?' Gretchen asked when they were alone again. 'Write up our report and go onto other things?'

Gorman glanced at Foley. 'No, I think what we should do is take a look at the scene. Maybe do a little more digging. It seems to me our job is to continue gathering information about Miss Anne Marie Steiner's actions, not of the other woman. Just possibly there's a link between the death of the two women. I wonder, do you think this new girl could have been part of the same system as the Steiner girl?'

'Well, we could check with Mr. Cochrane,' Gretchen said, 'but what about staying out of the police department's way?'

'Well, Miss Gretchen Bongiorno, I agree, we must take seriously the police order. However, if you continue to question people and the police take umbrage, you could possibly appease them by giving them this man Cochrane. Possibly that might result in something.' Glancing at the young woman, he smiled coldly. 'Anyhow, this is a good time for our friend here, Mr. Foley, to show you how getting around the police is done.'

Foley shook his head, remembering back when he had to juggle things, trying to gather enough evidence to put someone away while keeping the media or City Hall at arm's length. People didn't seem to realize the trouble they caused, getting in the way. With the reporters, the problem was he understood and often found them helpful. Just doing our job, they'd tell him. But much of an investigation had to be kept quiet and not give anything away. A hard thing to do sometimes. And now he had to teach his new partner how it's done? Impossible.

Staying out of sight of the official investigators and still get the right people to answer questions wouldn't be easy. As it turned out, the cops were already too close.

Chapter 17

STARING AT HIMSELF in the mirror while brushing his teeth the next morning, Brad thought about the visit from his former partner. He and Steve had formed, as most cops do when sharing the typical dangers of their profession as well as a patrol car, some very close ties. When the end came and they chose different directions, it had, for a time, been damn hard. His lips, with a little dribble of toothpaste on one side, curved in a slight smile around the toothbrush as he remembered those days. Not having someone to talk to about what was happening, he had taken to having long, silent conversations with himself. The more he drank, the more in depth the dialogue. Those silent talks ended when he stopped overdoing the drinking.

Until now. Gazing fixedly, toothpaste dribble forgotten, he realized it was starting again. He really missed the man's company.

Hearing the ringtone from his cell, Foley wiped his lips and went looking for the instrument, finally finding it in the kitchen, on top of the refrigerator.

'Yeah?' he barked, thinking it was too early to be nice and friendly to anyone. That was another memory. Steve's habit of always pasting a big smile on his mug whenever talking on a phone. The man firmly believed no matter how crappy he felt, whoever was on the other end would only hear the smile. Brad didn't believe it mattered.

'Are you out of bed yet?' He recognized Gretchen's voice. 'Or is this another sleep-in morning?'

'No, damn it, I'm up. Have been for hours. Just waiting for someone to call and kick-start my morning. Is this call rattling my cage to make sure I get over to the City before the sun has a chance to burn off the morning fog?'

'Nope. Just wanted to prepare you. I've just been told another woman's body has been found. She had been stabbed.'

He was silent for a moment. 'A third woman? Emma?'

'No. It's news of Sophie Grant's murder coming from a different source.'

'What the hell are you talking about? What "different source"?'

'I've got a friend,' said Gretchen, starting to sound as if speaking to a juvenile. 'Remember Danny Pan? The cop we talked to the other day? He's got the hots for me, thinks I'm cute. He'd called yesterday afternoon while we were talking to Emma. He left a message on voice mail. He wanted to take me to breakfast. So this morning I met him at Caffe Roma. About halfway through his ham and eggs, he mentioned a case he was working on. I thought he was simply bragging, you know? Like men do to impress the simple minded woman? Anyway, all he'd say was a woman's body was found, been stabbed.'

'And you think he was hinting around about Sophie Grant?'

'I don't know for sure, but I think it's likely. I mean, how many women get stabbed in this city? Are you coming in some time this morning?'

'Of course. I'll stop and get something to eat and be in the office in an hour or so. Early enough for you?'

The sarcasm went right past her. 'By then, I might know more. I asked Danny to call me first chance he had.'

Foley picked up a large coffee and an egg McMuffin from the drive-up window and ate breakfast while crossing the bridge into town, all thoughts of Steve and his "little job" of a search for drugs forgotten.

His new partner didn't have any more news even though her new cop friend, Danny Pan, had called. But, she added, something had changed.

'He wouldn't tell me anything and kind of, umm, well, bristled when I asked.'

'Bristled? Now there's a term I haven't heard in a long time. What exactly did he say?'

'You know what I mean. He sounded defensive. As if my questioning him was out of place. Anyway, he said he wanted to sit down with us. You and me. Had something he wanted to talk to us about. Asked if we would be here in the office at about eleven. Do you have anything planned for this morning?'

'Not a thing. Until you called this morning, all I was thinking about doing was how to puff up our reports for Gorman and try to see if we could add anything to make it sound like we'd really done everything we could.'

'Well then, let's do it anyway. Maybe by working on the reports, we can turn up something we missed before.'

'Uh huh. Fine by me. I think I'll start by going out and getting a real breakfast. C'mon, I'll treat you.'

'You mean you'll put it on the expense account.'

'Hey, it's all part of my mentoring you, making you a better PI.'

She didn't dignify his comment.

Foley's second breakfast was more filling, a Spanish omelet with toast and coffee. Gretchen ordered a cup of tea and sat and watched him eat.

'You never did come clean on why you were limping the other day.'

Having just taken a mouthful of food, he had time to decide what to tell her.

'Some old friends came by the house. They got a little rough and not getting what they came after, they got rougher. It's nothing to do with what we're doing. It all comes from before I moved to the Bay Area.'

'Mrs. Weems said you were in law enforcement but now you're not. What's that all about?'

'Nothing. Just as she told you; once I was in law enforcement and now I'm not. Let it rest, OK?'

'And so you don't have a PI's license?'

'No. I don't have a license because I don't want one. You got yours as part of your personal education. Didn't you say you plan on going on to get a law degree? Well, I've had enough of law. My working for DII is part time, extra money. Nothing more. I like keeping my options open. If I get antsy and want a change, I can just do it. I like the freedom and want things to stay just so. Now, enough questions.'

'If I'm your partner then don't you think I should know what kind of guy you are?'

'Don't go getting big ideas. We're partners on this one thing only because Gorman wanted someone to be able to keep him informed of what I'm doing. Plus it gets you out of everybody's hair while he figures out what kind of worker bee you are. Now, let me eat in peace, please.'

She didn't have time to pout; before she could try to continue the conversation, the two city cops came into the café, heading right for their table.

'They said over at your office you'd be here,' said Mazzucco, pulling out a chair and sitting down. Foley saw how Pan moved his chair so he was directly across from Gretchen.

'Good morning, officers,' he said, trying not to smile, 'why don't you join us?'

'Yeah, we have. Look, we don't have time for small talk. It's like this. Another dead girl has turned up,' said Mazzucco, then holding up a hand to stop Foley from speaking. 'Don't ask about it. At this stage you don't need to know. Read the newspapers. When they know, you'll know. OK? Here's the message we're here to give you. Stay a long way away from this. It's now a priority murder investigation and there's no room for a couple amateurs.'

'Priority? What made it important all of a sudden?'

'You two. Assistant Chief Lynch got the message from upstairs. With two women getting killed in the same manner, and both believed to be hookers, the top brass are afraid it's the first of many, a serial killer out there. The pressure is on and you're out.'

Foley nodded slowly. 'Does this mean your partner won't be staring daggers at my partner anymore?'

Officer Pan tore his eyes off Gretchen and shot Foley a look. 'Fuck you, Jack,' he snarled.

Mazzucco chuckled and pushing back, stood up. 'C'mon, Danny Pan, we got some patrol work to do.' Without looking to see if his partner was behind him, he strode out of the place.

'You weren't nice,' said Gretchen quietly.

'What was his beef? The stare you were getting was dark as sin.'

'He's upset because I won't go out with him. He asked me this morning and I told him I was already involved. Now I think he's pissed because he told me something out of school. Hinting about the second stabbing.'

'So, the second body saved the morning for you?'

'Don't be cruel. He's probably a nice enough man but I don't want to get mixed up with a cop.'

'Who's this guy you're involved with?'

'There isn't anyone. I just said there was to make him back off. Now, what are we going to do about these two women's deaths?'

'I don't see anything's changed. Chief Sands says back off, we talked with the cyber-cockman and warned Emma. Would it do any good to go have another talk with our resident internet pimp? I don't see how.'

'But what about our being told to back off?'

'Yeah. Can't forget the warning. Coming from both high and low. But we know something the cops don't. Actually, we know a couple things they don't; our friend King Cock and Emma.'

'So?'

'So I figure we can work with those two and the cops won't know about it.'

'What? I don't know. I don't care about your friendly pimp, but couldn't going back to Emma put her in more danger? Anyway, we'll really get in trouble if those two officers find out we're still on the case.'

'Naw, you heard the big guy. They've been sent back to patrol. The idea of a serial killer pushed the case up to the investigation bureau. And those guys don't know we exist.'

'I hope you're right.'

'So do I, lady, so do I.'

Chapter 18

Rex Cochrane's frown was deep enough to hide small cars in when he answered the door.

'What the hell, you said I'd seen the last of you two. Why are you back bothering me?'

'Simple,' Foley said, pushing by him and into the room. 'There's been another young woman found stabbed to death. We're wondering if she's another of your friends who used to work for you back when you were working on the street. This new death makes us have a couple new questions.' Holding his hands out, palms up, he smiled. 'Be satisfied it's us here, getting into your face and not the local police.'

'Another...' he started to say but stopped. 'Oh, shit. Not another of mine, for God's sake.'

'The latest has been identified as Sophie Grant. Did you set up a website for her too?'

'Sophie? Ah, God. Yeah, she was one of the best.'

Cochrane folded into his chair, his face white.

This was, Foley thought, going to be easy. 'Well, if we know about the tie-in between you and these girls, you can bet it won't be long before the cops are coming to talk to you. So you better have your story straight. Practice by telling us what we want to know and this time, leave out the bullshit.'

'C'mon, man,' Cochrane said, holding his hands up, 'I didn't lie to you before.'

Gretchen slipped in and settled in the same chair she'd sat in before. Foley, hands on his hips, glaring, stood facing the man slumped behind his desk.

'I think you did,' he said, his words clipped and hard. 'Maybe you didn't lie exactly, but you sure as hell didn't tell us everything. Holding back isn't going to work when the cops come busting in. You, more than anyone, should know what their view of pimping is.'

'Hey ...' Cochrane started to say before Foley, using his hardest tone of voice gritted out the words, 'No more bull, buddy. We heard all about it so tell us the truth.'

Cochrane slumped even deeper in his chair, shaking his head. Foley didn't let up. 'The big cop, Mazzucco, he said he remembered the girl 'cause he'd fallen in lust with her five or six years ago. He knew who she was, remembered her name. Same as he knew yours. So go ahead, tell us why everybody's lying to us or only telling us the headlines. It's the full story we're after. Now, this new dead girl, we're told she was everybody's dream girl. So, I ask again, what are some of the names of men who would be on both the dead women's client list?'

'I don't know,' said Cochrane, sounding distressed. 'Look, the way things are set up, the girls' clients aren't part of their sites. It should make sense even to you. Why do you keep coming back, asking for something I wouldn't know?'

'Because we don't believe you. The next people we talk to will probably be detectives from the investigative bureau and they aren't going to believe you, either. So, talk. Tell us about these two dead girls. They were yours back when you were King Cock, weren't they?'

'Oh, shit. Yes,' said the tall man. 'Yeah. Anne Marie, Emma and Sophie were just young girls when I found them on the street—'

'Wait a minute,' Gretchen cut in, 'didn't you tell us Anne Marie introduced Emma to you? Now are you telling us she was one of your original group of girls? And the other one was Sophie Grant?'

'Uh, yeah. I didn't know what you wanted when I talked to you before.'

Foley snorted. 'More bullshit you tried to feed us. Go on, let's see what else you've got to say. Be careful though, I've got my bullshit meter running and if we're not happy with your story this time, it's straight to the Hall of Justice we go.'

'Aw, c'mon. I told you those things—' he started but stopped when Foley held up a hand.

'Cut to the chase.'

'OK, OK. Look, when I met the girls, it was a long time ago. Hell, I don't think Emma was old enough to have a driver's license and the other two, well, if they were out of their teens, I'd be surprised. I found them walking the street and not knowing the danger. They had no idea the area they were trying to work belonged to other girls, girls with big, bad pimps.'

He stopped talking for a minute, as if catching his breath. 'They were together. I bought them coffee and explained how the system worked. Once they understood, they asked if I would look after them. Man, it was like manna from heaven. Things went along for a while. I found them an apartment and, well, took care of them. It was damn good for all of us until Fishbone Frank beat on Sophie.'

Foley didn't take his eyes off Cochrane. 'And now you're telling us there were three girls in this together. Tell us more about Sophie. Were they still close when they decided to go down to LA?' Cochrane nodded. 'OK. Tell us what happened. We want to hear about after they came back from the Los Angeles area.'

'There's not much to tell. I already had my website up and running. I got a phone call from one of them and, well, that was when we started. It wasn't long before they had their sites up and were back in business. Sophie isn't much older than Anne Marie or Emma but she was like an older sister to them. Well, like Anne Marie and Emma, Sophie has something special. A great appearance, good body and she's intelligent. They're all the kind of young women older men, men with money, like to be seen with and spend time with. Sophie Grant is tall; I guess I should say, was tall, with a willowy shape, dresses well and looks good in clothes.' He was having a hard time keeping his tenses straight. 'I always thought she could have been a model. There's not much else I can tell you.'

'What did she do when she wasn't working as an escort?'

'How would I know? Look, all I know about the girls, any of them, is they pay my bill on time and like me to update their sites every so often. That's all.'

'This,' said Foley after a long pause, glancing at Gretchen, 'doesn't really get us anywhere closer to knowing who killed them.'

Gretchen nodded. 'No, and now the police are concerned it might be the first work of a serial killer. Could it mean the killer is someone who doesn't have anything to do with Anne Marie? Just some weirdo? A creep who likes to murder prostitutes?'

Foley nodded. 'Hmm, yeah, I suppose it could be.' Looking back at Cochrane, he smiled coldly. 'Which brings us back to you. Face it, two beauties are stabbed to death. You are the main person linking them together. You and your websites. Now I wonder what the police will say if they learn about you.'

'Hey, now wait a minute. Yeah, I've been doing business with all three of these girls since they came back from LA. But I didn't have anything to do with them getting killed. Why would I? They are some of my best clients.'

'You know, Brad,' said Gretchen slowly, 'say it isn't a sicko out killing prostitutes but there is something we don't know tying those two women together. You could be right. Far as we know, the something could be Mr. Computer Pimp, here. But it could be something totally different. Something we don't know about.'

Foley nodded. 'Yeah, maybe. But that brings up another question … do you think Emma is in danger?'

This was a question Foley didn't want to think about. Of course the young artist was in danger. Two of her friends and work mates had been killed so why wouldn't she be next?

Giving Cochrane what he hoped was his most evil smile, Foley warned him to be prepared. 'Sooner or later the cops are going to remember you.'

'Oh, God. What'll I do?'

Foley didn't have to ask if Gretchen liked the thought of Cochrane the pimp being worked over by the police.

Chapter 19

Back on the street, Gretchen didn't argue when Foley suggested they hot-foot it over to Emma's to give her the news.

'With two of her friends killed,' he said, lifting a hand and waving down a cab, 'just maybe whoever is behind it has Emma's address. The least we can do is warn her, don't you think?'

Just as with Cochrane, Emma wasn't happy to find the two standing on her doorstep. They had hurried, taking a taxi to the O'Farrell address. Foley was sure his bruises had healed enough the walk wouldn't have caused any trouble but time was of the essence. Or it could be.

They were just going up the three steps to ring the intercom when Gretchen spotted the young woman coming down the street. She was walking with her head down, lugging a big handbag with an even larger colorful canvas bag hanging from her other shoulder.

'You lied,' she said, stopping to glare up at the pair. 'You said you wouldn't bother me anymore.'

'Emma,' said Gretchen quietly, 'we have to talk to you. Look, there's been another stabbing and we're afraid you might be in danger.'

'Me? In danger? Why?'

'Can we go in and talk about this? Trust me, it's for your benefit.'

'Yeah, trust me, I'm from the government and I'm here to help you. Aw, hell,' she said, digging in her oversized handbag for keys. 'C'mon. At least let's get out of the street.'

Inside she dropped the bags on a table and asked if they would like a cup of tea. Foley shook his head but his partner said she'd like a cup.

Emma poured water into a pot and got out cups and spoons. 'I've just spent the last four hours working on a project and I'm mentally whipped. A cup of tea and a sit down is all I'm good for right now.'

Nobody said anything until they were seated with cups in hand.

'OK, now why do you think I'm in danger?'

Foley sat quiet, letting Gretchen do the talking. 'You know a woman named Sophie? We have learned you, she and Anne Marie Steiner have been friends for a number of years.'

'Boy, I'd like to know where you get your information. Yes, we met here in the City a long time ago. When things got too rough, we all moved to the Los Angeles area and, well, worked. Anne Marie wanted to come back up here. I think she wanted to make amends with her father. I met him once. A real jerk whose only claim to fame was his family history. His past, which to hear him tell it, was more important than his daughter. But things aren't much better down there so we decided to move. Now what's this all about?'

From the look on her face, Foley thought she'd probably guessed.

Gretchen was more gentle than Foley had been. 'A woman the police have positively identified as your friend Sophie,' she said softly, 'was found dead, stabbed to death.'

'Oh, no. Not Sophie. She's the most beautiful one of us. The smartest one and the one Annie and I counted on the most. Are you sure?'

'Yes,' said Gretchen still softly, gently. 'It happened last night, late. The police are worried this could be something big starting and are putting a lot of effort into it.'

'But why would this put me in any danger? The three of us really haven't been together very much lately. I told you about the trip Annie and I took up to Seattle, remember? Well, we haven't worked together since then. Oh, she called a couple weeks ago; there was another of her clients wanting to take a trip. I had a series of exams to take. You know, end of the term. I've got the tuition but if I don't make it through the exams, I lose my place at the school. There's a waiting list of people wanting in and, well, I couldn't go with her.'

Foley cut in, frowning. 'Do you think Sophie went?'

'I'm not sure. To tell the truth I've been so busy lately, between my classes and my regular clients, I've barely had time to do anything else.'

'How many clients are there you consider your regulars?'

'Since I've been studying, I've had to cut back. Before I had about a dozen, but now, about half as many. I hated to lose them, the ones I had to drop. Most of them are really nice guys.' She stopped, noticing the look on

Gretchen's face. 'Wait a minute. You don't really understand, do you? You hear me talking about my clients and you think it's like I'm undressing for every Tom, Dick and Henry who calls. It isn't anything like that.'

'Then tell me what it's like,' Gretchen came back, ignoring her partner's frown.

'My website gets nearly a thousand hits a day. Can you believe it, a thousand people going to my site? How long has it been since you had a thousand men wanting to meet you? When I first started with this, I could pick and choose. A lot of the men I meet from there are looking for more than sex. Oh, sure there are some who want to meet at a hotel and we fuck and they go home to Mama or a wife who doesn't like sex anymore. Or whatever. But most of my clients are older, more relaxed about things. They want to have a young, pretty woman on their arm when they go out for dinner or the opera or... Look, these are, for the most part, businessmen. Some are retired. Men who believe they have earned the right to have pleasant company, not some woman with the same kind of aches and pains they have and want nothing more than to talk about them. Yes, Miss Straight-and-Narrow, I'm paid for my services. But the majority of the time, the dates I go on are not about sex, it's about companionship. The older men like to look, or maybe caress, but they don't always want to fuck.'

Foley chuckled. 'I have to ask, when you said you didn't undress for every Dick, was that a pun?'

Neither woman thought his comment funny, neither laughed.

'OK,' Gretchen said finally, putting her cup down, 'so maybe I don't know what your life is really like. All I've got to go on is what I've been taught. And what I see of life hasn't, so far, disproved it. But we're here about something more important. We came to warn you. There could be a serial killer loose. Or it could be someone with a bone to pick with the three of you. We don't know but we thought we should warn you.'

'The thing is, Emma,' said Foley, 'if it isn't a weirdo, it could be someone who is or was a regular customer of Anne Marie and, or, Sophie. And this could mean maybe one of yours, too. See what we're concerned about? Is there any chance of this being the case?'

'No, I can't see how. We never talked about our regulars, never shared them. Well, except for those times we teamed up. And we only did that a few times. Not often. No. And before you ask, I haven't taken on any new people, either. I just don't see how anyone can connect me with Sophie or Anne Marie,' she said, shaking her head side to side.

'Emma,' said Gretchen, 'think about this; we did. If we can, others might also.'

Emma continued to shake her head.

'Well,' said Foley, still smiling but thinking it was time to go, 'we've done all we can do; giving you some warning. I can't see anything more we can accomplish. We'll leave you alone. Please be careful.'

'Thank you for the warning. I really appreciate it. And,' looking at Gretchen, she smiled weakly, 'I'm sorry I got angry. I'm not ... what I do is not the dirty thing society thinks it is. I'm not being taken advantage of. And I do appreciate you're listening to my ranting.'

Showing them to the door, Emma held it open. Halfway through, Foley stopped and turned back. 'By the way, do you know who the man was? The client Anne Marie was trying to find another girl for?'

'No, she didn't say. All she told me was it wouldn't be Seattle this time.'

'Hmm, OK. I guess it's another dead-end. Take care, now.'

Again, more questions than answers. Could there be a weirdo with a big knife getting off cutting beautiful young women? What would motivate a man to do something like that? What kind of man, or woman, would kill just for the sake of killing? Man or woman. Most likely a man, Foley thought. It's well known that nearly all serial killers are men. Mentally shaking his head, Foley opened the outer door for his partner. No wonder, he frowned, men are considered by some women not to be worth spit.

Chapter 20

THE WEATHER HAD turned wet; a change not unexpected to anyone used to San Francisco. Foggy and dreary one moment, wet and drizzly the next.

Walking down from Emma's place, the two found themselves facing a very wet mist. Of course, there wasn't a taxi to be found.

'C'mon. Let's get a coffee and figure out what we do next,' Foley said, taking her arm, directing her quickly across the street to a corner espresso bar.

Foley's order was, according to the menu, a specialty of the café. With a name he couldn't pronounce, he found himself with a cup of rich-smelling, strong-tasting drip coffee fortified with a shot of espresso. Gretchen laughed and delicately sniffed the odor of chamomile tea from the steam coming from her cup.

Neither spoke for a while, sipping their drinks and thinking about what Emma had said.

'So,' said Brad finally, after sipping his concoction, 'the three of them come back to the Bay Area and get involved with the man who had once been their pimp, "Cock" Cochrane.'

'I wish you wouldn't use that stupid nickname,' Gretchen flared. 'It sounds so, oh, I don't know, so coarse. Little boy humor, you know?'

Foley smiled faintly and nodded. 'Anyway, the point is two of the three are dead and quite possibly by the same hand. So what do we do? Share this with our two uniformed friends, Mr. Mazzucco and your boyfriend Danny Pan? Or do we keep our mouths shut? And should we mention Emma, the last of the three Musketeers still alive and well?'

'You know, you sometimes piss me off, you and your smart mouth. Dan Pan is not … oh, never mind. I don't know if we should tell them or not.'

'I agree … I'm going to vote for not,' said Foley, after thinking about it for a moment. 'After all, our job was to find out what we can about Anne Marie Steiner, not do the police's work for them.'

'And this leaves us with what?'

'I'd certainly like to know who Anne Marie's client was.'

'Well, Emma said she didn't know. Plus, she didn't exactly say the other girl, Sophie, had gone to fill out the, what's the term for a threesome?'

'A good time.'

'No, some French word, something like ménage trio.'

'It's ménage à trois. Excuse my French.'

'Have you ever done it? I mean, been with two girls at the same time?'

'Oh, we're getting personal now, are we? To answer your impolite question, yes. Once, a long time ago.'

'It doesn't sound like something fun or enjoyable at all.'

'All I can remember is there were an awful lot of arms and legs and one or the other was always getting in the way. But maybe you should try it, as part of becoming a better, more knowledgeable investigator, I mean.'

'Not likely to happen. Just not my style. OK, let's get back to it. What do we do now, oh great teacher?'

'Like I said, there is just one dead end after another. The police have warned us off, we've talked to everyone who knew either of the two dead girls and learned little. I don't know. You're the licensed private investigator. You should be the one coming up with ideas. Isn't there a text book you can refer to in situations like this?'

'You're being silly. We could go talk to Mr. Gorman. Maybe he has an idea or two.'

'One would be enough. OK, drink up and let's find a cab.'

Back out on the street, Foley stopped, deep in thought. 'I think we should go talk to our favorite pimp again. Somehow there has to be more he can tell us. Maybe something he doesn't even know he knows.' Holding up a hand to stop her, he went on, 'Yeah, I know, it doesn't make sense. But so far about all we learned came from him. Unless we're ready to quit, finish with a couple reports and go on to other things, well, I think we should rattle his tree one more time. Hopefully before the cops do.'

'Wow. What's with you? Oh, I get it, you were once in law enforcement and the bug of fighting crime is kicking in again. Is that it?'

'Maybe. And maybe I'm afraid this knife-wielding killer is going to keep going if someone doesn't do something. And who's in a better place to stop him than us, huh? We're ahead of the cops. Or,' he slowed down, thinking, 'we could simply talk to your friend, Danny Pan, and tell him about Emma. And your other friend King Cock.'

Gretchen shook her head. 'No, I don't want to tell anyone about Emma. She's trying to make a life away from all this. I don't want to screw it up for her.' Frowning and looking down the street, she nodded. 'OK, so we keep digging, is that where you're going?'

Foley smiled. 'Yup. At least take Cochrane over the coals once more. I'd like to know more about Sophie's death but I can't see how. We ask too many questions and the cops know we're hanging around.'

'Understand me, Brad, I've had enough of that Cochrane fellow. As of right now, I'm going along only because I'm afraid for Emma. Do you really think we did enough by warning her?'

'I don't know what else we can do. She's either on the killer's list or she's not. The only thing I can think of doing. Once the cops follow up on whoever her friends and associates were, it might be too late. The best source we're got right now is Cochrane. I doubt we'll get more out of him but it's likely this will be the last chance we've got. C'mon. Let's find a cab.'

The ride didn't take long but it did give Foley time to think.

'You know,' he said, 'even without getting any closer to Sophie, there is one thing we learned.'

'What? Other than being told she was stabbed and probably with the same knife as Anne Marie, what did we learn?'

'No, it's more like we know something about the guy who stabbed her.'

'He's crazy. Is that news?'

'No. What we now know is, both women being stabbed in the chest. It's a good indication they knew and trusted him. Think about it, we have to believe Sophie's circle of girlfriends isn't very large. As a working girl, she'd most likely have more men friends than girlfriends. So the chances are it was a man. OK. Secondly, we have to assume, in many ways, she's a lot like you. Was a lot like you.'

'What do you mean, she's like me?'

'She's a classy lady. Classy ladies don't bonk in the nearest city park. Those girls only travel first class and stay in five-star hotels. Does this sound like someone who'd go for a romp in the bushes?'

'Uh huh. OK, did knowing that move us along in the right direction?

Or in any direction.'

'Maybe. I want another talk with King Cock. There must be a way to find out whose names are in the emails linked to Sophie's website. I seem to remember someone saying unless you toggle a certain place in the email page, in the tools section I think, addresses from messages imported are automatically added to your address book. Maybe there's something there.'

'Do we have to do it today? It's getting late and I do have a life away from Discreet Inquiries, you know.'

'Oh, yes, I remember you saying something about being involved. Got a hot date tonight?'

'No. I don't have a hot date and I only told Danny Pan I did to get him off my back. Don't you tell him, either. Uh huh. No date, but, unlike Sophie, I do have a large circle of girlfriends. One of whom is getting married and a wedding calls for a wedding present. So tonight a couple of us are going shopping.'

'Look out, San Francisco, the girls with plastic are on a spending spree.'

'While we're on the subject, there's something else bugging me. Whenever something is said about Sophie, Anne Marie or any of the street walkers, everyone calls them 'girls.' It's never women or even young women, always girls. Why do you suppose this is? Just men being sexist or what?'

'Umm,' Foley mumbled, trying to come up with an answer. 'I don't know. Somehow it's the way it is with girls who strip or do lap dances, or prostitutes. They're always girls. Guess I never gave it a thought,' he said lamely. 'OK, we'll carry on tomorrow.'

Leaning forward, he gave the cabbie directions to DII's office.

Chapter 21

Driving home was one of his favorite times of day, if he was able to miss the evening traffic. His Chevy seemed to know the way and almost drove itself, giving him an opportunity to daydream, or think of great and wondrous things which might be the same thing. This late afternoon wasn't so fine. His thoughts, for some reason, took him back to his being attacked by Anton and Cully. For sure, he'd have to become a lot more careful about things.

Nobody was waiting for him this time but he approached his little house from a different direction, taking his time driving up, being very cautious.

Home, he glanced at his cell and saw the little envelope icon; someone had sent him a text message. It was from Steve, saying he'd like to stop in tomorrow evening and talk, if Brad was going to be home. He'd left a number but Brad didn't return the call. Maybe it wasn't such a good idea giving his former partner his cell number.

He was in the office the next morning before Leonie Weems, which meant Gorman wasn't in his office, either. Gretchen found him at one of the empty desks, typing up a lengthy report on the previous day's work.

'Good morning, boss.' Her cheery mood was almost more than Foley could handle early in the day. 'What are we doing this fine morning?'

Trying not to sound grumpy, he continued typing, using the two-finger method. 'Don't tell me,' he said, not looking up. 'You just happened to run into an off-duty police officer and he bought you a drink or four last night.'

'You are starting to sound like a record stuck in one place. No. No off-duty policeman. No drinks, one or a dozen, and yes, it is a good morning, even if you're too old and decrepit to be aware of it. Now, as I recall, you

92

thought it might benefit us if we had yet another talk with our leading scumbag. Is having a talk with him still on?'

'Yeah. I can't think of anything else. OK,' he said, sitting back and showing the signs of a fake smile, 'it is a good morning and I'm feeling crappy. Due, I have to admit, to not knowing what else to do about this "little job" old Gorman laid on us. I can't think of a thing. And listening to the radio news, neither can the police. Of course, we all know how bright those radio jocks are.'

The young woman looked good this morning. Dressed for success, he thought. The tails of her polished cotton blouse, so pale pink it almost looked white, were tucked smoothly into the waist of her dark wool skirt which fit snug from the waist to just below the roundness of her bottom before flaring out in a series of pleats. The skirt was short and Foley wasn't sure if what she was wearing under the skirt would be called leggings, pantyhose or what. What he could see was black stockings disappearing up under her slightly lighter colored skirt. Her shoes were black patent leather flats. He remembered someone some time in the past calling them Mary Janes. Foley was never sure whether it was a brand name or what. On Gretchen, they made her feet look small and trim.

With her long hair falling in soft folds around her face, fanning over her shoulders, he had to smile. She looked good. Maybe too good, he thought, then quickly remembering the age listed on her PI license, he frowned, then smiled. Thinking about his new partner, he had to admit it: she sure looked good.

It wasn't far over to Cochrane's Union Street office and Foley felt really good for the first time since getting beat up, but he called for a taxi anyway. He didn't feel like screwing around with early morning traffic. Better, he thought, to put it down on their expense form and make it look like they're really doing something.

'You know,' he said, sitting back in the foul smelling cab, looking out of the side window, 'I doubt if we can make anything of it and I doubt it really matters, but if you marked where our office is, where old man Steiner lives, where Cochrane's office is, they'd all be within a dozen blocks or so of each other.'

A big, brightly colored hand lettered sign taped to the back of the driver's seat read *Thank you for not smoking*. From the odor, some recent passenger hadn't paid any attention.

'You're right, those kinds of thing can't matter,' Gretchen said, cupping her nose and mouth with one hand. Her words sounded muffled. 'Only in novels and movies does someone make such thinking work. It probably happens when the author doesn't have any other clue what to do.'

'Well, neither do we, Ms Sherlock. Neither do we.'

Breathing deeply as they crossed the sidewalk helped, but for Foley, riding up in the little elevator and breathing in the woman's perfume did a better job of clearing the air. Whatever she was wearing, it was effective. He decided when he had the opportunity, he'd better take another look at her, from the viewpoint of the partnership, of course.

The chic hallway with framed prints lining the walls was as quiet as an old fashioned library, the kind with a nasty old spinster ready to 'shhhh' every sound. The deep piled, soft burgundy carpeting probably played a part. Or, Foley thought, maybe nobody was at work behind any of the closed doors.

'Should we knock,' asked Gretchen, stopping in front of room 412, 'or just barge in?'

'If it's unlocked, I'd say barge in. If he wants privacy, let him lock the door.' Foley smiled and turned the brass knob, pushing the door open.

The stench filling his sinuses stopped him cold. All thoughts of sweet perfume vanished, halting him in his tracks.

'Well, are we going in or what?' Gretchen gently pushed against his back.

'No,' he said, pulling a handkerchief from a back pocket and holding it over his nose. 'Wait a minute.'

Not stepping into the room, Foley leaned forward as far as he could to look around the door.

'What are you doing?' she asked, instantly following up with a second question. 'What's that smell? Ugh.'

'Go back down the hall a little and wait. Don't touch anything. Go on,' he ordered when she didn't move.

'Well, you don't have to get huffy.'

Glancing to see she did as he said, Foley leaned into the room again.

He wouldn't have to go in to see what had happened. The curtains had been pulled back, letting in enough morning light, the sun sparkling dully on a big black shadow discoloring the carpet. Foley couldn't see the wound, but what he could make out of Cochrane's body, it wasn't lying naturally asleep. The smell made it clear, a mixture of human wastes and drying blood.

From where he stood, Foley could see someone had made a mess of a few of the servers usually neatly shelved along the wall. A couple of the gray aluminum computers lay scattered on the floor, leaving empty places on the shelves. Multicolored wires hung from where the electronic paraphernalia had been stacked. The big screen computer he remembered seeing on the desk was lying next to the body. The computer screen was cracked, looking like a badly broken window.

Scrubbing the door with his hanky where he had touched it, Foley pulled the door closed and carefully wiped the brass door knob.

'C'mon,' he said, hurrying down the hall, taking Gretchen's arm to hasten her along.

Stopping, she pulled her arm free and with her hands on her hips, turned stubborn. 'No. Not another step until you tell me what's going on.'

'There isn't time for this, not now and not here,' he said angrily, punching the button for the elevator. 'We've got to get as far from here as we can. Now move your pretty little ass.' Grabbing her arm again, he pulled her into the elevator and touched the button marked G. Before leaving, he used his hanky to rub against all the buttons.

The firmness of his actions, or maybe the tone of his voice, stopped her from arguing. Hesitating just long enough to glance up and down the street, she followed him as he hurried down and around the nearest corner.

Neither spoke as they rushed through the sparse morning pedestrian traffic. Finally, after cutting over two blocks, Foley slowed them down, matching the pace of everyone else.

'How about a cup of coffee?' he asked quietly, as if nothing had happened.

'Are you going to explain what happened? Why didn't we go in and talk to Cochrane?'

'Didn't you smell it? Someone beat us to the pimp. Someone let all the blood in King Cock's body escape. He's dead.'

Chapter 22

THE RINGTONE ON Foley's cell played its call before they could cross the street.

'Yeah?' he said abruptly, then listened for a brief moment, grunted a goodbye and put the phone back in his pocket.

'Old man Gorman. Says he wants us back to the office right now. Don't dawdle around, he says.'

'OK, but are you going to tell me about Mr. Cochrane?'

Foley glanced up and down the street. Not seeing a taxi, he motioned and they started walking back down toward Fillmore Street.

'Sure, if you'll tell me why when he was alive and working his pimping website, he was King Cock and now he's dead and suddenly became Mr. Cochrane.'

'I was taught to respect the dead. Tell me what happened to him.'

'Most of his body was on the floor behind his desk so I couldn't see much, but from the amount of blood on the carpet, I'd say he'd been stabbed. Another good indication was the amount of damage someone had done to a couple of the computer servers.'

'What do you mean? What does damaging his servers point to?'

Finally spotting a taxi, Foley stepped out to wave it down. It was a yellow cab, reportedly one of the lowest rated cab companies in the City. Better than walking, he decided, opening the door for Gretchen.

'354 Fillmore, please,' he said before settling back in the seat and answering his partner. 'Think about it, what reason would someone have to want Cochrane dead? Remember, two of the working girls he once pimped for and had set up their websites, keeping them in business, have been stabbed. So I figure the killer was afraid someone would be asking the right questions and coming up with what Anne Marie and Sophie had in common. The same questions we were going to see him about if you remember. The killer got there before we did.'

'Wow. We might have come in on Mr. Cochrane getting killed.'

'Hey, didn't you know, working as a PI could be dangerous? But no, I think he was stabbed last night. The blood wasn't bright red as it'd be if fresh. From what I could see, it was mostly black. No, I was more afraid someone would see us. Sooner or later the cops are going to bring their circus to his up-market office and it'd be a lot better if they can't tie us to him in any way.'

'Yes, I can see that. They wouldn't be happy to find us still involved, would they? I wonder what Mr. Gorman wants?'

'Guess we'll find out in a minute,' said Foley, glancing at the meter and handing the driver a ten dollar bill. 'I'd like a receipt, too,' he said, taking his change. The drive couldn't have been more than a mile but with the city's taxi commission fare schedule, the brief ride cost seven dollars. Frowning his displeasure, he didn't leave the driver a tip.

Upstairs, he held the door for Gretchen, looking over her shoulder at Leonie Weems, hoping she'd give some indication of what was happening. She didn't give anything away, simply waved them toward Gorman's office door.

'You go ahead,' said Gretchen. 'I'll go visit the ladies and catch up in a minute.'

Foley pushed through into Gorman's office. 'Come in,' said the older man, waving him forward. A man dressed in a lawyer's pinstripe three-piece suit sat comfortably in a client's chair, his legs crossed, hands folded on his knee. 'Thank you for responding so quickly,' Gorman went on. 'We've been waiting for you. Come in and pull up a chair.'

Foley didn't like it when the boss of DII tried to be just one of the boys.

'This is Robert Cisterio. He's with the California Attorney General's office and came over, he says, to help our little company out. Mr. Cisterio, Brad Foley. Now, why don't you tell us what we can do for the AG's office.'

'Yes, thank you. As Mr. Gorman said,' he started, speaking, Foley thought, directly to him, 'I'm with the Attorney General's office. As you may, or may not know, the AG's office is not directly involved with licensing private investigators. Such things are a responsibility of the Department of Consumer Affairs, Bureau of Security and Investigative

Services. However, my office received a query from yet another government office asking if we'd see if there were any improprieties going on with a certain case being worked on from this office.'

There was no question; he was aiming his remarks straight at Foley.

'And exactly which case would this be?' asked Gorman.

'According to the information we received, Mr. Foley and another agent from this office, a Miss Bongiorno, have been drawn into the deaths of two young women here in the City, Anne Marie Steiner and Sophie Grant. The local police investigative bureau has, we're told, requested Mr. Foley and Miss Bongiorno cease their activities in this matter. It is, after all, two felony murder investigations. Not something for private investigators to be engaged in.'

Before Francis Gorman or Foley could respond, Cisterio held up a hand. 'Whether you agree with it or not, the fact remains Miss Bongiorno just recently became a state licensed investigator while Mr. Foley is not so authorized.'

Gorman glanced first at Foley and then back at the attorney.

'Your information is only partially correct,' said Gorman, speaking with authority. 'We had been hired to find out what we could about the young woman identified as Ms Steiner. Her father wasn't convinced it was his daughter and at the time, even the police weren't sure of her identity. Ms Bongiorno, assisted by Mr. Foley, had barely started when it became evident the poor woman was only the first of what is apparently a double homicide. It was then Chief Sands asked my office to step away from our search for information concerning Ms. Steiner. I assure you, once the lady became part of the police investigation, we washed our hands of it. As far as Mr. Foley not being licensed, he has been employed by Discreet Inquiries, Incorporated for some time in a non-licensed capacity. With this case, he has acted only as support for Ms Bongiorno, doing only those things as a private citizen; he has every right. Whoever claimed differently has been given erroneous information.'

For the first time Foley liked the man, stilted rebuttal and all.

'Tell me, Mr. uh, Cisterio,' Foley said hesitantly, 'exactly which government office raised this complaint? You said it didn't come from the PI licensing bureau or from the AG's office, so where did it come from?'

'Well,' Cisterio said diffidently, 'I guess it doesn't matter. The query originated in the Governor's office. It's an election year, you know, and elections always means those higher placed incumbents work like the devil to guarantee that nothing goes on that might come back to bite them.'

Standing up and reaching across to shake hands with Gorman, the assistant AG smiled dryly. 'If what Mr. Gorman says is the case, then I'd have to agree this is a little bit of nothing.'

Shaking Foley's hand, he turned to the door just as Gretchen came in. Smiling, he nodded at the young woman and went out, closing the office door behind him.

'OK,' Gorman said when they were alone, 'what the hell's going on? Why would the Governor's office care about your not having a license or about the two of you not stepping away? Did you do something to piss any of Sands's people off? Have you been asking questions and getting in the cops' way? C'mon, gang, talk to me.'

Gretchen glanced to see what Foley had to say.

Foley took the lead. 'That gentleman you almost met, Gretchen,' he explained to the woman, 'came from the Governor's office to warn us away from the Anne Marie and Sophie murders.' Turning back toward their boss, he nodded. 'I don't know about why the state bigwigs would get on our case, and no, we haven't stepped on any toes. We haven't been close to any authority since learning about Sophie Grant's death.'

He didn't look to see if Gretchen reacted to what he'd said but went on answering their boss. 'The only cop we could have pissed off would be Officer Danny Pan after Miss Bongiorno here turned down his request for a date. I hardly think it would be enough for him to notify the AG's office, though.'

Gorman chuckled. 'Oh, you never know, Brad. Being knocked back by someone like our Gretchen might cause a young man to do something idiotic. OK, then,' again being serious, 'let's go on. What can you tell me about this Steiner thing? Is there anything I can take to Henry? Maybe we can get shot of this and let the cops do their job.'

'Well, there is one new wrinkle,' said Foley pursing his lips. 'What were Gretchen and I doing this morning, if someone should ask?'

'What do you mean, who would be asking?'

'Say, Chief George Sands or one of his people?'

'And why would they be interested in where the two of you were this morning?'

'There's been another killing. I think Rex Cochrane was stabbed, probably sometime last night,' Foley answered, going on to bring Gorman up to date.

Gorman sat quietly while hearing what the two had done. After Foley explained his thoughts on why someone would want Cochrane out of the picture, he turned to look out of his window, steepling his fingers under his chin.

'Whew, this does change things a little, doesn't it? I'm not sure if we shouldn't do as the state lawyer said; let the police figure it out. What do you think, Gretchen?'

'Don't ask me. I thought we should have walked away when the police department warned us off. If we'd done it then, maybe Mr. Cochrane would still be alive today.'

'Not likely, Ms licensed-PI,' Foley argued. 'Cochrane was killed and his servers broken because someone knew he was a link to the two dead girls … women. Someone wanted to make sure any investigation didn't lead back to them. I believe Cochrane was killed for the same reason the girls were killed. And I'll put even money on his death being caused by a big bladed knife.'

No one had anything to say. Gorman glanced up at Foley after a moment. 'What do you think the chances are the killer isn't thinking possibly of your involvement?'

Gretchen gasped and Foley nodded. It had already crossed his mind.

Not to make his partner feel better, but to clear his own thoughts, Foley shook his head. 'I can't see it. If we had learned something, anything, we'd have gone to the police. No, I think someone killed two young women, two working high priced escorts. The only reason making sense was that someone wanted to close their mouths. It's likely our someone merely wanted to ask Cocky the same questions we wanted to ask. And got a little carried away.'

'What exactly did you hope to learn from him?' asked Gorman, looking up from the clasped hands he'd been staring at.

'Well, for one thing, who the girls' last client was. Remember, Emma told us Sophie had called her about going on another trip out of town with some big spender. She didn't want to miss her classes and thought possibly Anne Marie had gone in her place.'

'And you think this guy could be their killer?'

'Dunno. But it's possible. I wonder what led the killer to Cochrane? We first heard about Cochrane from the cops. Did the killer do it the same way? I doubt it. I think he's too careful to get caught asking questions during an investigation. OK, has he been following us?' Glancing toward his partner, he smiled. 'Maybe you're right, Gretch, maybe we did show him the way. Or just as likely, the killer didn't need our help in finding them. It's just as easy to assume he, or she, it could as easily been a woman wielding the knife, knew them both. It's possible this person knows enough about the two girls to know about King Cock's business. What was it called, something eye candy.'

'SF-Eye Candy,' said Gretchen, nodding at what her partner was saying, 'but why would he or she kill Cochrane? Wouldn't he want to know more about the women the eye candy website serviced?'

'Ummm.' Foley hesitated.

Gorman was keeping quiet, his head moving back and forth between the two as if they were playing tennis. When the young woman had asked for a job, showing her PI license, he hadn't been too sure she could handle it. Sometimes, he knew, it took more than a pretty face or sexy smile to get the job done. From his own experience in the field, he knew it often took strong muscles or a hard head. Now, however, watching the interaction between these two, and listening to the reasoning they were doing, he was changing his mind. Maybe being smart, something he'd never have said he could lay claim to, was enough.

They were ignoring the man sitting behind the cluttered desk.

'Look,' Foley said after a moment of deep thought, 'let's think a minute about this. Prostitution as a money maker is right up there with drugs, right? OK, so let's say someone, someone like the big shot crime boss Mr. Gorman called yesterday, uh, Mane, Tolly Mane. Isn't he supposed to be mixed up with the drugs, prostitution and everything else? Now, say he or one of his underlings sees how this internet pimping is paying off. Mane wants a part of it. So what does history say happens when a crime lord wants to take over a neighborhood? Someone gets killed. Then if it's necessary, he moves one of his own men into the driver's seat. I think the murderer was interested in the business. If we wait and watch, see who opens up the King Cock's website, I think we'll know who the killer was—'

'Ah,' Gorman cut in, 'I don't see it. Look, I've known Tolly since we both stole milk bottles off the neighbors' porches. I'll admit he's the king rat in most of the area south of Market Street and it's true he's got fingers in most of the other pies making illegal money in this town. And it's also quite possible there are more than a few gentlemen sitting at the bottom of the bay because they stepped on Tolly's toes. But to destroy two women who are bringing in tons of money just as a tactic to take over the city's e-prostitution game? I don't see it happening. Not at all.'

'I don't know the man,' said Foley slowly, 'but it's reasonable to think someone is trying to get into the game. Makes sense, though, what you say about killing two of the high income producers. By the same token, would he do it by killing the man who put the cyber-prostitution websites together in the first place? Possibly. Whoever cleans up the office and continues with the website is going to have to know a lot about computers and the internet.'

Gretchen nodded in agreement. 'You think there aren't bad guys out on the street that could do the job? I may be holding a new license but even I'm experienced enough to know computer felonies are high on the list of the ever expanding kinds of crimes. Granted, most are non-lethal crimes but there's no reason for anything like crime to change. Especially if there's a lot of money to be made.'

Foley got up from the chair, throwing up his hands. 'Yeah. But remember, these are lethal crimes we're dealing with here. Three murders, to be exact.'

Gorman shook his head. 'Are you sure the death of this man Cochrane is linked to Anne Marie's stabbing? Didn't I hear you say you weren't able to see much of the body lying on the floor of his office? It might not have been him. I think we should wait until we know for sure it was Cochrane before we go mucking through the mud anymore.'

Foley had stepped over to stand with his hands in his pockets, looking down at the street. It was a well-known fact San Francisco had some of the best girl watching along the west coast. Even with all the fashion models and movie actresses down in La-La land, the average street scene in the City once described as Baghdad by the Bay was a voyeur's dream. Watching the short skirts, long skirts and bouncing hair-dos hurrying along the sidewalks down below was entertaining but it didn't stop him from listening and thinking. He turned to look over his shoulder at Gorman's words.

'I'd still like to know how the guy from the state capitol, Cisterio, heard

Gretch and I were working on the stabbing of those girls. Someone here has been keeping someone over in Sacramento informed. Wonder why?'

'Uh huh,' said Gorman, frowning. 'I wondered the same thing. There's a function at City Hall tomorrow evening. I think it's something to do with a restoration project. The drafty old building has been an eyesore since God was a pup but some of the old guard think it should be renovated. Anyway, Henry called and invited me to go along as his guest. I think he wants to know what we've found out without having to ask if we've found anything. He still has a hard time accepting the fact his daughter was a working call girl. So, I'm sure to bump into Chief Sands and maybe I can tweak him a little, find out who on his staff has ties to the state capitol.'

'Yeah. Meanwhile, I think I'll go have a late lunch over at the Caffe Roma. Maybe Gretch's newest boyfriend, Danny Pan, will drop by for a cup of coffee or something.'

'Damn you, Brad Foley,' she came back heatedly, 'Pan is an idiot and is not and could never be on my list of boyfriends. Mr. Gorman, I firmly believe your Mr. Foley is nothing more than a frustrated old man being eaten up with jealousy.'

Gorman snorted. 'Be careful who you call old, young lady. I'll have you know I've got more than a double handful of years on your partner and I don't consider myself old. I'm certain he hasn't been paying any more close attention to you than any other red-blooded man in this office. We're all dreamers, you know.'

'I don't know what you mean,' she sniffed.

Foley, trying to hide his smile and failing, waved a hand at the door. 'C'mon, let's go get a bite to eat. I'll buy.'

'I heard you, Brad,' Gorman called as they went out the office door. 'Your lunch had better not show up on your expense account.'

Chapter 23

OUTSIDE, GRETCHEN CONTINUED to make her case. 'I wish you'd stop with the teasing about Pan. I've known women who took up with cops and not one of them were happy. Cops are the worst people when it comes to non-cop things. They're on the job twenty-four hours a day, ten days a week. I mean all the time.'

Foley thought they probably looked just like a lot of other couples walking down the street, married and arguing about Gawd only knows what. He had no first-hand experience with such things. He'd never come close to getting married, it just never seemed like a good way to live. He had to agree with her, though. Marriage and police work just didn't mix. He'd seen it too often. But what did this young woman know about it? Damn it, he thought savagely, it wasn't fair. Didn't men who wore badges have the same right to happiness other men had? Men like bankers or car salesmen. It looked like wearing a badge was all right when you wanted protection from the baddies but would you want to marry one? No.

'And,' Foley went on teasing the young woman, 'it's your plan to marry some professional man in a less focused profession? Like what for instance?'

They had had to walk up around the block from the office to find a taxi. This time the cab Foley flagged down was a Luxor cab. He held the rear door for her to climb in and for the first time in a long while, didn't have negative thoughts about taking a cab.

'Down by the Hall of Justice, driver,' he ordered, ignoring everything except the ongoing conversation. 'Come on, tell me what kind of man you're looking for in a boyfriend or husband.'

'No certain kind. Right now I want to get my law degree which means I don't want to mess around with dating and all it'll lead to. And

I certainly don't want to get married. But if I were looking for Mr. Right, I definitely don't need your help in making my choice. You may think you're old enough to be my father but, thank heaven, you're not. So leave me alone. Please.'

'All right, all ready. You've made your point. No more teasing.'

Paying the cabbie, he tipped the driver a dollar and pocketed his change, forgetting to ask for a receipt. Deciding as he followed Gretchen through the door and into the Caffe Roma, he would claim this lunch on his expenses, no matter what old man Gorman said.

'Well, Danny Pan, look who just walked in,' Muzzucco's voice barreled out of the bottom of a barrel, 'if it isn't our favorite Sam Spade and his girl Friday. C'mon, there's an extra chair or two here at our table.'

Foley noted the sour glance Gretchen flashed his way but overlooked it and pulled out a chair. 'You know, we were hoping to run into you here. We just had an interesting conversation, one that left us with the feeling we're being had. Maybe you can help us clear up a couple things.'

'Oh, you want our help on one of your big deal cases? What, can't figure out how to focus the camera so the photos through the hotel window will turn out? You do a lot of work with cameras and windows, don't you? And now you want our help? Am I right? You want our experience to help you to catch some poor sucker with his pants down so his long suffering wife gets both cars, the house and a check every month? Do you see, Danny Pan, this is what happens when they take your badge away from you. Skip tracing, process serving and for excitement, catching the foolish philandering husband.'

Foley frowned. 'Who have you been talking to, Muzzucco?' he asked, leaning forward and looking hard at the rotund uniformed man. 'Someone's been telling tales out of school.'

Muzzucco held his hands up in surrender. 'Ah, well,' he said soothingly but letting his smile send a message different than his words. 'You know how it is. People talk. No reason to get all huffy.'

'What are you two talking about?' asked Pan. The younger officer had watched Gretchen, hoping she'd look at him, give him some sign he wasn't being ignored. She wanted to know too, but was making sure she kept her eyes on Foley. Neither of the two men offered to continue with the topic.

'But what did you want our help with? Not anything to do with the girl what got herself stabbed, I hope.'

Foley waited until the waitress came and took their order before answering. When he asked for a cup of coffee instead of the lunch menu, Gretchen followed suit, ordering a pot of Earl Grey tea.

'OK, first things first,' he said, 'this morning, we, Gretchen here and I, were questioned by some suit from the state Attorney General's office. He said he was responding to a complaint from the Governor's office. I tend to believe he was simply someone's errand boy, sent to give us a message. He covered up by asking me if I, working for a private investigator's office but without obtaining a license, were doing things I shouldn't. The AG's man touched on the recent deaths by knife but only vaguely. He knew we had been warned off as it's a full blown murder investigation. Now my question is, who's been talking about us, me specifically, to the state people?'

Muzzucco glanced at his partner and gave a quick head shake. If Foley hadn't been watching, he'd have missed it. The four sat for a long moment silent, waiting for someone to speak. It was Muzzucco who broke the silence.

'And you think it had to come from the department?'

'I know it did. This guy knew things. Things only you guys would know. Things like our being told to leave the murders to the experts. What he was really doing was making sure Discreet Inquiries is not spending any time on doing police work. I had the feeling his comments about my not being licensed was part of the window dressing. Who in your department is popular with the state government over in Sacramento?'

Nobody said anything as the waitress put Foley's coffee in front of him, and placed a small white tea pot, a thin tea cup, a miniature pitcher filled with milk and a sugar bowl on the table for Gretchen.

'There be anything else?' she asked, looking directly at Gretchen, ignoring the men at the table. Gretchen smiled and shook her head. As soon as the tired-looking waitress turned away, Pan took up Foley's question.

'It'd have to be Lynch,' he said before Muzzucco could stop him.

'Shut up, Pan,' the other cop growled. 'You're talking about things you shouldn't be talking about.'

'What, everybody don't know the fool is working at getting a job with the state government? Shit, excuse me, Miss, but bullshit. He's the local spy, Foley. Lynch's got a direct line to some turkey over in Sacramento. Someone working for the Governor—'

'OK,' Muzzucco cut in, scowling at Pan before turning to Foley, 'now what does knowing about Lynch tell you? What good does knowing who it likely was do you? So someone on the Governor's staff gets a tickle you're over here, getting in the way of the police in a murder investigation and you don't have a license to be involved? Is this so bad?'

Foley shook his head. 'Makes me wonder why, though.'

'Ah, hell, I don't know,' the big cop said, looking down at his cup of cold coffee. 'When Lynch got told by the Chief to give you what we had on the Steiner woman, he told us to keep an eye on you two. We thought it was in case you turned over a rock and learned something we'd missed. You know, protecting the department for getting blamed for not doing anything. Now maybe I think Danny Pan is right on the money. There's someone in the Governor's office Lynch is trying to stroke. Everybody knows the assistant chief isn't happy being the assistant anything. Look, we weren't trying to cause you guys trouble. Hell, I didn't even give it a second thought, not after the second girl got killed.'

'Well, I wouldn't worry about it,' said Foley after a pause. 'The state lawyer went away satisfied. No reason he shouldn't. We've stayed out of your way, haven't we?'

Pan glanced sideways at Muzzucco before answering. 'Christ, we wouldn't know. The case was taken by the investigative bureau. Which means if we get anything about it, it'd only be scuttlebutt. Once a uniform passes the test and gets his gold badge, he forgets his old buddies and don't talk to us anymore.'

Muzzucco chuckled, a sound Foley thought like you'd get if you rolled golf balls around in a tin bucket. 'Don't pay any attention to my partner, guys. He's just jealous 'cause he's got another six months before he qualifies for the detective exam. But he's right. We found the first one and it was a uniform got the call on the second one. You think any of those dickheads'll let us know what's happening? Only way we get anything is to read it in the papers.'

Foley glanced at Gretchen, who nodded. 'Well, Gretch,' he said, pushing his empty coffee cup away, 'think it's about time we got back to what we're supposed to be doing? Look,' he said, looking back first at Pan then at Muzzucco, 'thanks for explaining about Lynch having you watch over us. I just wanted to know who had put the bug in Sacramento's ear. No big deal, I guess.'

'Yeah, well, you know how it is. The assistant chief doesn't tell his

Indians anything, just what to do. But from what I hear, there hasn't been too much new on those girls. So what do they have you two working on these days?'

'Oh,' Foley said dismissively as he pushed away from the table and stood, 'mostly serving court documents to scumbags. A couple ripe divorce cases. Complete with photos, not only in color but with surround-sound. You know, the usual stuff.'

Chapter 24

'WELL, WE DIDN'T get lunch,' Gretchen complained as they reached the street. 'And it didn't look to me like we learned very much.'

'Oh, I don't know. We know someone over in the capitol is following the murder case. We don't know who or why, but it's clear someone's interested. And we know if they know about it, they're playing Cochrane's murder close to the vest. We know, as far as the police are concerned, we aren't tied to it at all. Now, as you're concerned about starving to death, how about we walk up the street a couple blocks? I seem to remember a little Italian place with a great lunch menu.'

About an hour later, they left the little hole-in-the-wall restaurant Foley had taken them to feeling full and content. Actually, Foley felt like it was time for a nap.

'Thank you for the lunch. It was good,' said Gretchen, as they stood on the sidewalk outside. 'Now, what do you have in mind for this afternoon?'

'There's not much else I can think of. Gorman said he'd be talking to people tomorrow evening. Unless you can see something I'm missing, I'd say we've reached another dead end.'

'Don't say dead end. The last time we said it was just before we found Cochrane's body, remember?'

'Yeah, and we don't want any more dead people. Look, the city bus will take us back up through the Haight District. I think it'll drop us about a block or so from the office. I'm thinking of calling it a day. Fact is, until the old man comes back with something, I don't know what else we can do. Steiner is just going to have to accept the fact his little daughter was a working girl or not all on his own.'

'So I'm to go back to the office and...?'

'And do whatever it is you were hired to do. Now, c'mon. I'll even pay your bus fare.'

Getting back to his Chevy, Foley remembered Steve's message. Before pulling out of the parking space, he called his former partner on his cell.

'Hey, I'd just about given up on you. Where are you? You're breaking up.'

'Yeah, I'm down in the company parking garage. I'm taking the rest of the day off. Want to meet somewhere for a beer?'

'Sounds good to me. I'm over here in Sausalito. You familiar with the town?'

'I've been through there a couple times, mostly trying to dig dirt on a skuzzy used car dealer who was trying to hide some high-end cars from the repo man.'

'OK, there's a good place over here where we can talk and not be bothered. Henry's Bar and Grill. I'll meet you.'

It took Foley the best part of an hour getting out of the City and across the Golden Gate Bridge. You'd think traffic would be light this time of day, he groused, slowing down behind a semi-truck rig. With no break in the traffic, he was stuck behind the big rig until taking the turn off and dropping down into Sausalito.

Finding Henry's wasn't hard; there was only one main business street, Bridgeway Street, in the bay-side town and the bar and grill sign was big and colorful. Steve was waiting at the bar, nursing a tall glass of draft beer.

'C'mon, let's take a table,' he said after Foley ordered. 'Thanks for coming over, Brad. I wasn't sure you would. The other night when we talked, you didn't sound too sure about working with me again. Say, you ever been here before?'

Foley shook his head.

'I get in every so often. They've got a good hamburger, made with real beef, not the kind of stuff you get over in one of the fast food places.'

Obviously Steve wanted to work around to what he had to say. Foley didn't interrupt.

'The owner's name is Dennis. I asked once but nobody has any idea who the original Henry was. They weren't even sure there ever was a guy named Henry in the first place.'

Foley sipped his beer and carefully placed the glass back in the wet circle left on the table. He'd had enough small talk.

'OK. So, Dennis owns the place, makes a hamburger McDonald's couldn't make and Sausalito is a nice, quiet little town. Now, tell me what you wanted to talk about.'

'Damn it, Brad, you haven't changed a bit. Still taking the serious view of life. All right. Here it is. Remember I said I was working out of a state senator's office? From what you say, we're doing about the same thing; you with your private investigator and me with the senator, doing the dirty jobs the suits in charge can't or don't want to do. In my case, most of the work is what the pollies can't be seen having anything to do with. So, not so long ago the state highway patrol pulled over a pickup towing a U-Haul trailer. Some kind of minor traffic violation. I don't know what it was and it doesn't matter.

'As they do, the officer quickly ran a license check and found the truck's owner before parking behind the rig. Later, he said he thought he smelled something familiar as he walked up the side of the truck. He checked the license of the driver and it was for the registered owner. Everybody smiling innocently, you know how they get, all chastised and repentant. The CHP officer either wrote out a ticket or didn't, but turned to go back to his patrol car and once again, thought he caught an odor. This time he remembered what it was, the aroma of lush, green marijuana plants. Once smelled never forgotten, right, Bradford?'

Foley tried not to give anything away, working to keep his poker face. Knowing what Steve was talking about, he finally had to give it up.

'Yeah, damn it,' he said, letting a little smile lift his lips.

For a time, he'd been madder than hell and wouldn't even speak to his former partner. To a degree, he still was. It was all because of when the two of them had been kicked out of the county sheriff's department.

For a long moment, Steve didn't speak, only watched his former partner and smiled. Finally, chuckling, he went on with his story. 'Anyway, the CHP officer did the smart thing. He didn't bother the men in the pickup but got back in his patrol car and as the truck and trailer pulled out into traffic, called in his report. A road block was set up a few miles ahead and the men were arrested.

'It was a good bust,' said Steve. 'Almost a hundred plants were in the trailer along with the equipment to use for a large grow. As you might guess, everybody got into the act; the CHP presented an award to the officer, the California Drug Enforcement Administration bragged it up in the major newspapers, and by doing so asked for and got a huge increase in their departmental budget.'

He paused to empty his beer glass. 'All this talk is drying me from the inside out. You want another?' he asked, getting to his feet.

Foley nodded. So far, he couldn't see where all this was going. To tell the truth, he was feeling pretty good, sitting over a beer with his old friend and partner. The last vestiges of anger over what had happened getting them fired had faded. He had to smile to himself. This was as good a way to spend an afternoon as he could think of.

'Now, where was I?' said Steve when he came back carrying two glasses of beer and a bowl of mixed nuts. 'Oh, yeah. Well, everybody who could got in on it. Happens a lot, I suppose. But it was the bust that triggered the idea in the Governor's office. Now, you know there's an election coming and the incumbent Governor wants another term. Hell, rumor has it he plans on the US Congress after he's term limited out here. So what happens? His right hand man, a guy named Curtis Lee Owens, figures if at the right time in the campaign there were to be another major drug bust and his boss could be seen to be involved somehow, it'd help him win his election. That's where we come in.'

Foley frowned. 'What do you mean, where we come in? Are you suggesting that we ... oh, wait just a minute. I remember. You want us to go out in the woods to bird-dog a couple major plantations.'

'You got it in one. You, me and a couple other guys I found who know a lot of the forests up in Humboldt, Klamath and those counties right up on the California-Oregon border. It'll be like a week or so hunting trip. Only the game we're after has two legs, not four.'

'What's this guy, Owens, like? I started the morning off being quizzed by a lawyer type from Sacramento and didn't think much of it. You trust a politician or someone who's appointed by a pollie and you're putting your soul on the line.'

'He's smart, there's no doubt about it, smart and driven. But when it comes to street smarts, I don't think Owens has the common sense God gave a goose. He's the kind of guy who'll take advantage of anyone without a second thought. And watch out if anyone is caught standing in his boss's way. Not the kind of guy you'll ever see making the headlines but the guy standing right behind the one who does, propping him up. You'll meet him. Just look for the one who reminds you of a weasel.'

'And you like working around this kind of people?'

'No, not really. Look, the senator I'm working for has treated me OK. It happens he's a friend of Governor Vasconcellos's. Now if he can be seen as helping get the Governor re-elected, then everybody benefits. It's politics at its very best; you stroke mine and I'll stroke yours.'

'And you, I and your gang of forest hunters get a good payday out of it? What are we talking about, exactly?'

'Basic flat rate per day plus expenses. If no, when we're successful, we get to share the reward the state DEA has for whistle blowing. The amount is based on the estimated street value of the drugs taken out of production.'

'You figure it'll take a week?'

'Uh huh. At most. Maybe ten days. There's a lot of country up there, but if we do it systematically, we should be able to cover the areas we want in no more than that.'

Foley sipped his beer and nodded. 'Your little job brings up two questions. First, are we carrying on this trip?'

'Yeah. I've been sworn in and can carry. Got a badge and everything. You and the others would be the same. What's the other question?'

'Recall I mentioned a guy we once knew, Freddie something? Uh, oh, yeah, Freddie Isham. Anyway he called me a few days ago. Wanted to warn me there was someone wanting to talk to me about some drug money someone had apparently stolen.'

Quickly holding up his hands to stop Steve from asking questions, Foley went on.

'The only trouble was the men had already talked to me about it. There were two of them, Anton and Cully someone or another. Yeah, as I recall way back when, Anton was buddy-buddy with Hubert Ralston. They came looking for me and found me. Those two worked me over pretty good. I've still got a purple spot on my thigh and there are twinges of muscle spasm elsewhere once in a while if I overdo it. Now, I'm telling you this because if I go along with you on this and we're out there and I get the chance, I'm going to leave either or both of those two where I find them.'

Steve shook his head. 'I don't think anyone will mind, as long as you don't do something that'll screw up the prime reason we'll be out there. First and foremost, it's evidence of a couple big marijuana plantations we're after.'

'Hell, we could find a new one every day and your senator and his friends could come in and make the big arrests but it wouldn't make a dent in what's growing back in those mountains.'

'The whole point is not to try to get rid of anything, never happens, Joe. Uh huh. We're merely doing our bit to get certain people looking good for the election. Now, are you part of it? Remember, there's gonna be a good payday coming.'

Foley's smile was small and humorless. 'Yeah, why not? I'll have to let Gorman know I'm taking off for a week or ten days. He won't care. The thing I'm working on now has reached a dead-end.'

'OK. So it's on then. Today is Friday. How about we get together on Monday? I'll pick you up early and we can take a run over to Sacramento and get things started. We'll take a couple days to get our gear together and get up to our jump off point. Figure we can start our canvas early on Thursday or Friday. Sound good to you?'

Foley nodded his agreement. All the way out to his car, his mind was churning. Was his drive to get back at Anton and the other turkey going to get him into the deep and dirty? The idea, while sitting with a beer in hand and friend Steve across the table was one thing but once out the door, the doubts settled in. Hoo-boy, what had he let himself in for?

Chapter 25

SITTING BEHIND THE wheel, he mentally shook his head. Better to think of something else. Maybe while he was still under the impact of the beer, it would be a good time to talk to Gorman. He certainly didn't want to, but the only way to go about it, he figured, was to drive back into the city. Traffic in that direction, as it turned out, was light. Typically, most everyone else was starting their weekend early and rushing to get out of town. One of the things he always found himself wondering was where everyone was going. Back in the City, traffic on the downtown streets didn't seem lessened. What happens, he concluded, was come the weekend and all those people who rarely left their house or office came out. Like vampire bats coming out only after dark. Another of life's unanswerable questions.

The half hour or so it took to get back to the office gave him time to think of such things. And of the Steiner murder. Unless the old man came up with something new at his party at City Hall, there wasn't much more Gretchen and he could do about the Steiner case. Spending a few days tromping around the forests with his old hunting buddy wasn't a bad thing, especially if there was a good payday at the end of it.

Leonie Weems gave him a shake of her short gray head.

'Yes, Mr. Foley, you just caught him. Another two minutes and he'd have left. Now don't do anything to delay him. He needs to get away from the office so he can relax.'

She called everyone by their last name. Foley had thought at first it was because she was being over polite. Only thinking about it later did he realize she was building a barrier around the old man with herself right in the center. To look at her, a stranger would think Leonie Weems was somebody's grandmother. She had the plump old woman build and wore the kind of dresses most associated with older women. At least Brad Foley judged them as being old women dresses.

Today her dress was white, decorated with huge red flowers. Sitting behind her desk, he couldn't tell but he made a mental bet with himself about her hemline. Big money, he told himself, said the bottom of her dress stopped six inches above her ankles. She may dress old style, wear her hair in the fashion of the mid 1970s but that look was deceiving. If you looked close it was clear, Foley saw, she wasn't much older than he was. He figured she had fallen in love with her boss as a young woman on her first day and nothing had ever changed. For the past twenty years, she had grown to be at least twenty years older than she was. Just for the old man.

Foley bet Gorman had never realized it. Too bad, under the woman's stern, no-nonsense outer casing, Leonie Weems was probably a real goer.

A goer; he almost laughed out loud. The label people, or men at least, used to give call girls who looked hot. Another memory of back when he was young.

'I'll tell him you want to see him,' she said, leaving no doubt she'd be happy if Gorman said no about seeing him. She frowned at the man while picking up the phone.

'He says go right in. But remember, keep it quick. For his sake.'

'Yes, Mother,' said Foley, taking the sarcasm out by flashing a big smile.

'Brad, come in and tell me what brought you back to the office. Ms Bongiorno said you'd left for the weekend. By the way,' he went on, motioning Foley toward one of the wood client chairs, 'what do you think of her? Think she's going to make a good investigator?'

Settled, he gave the question some thought. 'She's smart enough,' he said slowly, 'a little naïve, maybe, not big in street-smarts. But give her time. I think she'll learn quick. But, hey, we've only been working together for a few days. I'll hold back making my judgment for a while, if it's OK with you.'

'Certainly. Take your time. I want a good reading. Now, what can I do for you?'

'As I understand it, you're going to try to learn what the police are doing as far as the two dead girls and our dead computer pimp, Cochrane. Didn't you say something about a party Saturday evening?'

'Yes, it's a fundraiser of a sort, I believe.'

'Well, from where I sit, it looks like there isn't much more Gretchen and I can do about the Steiner girl unless you learn something. Now, I've been offered a week's work up in the northern part of the state. Strange as it sounds, the work has to do with politics and illegal marijuana growing practices. Nothing to do with any of the stabbings or with DII. But I thought, before I take it on, I'd better touch base with you.'

'Ummm, well, I can't see how anything Chief Sands can tell me could change anything. To tell the truth, I'm about ready to tell Henry Steiner we've done all we can about his daughter. If we're done with it, I'd have to put Ms Bongiorno on with one of the other investigators. It'll have to happen sooner or later anyway. Tell me, Brad, you know them all, who do you think would be the best one to work at bringing her up to speed?'

Not Carl Dallas, he thought instantly. He'd do his damnedest to get Gretchen's panties off her. Mentally he shook his head, hearing the little voice of his conscious reminding him he wasn't her father. Let her fend for herself.

'Oh, I don't know,' he said pensively, 'probably one of the older, more experienced men, I guess.' Better be safe than sorry.

Gorman nodded. 'I'll give it some thought over the weekend. How long do you expect to be out of the office?'

'Ten days at the most.'

'OK. Call when you're coming back and I'll see what we have for you.'

Gretchen was sitting on the edge of Leonie Weems's desk as he came out of Gorman's office, laughing at something the receptionist had said.

Just like the first time he saw her, he liked what he saw. The black pantyhose she wore interested him. The leg coverings had to be pantyhose. He didn't think modern women her age even knew about garter belts. Too bad, he mused silently. Unknown to most women, the little bit of lacy harness was a sure-fire way to a man's libido.

'Hey, Brad,' she smiled, 'thought you'd gone home for the day.'

'Did. I had to come back to talk with the old man, though.'

'He's not the "old man,"' said Leonie Weems, all signs of fun and frivolity leaving her face. 'It wouldn't hurt you to give the man some respect, you know.'

'Of course, you're right. I'll do my best to remember. Thank you for correcting my oversight, Mother Protector. Want to grab a My-God-I'm-Glad-the-Week-is-Done drink, Gretchen?' he said, turning to the other woman and not giving her a chance to interrupt. 'Of course, you're welcome to come along, Ms Weems. I'd enjoy the company of two fine looking women.'

'Not on your best day, Mr. Foley. Not on your best day, if you ever are lucky enough to have one.'

Gretchen stood up, laughing. 'Stop it, you two. You're sounding like a couple of children. Sure, I'll let you buy, Mr. Foley,' she said, putting the same emphasis on the mister just as Leonie Weems had done.

Following her down the stairs and outside, he chuckled. 'I didn't think old Weems would come with us and thinking back, I don't know what I would have done had she accepted my half-assed invitation.'

'You would have bought both of us a drink and been a gentleman about it. Why, didn't you mean it?'

'Nope. My idea was to buy you a drink, talk a little bit about DII and Gorman, buy you another drink and talk a little bit about you, buy you another drink and…'

'Stop right there with the drinks. Two is my limit. After two, I always lose track of things. Which means you'll only buy me one. Now, what about Mr. Gorman and his company?'

Having the door to the Westside East Restaurant and Bar handy made it easy. The place, Foley saw as they pushed through that door, was only about half full. Probably too early for the TGIF folks to get away from their offices.

'How about over at that little table?' he asked, pointing.

'How about at the bar?' she said, not waiting but walking down to take the bar stool at the end farthest from the door. 'You said something I'm paying attention to. I feel a lot safer here where the bartender can keep an eye on you.'

'Now what did I say that made you feel unsafe?' he asked after they gave the bartender their order, a glass of white wine for her and a dry vodka martini for him.

'It was something about buying me the third or fourth drink and talking about me. I'm not sure what you think being partners on a case covers.'

'Ah, Gretchen, you don't think I'd be coming on to you, do you?'

'Yes, and so does Leonie. She warned me to watch out for you.'

'Mistress Weems shouldn't be poking her nose into our affairs.'

'We're not having any affairs. And Ms Weems is only looking out for my best interests. She likes me.'

'Now, looking out for your best interests is what I'm doing. Isn't it? If you recall, Gorman ordered me to mentor you.'

'So, mentor me by telling me about Mr. Gorman and the company.'

'I give up. OK, I'll be gone for a week or so. The Steiner thing will have to wait. There's not much more we can do about it anyway, unless the old man brings something back from the party he's going to tomorrow night. I came back to the office to tell him I was taking some time off. He's OK with my being gone and we both agreed on what to tell his friend Steiner.' He waited until the drinks were served. 'He also asked me to suggest which of the investigators he should team you up with. To continue your orientation, I mean. Uh, he means.'

'You haven't even had one drink yet and already you're talking confusion. So, what did you tell him?'

'Be nice to me, he also wanted my opinion on who you are to work with.'

'Stop teasing and tell me what you said. By the way, where are you going, taking a vacation?'

'No. It's a little job up north. And I told him you were looking pretty good.'

'Back to flirting. More importantly, what am I going to be doing while you're gone? What happens if something comes in about the Steiner case?'

'If it does, it'll come from Gorman. He'll know what to do.'

Chapter 26

DRIVING HOME AFTER leaving Gretchen, Foley thought about how good she looked. She certainly was a fine looking young woman and there was the trouble – the young part. That big gap in their ages and experience. The gap became evident whenever they talked about non-work things. Like music, politics and, he was afraid, personal attachments. Ms Gretchen wasn't a one-night affair. She'd been clear about it. She wanted a law degree and then maybe marriage. Degree first, marriage second, with marriage in the 'someday' bracket.

Ah, well, he decided, he could still look and lust. About all he could do anyhow.

Maybe a walk in the woods away from big city life would clear the cobwebs from his mind and his life. Maybe, but he doubted it.

Saturday morning started out nice and quiet, the way he thought things would be in paradise. It began when the early morning sun finding a thin opening in the bedroom curtains woke him up. For the first time since being visited by Anton and Cully, he stretched and got out of bed without feeling the least little pain or stiffness. Life was good.

With nothing to do until meeting Steve on Monday, Foley took a long time over breakfast, savoring a second cup of coffee on the back deck. Looking out across the empty stretch of beach, he saw how the ocean was flat, sparkling in the early sunshine. The beach, all the way down to the mouth of the lagoon, had become a favorite part of his world. Walking to the end of the spit was about as spiritual as he could get.

It was interesting how his morning walks helped clean out his mind. And the physical benefit of the walk, especially after a night of too much wine.

This morning, he decided, would be just right for a health-restoring walk.

The next day was a day of housework, reading the Sunday edition of the *San Francisco Chronicle* and generally lazing around. When Steve pulled up early Monday morning in his big 4WD truck, Brad was ready.

'What's on the agenda this morning?' Foley was dressed for business, wearing cleaner's-pressed summer-weight wool slacks, a pale blue cotton shirt kept in place by a matching tie. After looking to see if the interior wasn't as dirty as the outside of the rig, he laid his two-button blazer on the back seat. Steve, on the other hand, was looking like he was ready for the hike; clean Levis, the legs covering the tops of his lace-up leather boots, a plaid shirt and a black leather jacket.

'I figure breakfast at a place I know then go on over to meet with some people in Sacramento. Remember I mentioned a guy named Owens? He's the one putting this deal together. Anyway, he wants to meet with us right after lunch.'

'Who's this "us" you keep talking about?'

'I've got four other guys. They're familiar with the country up along the Klamath National Forest and on up toward the state line. I figure they'll take that area while we head over into the Six Rivers National Forest. Anyway, first things first. Owens wants to meet and give us a pep talk. I don't doubt the message will be along the lines of whatever we do, we make sure he and the Governor are front and center when it comes to getting in the public eye.'

Politics and politicians – already Brad was wondering if he had made the right decision. Already he was almost wishing he was back searching for answers to the Steiner murder. Almost.

Curtis Lee Owens was not what Foley expected. Somehow he'd had the vision of a sneaky little rodent of a man. What he saw standing at a whiteboard in the conference room they were shown into was just the opposite. Waiting for the last man to arrive, Foley studied the Governor's right-hand man. Standing at a stiff parade rest, he looked tall and thin, with a long solemn face looking almost bleak, as if a smile had never passed over it. Thick black hair, a wide, equally black eyebrow barely thinning in the middle. His beady little eyes looked sunken deep in their sockets. Owens stood and waited until everyone was seated and quiet before starting.

'All right, then,' he said finally. 'Gentlemen, this is the plan. We all know there is a lot of marijuana growing up in the northern part of the state. For years, law enforcement agencies, federal, state and local, have tried to stamp it out and failed. It's just too big an area and as you all know, too mountainous. Stopping this illegal activity is impossible but we have to keep trying. This is what this task force is all about. We've labeled it Ground Strike.'

He stopped, looking at the six men one at a time. Probably, Foley thought, looking for someone to laugh. Nobody did.

'OK then. From what we in the Governor's office can tell, in recent years there has been a marked increase in the number of illegal outdoor and indoor cannabis grow sites in this part of the state. There has also been an increase in the violent confrontations between law enforcement officers and cultivators, particularly during the September and October harvest season. That's why we chose this time of the season for our concentrated effort.'

Ha, Foley thought. It all has to do with the seasons, not the coming election. Uh huh. Sure. Again nobody said anything.

'Mr. Tichenor has sectioned off the area Ground Strike will focus on. Three teams of two men each will canvas certain isolated areas, pinpointing what we believe are the location of targeted plantations by use of GPS satellite technology. The information you will come back with will determine exactly which plantations will be eradicated.'

Not all, just certain ones. Without looking, Foley knew the other men were keeping straight faces, not letting anything show.

'You won't be going in blind. We have intel from a state group code named CAMP. Campaign Against Marijuana Production is a task force funded by the federal government's War on Drugs program. They are the outfit flying helicopters all over the state looking for pot groves. From this intelligence we can reduce the area of terrain to be searched.

'Let me be very clear. This is serious business. In California, possession of under an ounce is a misdemeanor which carries a $100 fine. Since the passage of Proposition 215 in 1996, people with medical conditions are relatively free to smoke, possess and grow pot as long as they have a doctor's note. For everyone else, it's still naughty. However, much of society seems to regard pot as an entirely different drug than cocaine, methamphetamine or heroin. There is not much we in the government can do

about it. What we can do, however, is wipe out as much of the illegal production as possible.'

Once more, Foley wanted to jump up and say he agreed and ask the
question he'd been framing in his mind. 'C'mon, cut to the truth, nobody
but the cops and you politicians really care about dope. The cops because
they've been fighting the so-called war for so long it's all they know. And
for the pollies, it comes down to votes.' He thought the thought but kept
his poker face and listened.

'OK, there's not much more to say. Gentlemen, thank you for taking
this task on. I have every expectation the end result will be what we all
want. Now then, Mr. Tichenor, if you'd stay a few minutes, I'd appreciate
it.' The group had been dismissed.

'Hey, Brad, I'll catch up with you,' Steve said, turning away to see what
the man had to say.

Foley followed the others, none of them saying anything and everybody going their own way once they came out into the sunshine. Steve had
parked in the section of the parking lot marked for visitors but hadn't given
Foley a key. Finding a park bench in a little patch of shrubbery overlooking
the parking lot, he settled in to think about what he'd gotten himself into.

A comment he'd once read poked into his thoughts. Something Willie
Nelson was quoted as saying. "I think people need to be educated to the
fact marijuana is not a drug," the singer had said, probably on leaving a
court house somewhere after answering to charges of possession of the evil
weed. "Marijuana is an herb and a flower," Nelson went on to say, "God put
it here. If He put it here and He wants it to grow, what gives the government the right to say God is wrong?" The man liked to thumb his nose at
the government, all right.

Brad Foley felt he was, for the most part, in agreement with the nasally
voiced musician. Old Willie wasn't alone with his live-and-let-live views
on marijuana. It was an accepted fact after alcohol and tobacco, pot was
the third most popular drug in the country.

Thinking back to when he and Steve were deputies, he could remember
other members of the department, not the sheriff, of course, but others
wondering how long it would be until dope became legal. Now, a few
years later, here they were, about to go out and roust a half dozen or so
plantations just so a couple politicians could look good to the up-standing
electorate.

The sun felt warm on his shoulders and relaxed as he was, he had almost dozed off when Steve came around.

'Hey, there. C'mon, it's time for a beer before we go to work.'

'What'd your friend want? Information on where we're going?'

'You know, I'm not sure what it was all about. When my contact in the senator's office introduced Owens to me, I was told to organize enough men to form three search parties. Now he's questioning my choices.'

'He's not happy with your little dope army?'

'Well, he wanted to know how I came to pick two members of our little group, you and one other guy. The thing that bothers me is the fact the other guy has a long history of working with the state's MET people. And you, well, you haven't been doing something you should be doing, have you?'

'Not anything to get his nose out of shape. What's MET?'

'It's a fairly new program set up to take advantage of federal War on Drugs funding. The sheriff's departments in each county have formed a Marijuana Eradication Team. Some of them actually do go out and try to destroy grows in their areas.'

'So how come your little army is called in? Why not use the MET people?'

'Ah, now we're back to the political way of thinking. If the Governor is seen merely to rely on teams already supposedly doing the job, there wouldn't be the big headlines. Not as big as if he himself got involved and formed a special team of experts. This means us, the Governor's own special team of experts.'

'Uh huh, and what'd he want you to do, cut me and the other guy off the special team?'

'No, he said he just wanted to know more about the two of you. I told him you and I had been partners way back when and reminded him the other guy was an extra special expert in the field. He's satisfied. Now, it's beer time.'

Chapter 27

GETTING THEIR GEAR together didn't take long. Both men simply dug out the camping equipment and hunting clothes, aired out their sleeping bags and loaded up on freeze dried meals. Foley spent a couple hours working Mink Oil into his high-top leather hiking boots. The shoes had sat on the floor of his closet behind everything else since the last time he'd gone deer hunting and were dusty and stiff. A couple days later, when Steve picked him up early in the morning, they were both ready.

'Just like one of our hunting trips,' Steve said, driving north up the Shoreline Highway. 'You done any hunting since moving down here?'

'Nope. This'll be the first time I've been north of the Bay Area in a long time. Somehow I lost the taste for tramping through the woods.'

Sipping coffee poured from a thermos, the two let the miles go by without further talk.

Sitting back, feeling the warmth of the morning sun, Foley was relaxed. It had been a long time since he'd ridden anywhere with his old partner and it was as comfortable as it had been back when they were in a patrol car.

As Steve had said, it was just like going hunting. Wearing well-broken in Levis and soft cotton shirts, the typical outfit worn on such trips, helped bring back the familiar feeling. They had been partners too long and Foley was a little surprised at how he had missed the companionship. Just like a couple who'd been married fifty years, he mused silently, so used to each other they didn't need to talk.

Steve Tichenor had mapped out the areas his three teams would cover. Each area had been overflown by CAMP helicopters armed with infrared heat detecting hardware. The aerial maps Steve had handed out had been marked with suspected plantations. The plan was simple, each team would trek in to those sites, check them out, discover the danger potential and report back.

Steve and Foley had expected to stay out no more than a week and, just in case they ended up not being near a restaurant, packed enough freeze dried meals for that long. As it turned out, they were only on the road for part of the time and never once had to rely on the tasteless packaged food. Before heading back to Sacramento, they had come across four cultivated areas, three of which had been marked by the air surveillance, and made the decision to report only two of them.

The first one they decided wasn't what Owens and his boss would be interested in. They heard about it when stopping to talk to a couple of men fishing on the Trinity River near the little town of Willow Creek. Two of the places marked on the map Steve had were in the Six Rivers National Forest. Willow Creek lay smack dab in the center of the forest.

'Hey there,' Steve called out to the man standing on the river bank. The man had been intense, tying a fly onto his leader and hadn't paid any attention to Brad and Steve's approach.

'Good morning. You two going fishing?'

Neither man was carrying fishing poles.

'No, 'fraid not.' Steve answered, pasting a big, friendly smile on his face. 'You doing any good?'

'Oh, had hits from a couple steelhead but I wasn't able to land one. My son, down there, he's taken the only trout so far but I'm about to enjoy a change of luck.'

'We stopped in at the cop shop back in town and they sent us to look for you.'

'Yeah? Now why would they send you to me?'

Steve flipped open his leather wallet and showed the fisherman the shiny gold badge. 'We're working a special investigative team. Trying to get a handle on a couple pot farms reported up in the forest. When we let the local law know we were in the area was when we were told you'd had some trouble.'

'Guess it'd be my brother-in-law talking. Most useless cop on the force, but there you are. Yeah, we had some trouble. My oldest boy down there, Jimmy, drives a school bus. When he's not working, he spends a lot of time hiking our property. Wants to write a book about the ranch. It's been in the family for, well, he'll be the fifth generation. He's found a lot of Indian artefacts and even came home one time with a silver spur. Broken and all tarnished. Couldn't tell what it was even, until we got it cleaned up. Got him all excited. He did some research and believes it was likely lost by the De Anza party back in the eighteenth century. Anyway, he spends a lot of time hiking and hunting with his son, my grandson. Lately, though, they've had to back off those trips. They kept coming across foot trails in places where nobody should be.

'First time he told me about it, I called Leroy, my brother-in-law. Jimmy took Leroy and a couple other officers to one of the trails and sure enough, after they followed it about a mile, they came to a well-equipped campsite littered with trash. Leroy said nearby was an old pot garden. Well, since then, everybody has pretty much stayed away from those parts of the forest. Never know what those assholes'll do.'

'Uh huh,' Steve agreed, 'I'd agree it's probably the best thing. Can you show me on a map where this garden was?'

'You got a map of these woods, I can.'

Following the trails marked by the fisherman, the two walked in and were at the campsite before the sun had much more than passed overhead. It was evident there were more than a few men spending some time living there. Piles of tree boughs, the needles still green, indicated where at least three men had put their sleeping bags. A rough rock-lined fire pit had about six inches of cold, black ash in the bottom. A galvanized bucket lay half submersed in a nearby creek.

'Yeah, and what'd the fisherman say? There's a garden nearby? Let's see if we can find it.'

The plot they found was up-stream from the camp, water from the same small creek was used to irrigate a roughly cultivated smallish clearing. Off to one side, a couple of rusty shovels had been tossed after being used to turn over the rich forest loam. Narrow shallow ditches had been dug, taking water from the creek, flowing down the slope through rows of healthy looking marijuana plants.

'Now what'll we do?' asked Foley. 'This grow isn't indicated on your map.'

'It's too small to show up or to interest the Governor and Mr. damn-fool-Owens. But I'd hate to just leave it. Normally I wouldn't bother, but if these farmers are causing trouble, then, well, it isn't right.'

'Looks to me to be about an acre of the stuff. I suppose if I took one of these shovels,' Foley said, picking up one, 'and cut the plant like this,' and using the blade chopped through the tender stalk, cutting it off just above the dirt, 'it wouldn't take long to destroy this little bit. What do you say?'

Steve nodded and picked up the other spade and the two men went to work.

They finished long before dark. Leaving the clearing empty of growing plants, they then destroyed the campsite as much as they could. They carried the shovels down the trail from the camp to where it joined the well-traveled hiking trail. After breaking both long handles, they jammed the shovel blades into the pot growers trail as a warning and headed back to the van and back to town.

'It seems to me foolhardy for someone to go to all the trouble of planting such a small grow,' said Foley later as the two men were eating dinner.

'Oh, I don't know. According to the state experts, each mature pot plant will produce as much as a pound of buds. The going rate for a pound of dried pot is said to be about $5,000. Now, how many plants do you think we cut down today? A hundred? Five hundred? If there were a hundred, there would be a hell of a lot of money to be made for someone.'

'Hmm, maybe we're in the wrong business.'

Chapter 28

THEY STAYED THE first night in a Super 8 hotel, had breakfast the next morning and left Willow Creek. The next two days were spent hiking in the Trinity Alps, a huge, rugged, mountainous, federally protected wilderness. Back when the two men lived and worked over on the coast in Humboldt County, they had come over to the western side of the huge forest for some small stream fishing. The western side of the mountainous wilderness was made up of gentle sloping terrain, filled with uncounted and unnamed creek and streams. Most of these made perfect rainbow trout fishing. All of them could be used to irrigate hidden plantations.

'We'll have to be careful,' Steve said unnecessarily one morning. They had driven the van as close to where the mapped site was as possible and had taken off walking. Taking their time and being careful not to barge into anything, they stopped to catch their breath.

'Anyone this far off one of the old logging roads has too much invested to think kindly of us barging in,' he pointed out. 'I don't want to just barge in on anyone. If the map is right, somewhere down there,' he pointed to the next little valley, 'probably over on the north slope is where what we're looking for will be.'

Foley didn't say anything, remembering another time and another place.

'Uh huh, I seem to recall you and I almost getting into a situation in a similar place. Remember the time we ran into a fella who was protecting his grow? The same guy we ran into a little later. Remember I told you about getting a call from him? Freddie Isham?'

'Oh, yeah. This is the second time you've mentioned him. Back the first time I had to think about it a little. So what brings him up now?'

'Yeah, all you were thinking about was getting me involved in this dope hunt. Didn't pay any attention to what I was saying. No, I wasn't exactly thinking about him just now. Possibly coming up on a protected dope farm reminded me. You know?'

'Yeah. And thinking back, I somehow recall when you talked about him, you got all smiley-faced. I'm thinking you're anxious about making this hiking trip to get you close to old Anton. That's what you're after, isn't it; getting first dibs at some of our old enemies. Well, we can hope we run into him up here. But I doubt it. He's most likely to be over nearer the coast, don't you think?'

'Yep. I figure he's still working with the other young fool, Hubert Ralston, and that would put them over closer to the old man's forest.'

'Well, maybe we get through over here, we should drop in over there. There's nothing on our map about the coastal area but maybe we could get lucky.'

Foley nodded. He liked that idea. Revenge, and while on the state payroll. How good is that?

They had driven up the rugged dirt road as far as they could, following the track indicated on the US Forest Service topographical map. The map wasn't really needed, though. Tracks left by other recent visitors were plain to see. From the width of the tire prints and the depth the tires had sunk into the dirt, the two men knew the vehicle had been big and heavy.

'Probably one of those Hummers,' Steve mumbled at one point, 'you know, the Army's modern version of the jeep? Just what you could expect from any backwoods pot farmer.'

Brad Foley didn't bother responding.

It was obvious where the Hummer, if a Hummer was what it was, had at one time been parked. Steve pulled around the next bend, looking for a place to turn around. Backing and filling, he finally got the van pointing back the way they'd come. Parking, they locked it up and started walking.

Usually, Steve said, growers wouldn't plant their product very far off a trail. The farther into the timber they went, the longer they had to carry their gear in and the dope out later. Whoever made the faint trail they were following to a patch indicated from the air, they could have used pack horses. There hadn't been any sign of pack horses but you never knew.

Stopping before breaking over the ridge, they'd been climbing to take a look at what was ahead, it wasn't the sight of the brilliant green plants telling them they'd found their plantation, it was the odor of pot being smoked.

'Hey, grab a whiff of that and tell me it isn't high grade dope,' whispered Steve, dropping back a few yards from the ridgetop. 'Those damn fools are sampling their own product.'

'I doubt it. Too early in the season for good stuff to be ready to smoke. But what do I know about it?'

Steve glanced at his friend and smiled. 'Just like me, you've smoked enough to know. OK, what say we make our way up this ridge a few hundred yards before crossing over? Maybe we can get lucky and come out above the plantation.'

'Fine by me. Lead the way, Captain.'

'Uh huh. C'mon.'

A little higher up, the amount of brush cover thinned out, opening up wider spaces of clear ground between the trees. At this elevation, it was mostly pine with a few hardy cedars mixed in. Taking their time and moving cautiously, they came down through the trees until reaching the edge of the field.

'My God, will you look at that? There must be ten acres out there.'

Foley could only smile, thinking back to the $5,000 for a pound of pot figure. The plants had been planted in small bunches of five or six in each group and were partially hidden in the trees. From the air, it'd be difficult to pick them out, spread out as the plants were. Sitting with their backs to a huge pine, even with the binoculars Steve had brought, they couldn't see the other side of the large, gently sloping hillside below them.

Faintly, Foley thought he could make out the soft voices of men talking. They were too far away to tell what the discussion was about or even how many there were. Masking the hum of their conversation was the continuous sound of the breeze gently blowing through the tall timber. Not having been in the woods for a long time, he found himself relaxing, feeling very comfortable.

'I'm going to crawl around that way a little,' Steve said pointing, 'and try to see just who we got here. Stay here and I'll be right back.'

He wasn't gone more than five minutes.

'Shit, it's what we're looking for. There are three of them. From the looks of the camp, they have set up back in the trees over there, they've been living here for a couple weeks. There are cardboard boxes stacked around all over the place with camouflage colored tarps strung up between the trees. I suppose it'd be damn hard to see them from the air.'

'Yeah, especially with the plants hidden by the trees. So, what now?'

Taking a handheld GPS receiver from his day pack, Steve punched a few buttons. 'We do what Mr. Owens wants. Get a precise reading on this place and then get the hell out of here. This will be just what he's wanting, a major stealth operation. It'll make great photos in the bigger newspapers.'

Ah, yes. Politicians and the media mixed in correct proportions, and the outcome would be votes.

Chapter 29

ACCORDING TO OWENS's aerial map, the next suspected plantation was north of Willow Creek, on the eastern edges of the huge Redwood National Park.

It was a part of the north coast that neither man had ever been in before. Going back to the Forest Service topo map, they saw that the closest road was off the State Highway 289, the most direct link to the coast's Redwood Highway called the Bald Mountain road. Taking to the dirt road, it soon became obvious how the road that had started out life as a logging road got its name. Following ridge line after ridge line, the narrow road took them through steep sloped mountain sides that was barren of timber.

'Christ, will you look at that?' asked Steve, disgustedly. 'Makes me wonder how those fools didn't realize that clear cutting all the timber would mean leaving behind a huge opening where nothing worthwhile will ever grow again.'

'Clear cutting was thought to be the best method, back when this was area was harvested.'

'Yeah, makes sense, doesn't it? Timber growing slowly hundreds of years and then taking only a couple weeks to be cut down? Has to make the best of all possible use of the forest.'

'C'mon, getting pissed over the stupidity of people isn't worth anything. Where the pot farm we're heading for, according to Owens's map, is down there somewhere close to a little river. And,' Foley said, picking up the topo map, 'down there it is; Redwood Creek. Flows out to the ocean about fifty miles from here as the crow flies. From up here it looks like it'd be good trout water.'

'OK, you got the map. How do we get down there?'

'Another few miles more and there's a road takes off to the left, I don't see a name for it. Probably another old logging road. Lots of twists and turns but ends up running right close to the creek for quite a way. Owens's map shows the grow is along there.'

It was obvious when the boundary of the Redwood National Park had been reached. Dropping down off Bald Mountain Road, they could see where the loggers had cut right up to an invisible line. The slope rising behind them had been shaved of every tree. On the other side of the unseen boundary, the slope was covered in tall old-growth timber.

'Damn fools,' Steve mumbled but didn't lecture anymore on the subject.

Unlike the other plantations indicated on Owens's aerial map, this one was easy to find. Steve pulled off on the first dirt track they had reached since leaving the top of the clear cut.

'Can't be too far,' Foley said, studying the topo map, trying to estimate distance using the one inch to a mile gauge along one border. He needn't have bothered.

'Good Gawd,' exclaimed Steve, getting out of the van and looking down.

The rutted dirt road ended at a packed yard a bit farther along. From where they stood, the creek, running fast and furious, was only twenty yards or so below. A shabby looking camper trailer complete with a ripped canvas awning sat on tree stump blocks on their right. It was the culti-vated field on their left grabbing their attention.

All ground hugging bushes had been cleared out, leaving the forest canopy to filter the bright sunlight shining on nearly mature marijuana plants. It appeared the plants had been planted three feet or so apart and had reached the stage of their growth to where some of the leaves were overlapping. Black plastic tubes ran down alongside the rows, part of a drip-irrigation setup.

'Now there's a nice little plantation,' Steve said, scanning the area with his binoculars.

'Hey there,' called a man coming from back behind the sorry looking camper. 'Welcome to the Blitz Farm. We weren't expecting company or we'd have baked a cake. I'm Aaron Blitz. My wife Annie is down at the creek trying to get our little irrigation pump working.'

The man stopped, putting his hands inside the sagging front of his bib overalls. The skin of his cheeks had tanned chocolate brown, looking like smooth leather. His smile broke through the full beard hanging down from his face, hiding his neck. The man hadn't seen a barber or razor blade in years by the look of it. Clear, steady blue eyes sparkled under dark, heavy brows. His sun bleached long-sleeved shirt had once been some shade of red but was now faded to a mottled light pink hue. Foley, if asked, would have described him as one of the old style hippies got to pot.

'And would your cake have any of your product in the recipe?' Steve laughed.

'Nope. Afraid not. But what can we do for you? Don't mean to be inhospitable but we don't get too many visitors and don't really know how to deal with them when we do.'

'With a farm like this, out in the open and all, I'd bet you do get a visit now and again. This is the kind of thing most small town cops love to see.'

The man chuckled. 'Oh, they leave us alone. We've been up here since the state passed Proposition 215, the medical marijuana act. What you see there will be harvested in a month or so, dried and sold to a number of legal shops. Anyone with a doctor's prescription can legally purchase it for their health reasons. What're you two doing up here in the back country, anyhow?'

Foley smiled at the way he'd slipped his question in. 'To tell the truth, we're looking for an illegal plantation,' he said, stepping forward and sticking out his hand. 'I'm Brad Foley and my partner is Steve Tichenor. We're advance agents for a state enforcement agency. Your little farm here showed up on one of the maps we've got.'

'Ah, don't tell me we're going to be raided again. Damme, every so often they'll come in, all dressed up like we were terrorists or something. Pull up our entire crop, then take us off to jail, only to discover we're a legal enterprise.'

Steve stepped over to finger the immature bud topping a near plant.

'Well,' said Foley slowly, 'your plot shows up on our map so I imagine others get the same information. I'd say it was just part of doing business in this type of venture.'

'Yeah, well, maybe. But we try. Every year for the past five or six years, before anything is planted, I draft a letter to the county Board of Supervisors, the local Sheriff's Department, the District Attorney and the County Council. This year we even sent copies to the Attorney General and Governor Hugo Vasconcellos, letting them all know who we are and what we're doing. Sent with copies of our permit. No one pays any attention. I keep hoping, though, someone will get the message and leave us alone.'

Steve came out of the patch, sniffing the tips of his fingers. 'From the smell and the stickiness of the bud, I'd say you've got a crop of high grade marijuana.'

'Nope, to be precise, it's cannabis. Marijuana is the true name for the dried flowers. At this stage it is simply cannabis sativa, one of a group of cannabinoids which produce substances structurally related to tetrahydrocannabinol, or THC.'

'Now,' Steve said, chuckling, 'you've stopped sounding like a backwood's hippie and started talking like a university professor.'

Foley laughed. 'And now you're up here, growing medical pot. Sounds to me like a good life.'

'Oh, we're only here from spring until we harvest in late summer. During the rest of the year both Annie and I teach. You hit it pretty close to the head a bit ago. I teach at UC-Berkeley. Phytopathology is my field, the study of plant diseases. It wasn't a huge step from there to attempting to grow a better, more potent marijuana product. Annie is an instructor at the UC-Berkeley's Women's Center where she advises on non-traditional education.'

'Well, I'd say we got some wrong information, Mr. Blitz,' Steve said, looking at the tops of the plants gently moving in the afternoon breeze, 'and for what it's worth, we'll make a note of it in the report we'll be expected to turn in.'

'Hey, anything you can do won't hurt. I'd invite you back, but, well, we'd rather people didn't make it a habit. Coming in here, I mean. Too many people like to raid small, out of the way places like this.'

'Oh, we won't tell the wrong people. Just add a note to our map. Those folks back in Sacramento have this down as one of the larger plantations.'

Walking out, Steve glanced back down at the creek. 'Wouldn't mind coming back to see what the fishing's like down there.'

Chapter 30

THEY HAD BREAKFAST the next morning over on the coast in Eureka. Foley hadn't seen the town since leaving the sheriff's department but with the exception of colorful spring flowers blossoming in new planter boxes attached to a number of light poles, it hadn't changed. Steve said something about having come through town a few weeks back, but didn't say anything else. Brad wondered if there weren't a lot of things going on in the man's life better left unmentioned.

In almost every community, there is one café or restaurant where the city's movers and shakers meet for breakfast, coffee and talk. In Eureka, the place was Adel's Restaurant. Normally most customers wouldn't notice the half dozen or so men seated around the largest table, typically round and nearly always close to the back wall. It was here those decision makers, not the mayor or city manager, but their assistants and generally one or two of the members of the city council would meet for breakfast and talk.

Much of the talk would be light-hearted banter, teasing first one person then another about this or that. Someone's golf score at last weekend's city tournament would be good for ten or fifteen minutes of joking and laughter. Voices would drop a little when someone mentioned the dress one of the secretaries over in the budget department wore to the charity ball Friday night.

In between all the jocular chitchat, one of the men might mention the proposal for expanding the city's main sewer plant. Another might nod and comment on the quality of work a certain construction company was doing on a sidewalk project. Thursday evening during the regularly scheduled planning department meeting, someone would make a motion to put out to bid the sewer plant improvement job. After much discussion, the motion would pass and a few weeks later, a certain construction company's bid would be likewise approved.

This type of informal breakfast meeting was not illegal. Under all accepted open meeting laws, discussion of motions and decisions on them can only be made in a scheduled public meeting. No decisions were ever made at these morning get-togethers. Anyway, anyone could come in and take a seat. The restaurant or café was, after all, a public venue, wasn't it?

The morning coffee klatch wasn't advertised and rarely, if ever, mentioned by anyone. Being in a popular restaurant didn't mean that reporters from the local paper would be made welcome, though. No. And if one of the members of the opposing political parties came by, the talk would never get past the short skirt on the girl from the budget office. Those sitting at the back table didn't pay any attention to Steve and Foley when they took a nearby table.

Foley had questioned going in to Adel's, thinking someone might recognize them. After all, they'd been very visible members of the sheriff's department for more than a dozen years. He pointed it out to Steve when talking about where to have breakfast.

'Not a problem,' he said smiling. 'Look, you and I both know Hubert's been in the business since he came home after getting kicked out of college. How many times did we try to nail him? OK, back then nobody'd talk to us. We were cops. And the Ralstons were creating jobs. Trust me, things are different now. Old man Ralston isn't the power in this part of the state he used to be. He made the wrong people mad. I don't want to say too much, but I was up here a few months ago. Talked to some people and … well, let it go. Trust me. Nobody is going to pay us any attention.'

Steve's incomplete explanation bothered him, but it was clear they would need some help locating any plantations Ralston was working. Owens's aerial maps hadn't covered this part of the state. Anyway, either they'd be recognized or they wouldn't. Either way, Adel's used to serve a good breakfast. The place was about half filled when they walked in so Foley figured it still did.

Steve led the way, going to a small table near the back, taking the chair closest to the men at the round table. Nobody at the nearby table looked up and their conversation, broken at times by laughter, continued.

Foley and Steve didn't talk except to order their meal. They were eating when Steve heard a brief pause in the table discussion behind him. Not taking his eyes off the plate in front of him, he turned his head to whisper a few words over his shoulder.

'A state task force is about to raid a Ralston pot farm,' he said quietly, not looking to see if anyone was listening.

Both Brad and Steve continued focusing their attention on the ham and eggs they'd ordered, not paying any notice to anything around them.

Talk at the table flowed on as it always did, touching first on this rumor or another before someone mentioned H. Fredrick Ralston's name.

'Anybody seen anything of old man Ralston lately?'

'No, not since the city department of environmental control turned down his plan to fill in the mill pond out at his old sawmill.'

'Well, hell, it was to be expected. After all, the pond's been there for, what, thirty years? Forty years? God only knows what's growing down in the bottom of it.'

'More like fifty years, Jake. My dad worked out there back when H. Fredrick's pa ran the place and that had to be at least fifty years.'

Talk around the table died while the men thought about it.

Finally someone asked a question. 'What'd old Ralston want to put on that site, anyhow?'

'Oh, he had great plans for a shopping center. You know it's a good thing old Silas Ralston's dead in his grave. Wouldn't he be pissed if he saw the way that son of his has let the fortune drain away?'

'The big problem,' another man said quietly, 'is Silas's grandson, Hubert. Fredrick Ralston just isn't strong enough to put that boy of his down. No controlling him at all.'

'Runs wild, young Hubert does. Rumor has it that the boy is one of the big guns in the local drug scene. Of course, the only time anyone came close to catching him, the old man sent him out of the country quick as a shot. Claimed Hubert had been out of town and nobody could prove different. I heard he flew him south in a private plane so there'd be no record of when he left.'

'Hey, Carl, you were up there scouting the deer herd last month, weren't you?'

'Un huh. Got as far as the Forest Service turn-around at Fern Canyon. Was planning on hiking in from there but there's a new gate across the trail. I checked it out and by golly, it turns out that the Scotia Lumber Company owns the land from there on over who knows how far. All part of Ralston timber, you know.'

'Isn't that the way it goes? The rich get richer even when they've got idiots for offspring.'

Steve finished sopping up the egg yolk with a piece of toast before picking up the check.

'Hey, Brad. You about finished? Let's get going. We've got some miles to go before lunch.'

Not paying any attention to those sitting at the round table, the two men paid and walked out into the morning sun.

'Well,' murmured Steve as he stood looking up and down the street, 'that worked pretty good. I was afraid none of them would remember us.'

'How'd you know those guys would tell us anything?'

'Ah, well, I learned a long time ago there are certain people in this town don't exactly like the way old man Ralston does business. His Scotia Lumber Company ruled the roost for too many years and now he's lost favor, they're all ready and willing to make sure he's down and stays there. C'mon. Let's get some gas and go for a drive up toward the Fern Canyon trailhead.'

Chapter 31

THE SOUTHERN END of the Redwood National Park, compared to the rest of the park, was generally flat although with the towering redwoods, giant Sequoia and Ponderosa Pine trees, it's hard to believe it. The old-growth forests were what made the park one of the most popular along the northern Oregon coast. It had been long enough since the last rainfall and the dust on the unpaved road left a cloud behind Steve's truck.

The dirt road was gravel in some places, letting Steve and Brad know the county did maintain it somewhat. Probably not going over it more than once or twice a year. After all, who'd make the trip except for hikers, horseback riders and, in season, deer hunters? Oh, and those intrepid state hunters of dope farms.

'You know,' said Steve at one point, 'driving through forests like these is a lot like walking down the middle aisle of some huge cathedral.'

'How would you know? The first time you ever set foot in a fashionable house of worship it'd scare God so bad He'd have to react with a bolt of lightning.'

'Funny man. But look at it, some of those trees have to be hundreds of years old. Those redwoods could even be older.'

The spectacular old-growth they were going through was something. Huge trees reaching hundreds of feet toward the sky, making the ground dark with shadow. It was easy to imagine Daniel Boone or one of those old-time hunters creeping silently through the trees, sneaking up on an elk or deer. Foley was watching out his side window but so far hadn't seen any hunters or animals.

'I don't ever remember hunting this far south. Did you?' he asked, not taking his eyes off the scenery.

'No. About the only time I ever came down to this end of the county was when someone called in a report of there being a still cooking up in the forest. As I recall, you were tied up in court and Sheriff Millard wanted to get out of the office so we came up to take a look. Turned out to be a bunch of kids from the Seventh Day Adventist Church holding some kind of youth retreat.'

Foley chuckled, thinking about how the sheriff would have reacted, him being a staunch Catholic.

The road ended in a clearing big enough to hold a half dozen pickups and horse trailers. It was empty.

'You know,' Steve said, getting out and reaching back to take his rifle out of the rear window rack, 'I remember people complaining about the damage horses were supposed to be doing to the hiking trails. Personally, I always figured the horses left behind some good fertilizer to make up for it.'

Foley thought about it a second and left his rifle in the rack.

'You're not taking your weapon?' When his partner shook his head, Steve smiled, hung his Remington back on the gun rack and handed Brad the daypack. 'Then I'll let you carry the bottled water and binoculars.'

A huge sign at the trailhead had a map showing the various hiking trails. Beyond a point, the wide trail separated out with smaller paths going in slightly different angles from the parking lot, all quickly disappearing into the forest shadows. Only one trail wasn't on the map, one with a single bar gate across it. Painted a bright yellow, a black sign read PRIVATE in bold red lettering.

Steve chuckled. 'Got to be the boundary of Ralston's land. Come hunting season, bet the deer know they'd be safer up past the sign.'

Not hesitating, the two men walked around the post the gate was attached to and started up the faint trail behind it. Pine needles and other forest debris covered the path, making it impossible to tell if anyone had been up there recently.

The trail climbed gently, turning one way and then another, snaking around the base of the huge trees. Hearing the silence of the forest, Foley thought of Steve's comment about being in a church.

'That'll be far enough, boys,' a hard voice called out from somewhere to the right. Both men stopped, holding their hands palms up and away from their bodies as a tall man in dark, well-worn clothing stepped out from behind a pine tree. It was hard to make out the man's features; most of his face was in the shadow of a floppy slouch hat. The one thing they could see, though, was a full dark beard. 'Didn't you read the sign back there? This here is private land you're on. The park is back there.' The man was carrying a short-barreled rifle. The rifle wasn't exactly pointed in their direction, but Foley saw it wasn't far from it.

'Yeah, we saw the sign,' said Steve. 'We didn't expect to find a gate keeper, though.'

Foley thought he knew the man. 'Say, aren't you Freddie? Uh, yeah, Freddie Isham? You tried to warn me of things a few days or so back.'

'Damn, is that you, Deputy? Gawd, you look a lot different without your sheriff's uniform. What the hell you guys doing up here, anyway?'

'Freddie, as I recall, last time we talked you mentioned something about looking for a different kind of work. But here you are. How come?'

'Ah, hell. No, I been thinking about it, but, well, things ain't much different back then when y'all were wearing badges. Except I'm not drinking as much as I used to. Can't, being up here five or six days a week without a break. What're you two looking for, as if I didn't know? Hell, you're not with the sheriffs anymore, are you?'

Steve relaxed, letting his hands fall to his side. 'No. Those days are long gone. But we're still doing the same thing, hiking the back country, only now instead of looking for good hunting camps, we're searching out dope plantations. Heard back in town something about your buddies, the Ralstons, have a going project up here. Thought we'd better come take a look.'

Leaning his rifle against the side of the tree, Freddie took a packet of cigarette papers and a sack of tobacco from his shirt pocket and started rolling a smoke.

'Hey, Freddie,' Foley said, watching the man's fingers as they expertly made up the cigarette, 'when you called, you said something about money going missing and you were being blamed. Didn't you say it was Hubert's partner, Anton, who'd taken to beating on you to find the money?'

Freddie twisted the end of his cigarette and struck a kitchen match with a thumbnail. 'Yeah. It was Anton and another guy, name of Cully, they worked me over pretty good.'

'Uh huh. I got some of it, too. Your phone call was a little late getting to me. But if they beat on you, how come you're working with them?'

'I'm afraid not to. If I take off, they'll for sure think I took the money.

143

Anyway, I ain't got a lot of other places to go now, do I? They pay me pretty good for sitting out here all day, warning people off and ready to give them what's working on ahead some warning if I see something like you two coming to raid them.'

'But you didn't warn them about us, did you?'

'Naw. But now I see who it is, well, makes me think. You know? Ever hear of the old saying, what goes around, comes around? Maybe whatever you're up to might be of interest to me. Know what I mean?'

Foley smiled. 'Yeah. So tell us about what's growing up ahead.'

'It's mostly up along the slope. They've tapped into a spring and are using the water from there and from the creek to irrigate the plants. The creek is pretty good sized, stretches out into the forest quite a ways. Been three or four men working on it regularly. Gawd, they're a messy bunch. Leaving their empty food cans and wrappers wherever they drop them. Plastic water bottles and other jugs are scattered all over the place. It's a real mess, mostly empty fertilizer sacks and what other stuff came in. They packed it all in on their backs. Just wait until there ain't any hikers down at the trailhead and hump it on up.'

'How complex are their irrigating systems?'

'Oh, they dug a couple big pits and lined them with black plastic tarps there by the spring. They got a couple pumps taking water up from the creek down below, too. I'll say this about them, for dope growers they're hard workers.'

'You say the plantation is just up the trail a ways?'

'Yeah, another quarter mile or maybe a little less. Not far.'

'Brad, I think one of us should go take a look-see.'

'Hey,' said Freddie quickly, 'you be damn careful. There's a couple booby traps along the way. Hubert damn near set off one of them the last time he was up. Anton wired a sawed-off shotgun to a little tree just where the trail comes out into the opening. He strung a trip wire down across the trail and in the shadows you'd never see it. Old dumb Hubert came along and run into one up there not long ago.'

'Another shotgun? Hubert didn't get killed, did he?'

'No such luck. No, there're a couple noise-making sets down at this end. The dumb kid tripped one. It rattled a lot of cans down in the camp. Anton got up there just in time to keep the fool from going on and getting a gut full of buckshot.'

'If I stayed up hill above the trail and went beyond,' asked Steve, pointing, 'say a couple hundred yards, I'd be OK, wouldn't I?'

'Well, maybe. There's two of them warning wires across the trail between here and where the trail drops down off this little ridge and into the camp. It's about where it comes out of the trees is the shotgun. Be best if you went off up there,' he pointed over his shoulder, 'and stayed high up on the ridge for a good quarter mile or so. Come down slow and careful and you should be at the far end of the field. But be damn careful. They have a couple guns and I don't doubt they'll use them.'

'OK, then. You guys stay here and I'll go see what's what. Won't be gone long.'

Foley watched as his hunting partner disappeared up into the trees. Settling back against the pine, he and Freddie sat and waited.

'There's something else, Mr. Foley. If you guys are still in the law business, does it mean there'll be a raid up here?'

'Sooner or later, I'd say. All we're doing is checking some possible sites. It'll be up to some other people to decide what to do with the information we take back. It almost looks to me like unless the grow is especially big, they won't do much about it.'

'Well, there's more to it than just marijuana growing on up there. Fact is, the dope is kinda like a cover. There's a full blown meth lab on the other side of the creek.'

Foley was stunned. This was looking better and better all the time. News of a meth lab would likely be all it'd take for Owens and his crowd to come storming in here.

Freddie wasn't finished. 'They got some big bad looking dude to do the cooking. It hasn't turned out anything yet, but from what I heard Hubert and Anton say, they expect to have a load to go south about the same time they're harvesting the pot. The plan is to have any cops what get too close find the bundles of bud, figuring they'll be satisfied and the meth can slip by.'

Brad picked up a little stick and sat digging in the dirt. 'Knowing about a meth lab could change things. But how come you're telling me all this?'

'Well, you helped me once and I feel kinda bad about giving you up to Anton and Cully. Anyway, see what they did to me,' he said, pulling his hat off and turning so Foley could see the side of his head. 'When they cut my ear off is when I told them the first name I could come up with, yours. They'd already cut off my ear lobes and boy, talk about hurting. Like nothing ever did before. But when they took the whole damn ear, I thought I'd been hit by lightning.'

'Jesus, hurts me to look at it.' Foley said softly, looking at the puckered scar tissue surrounded by greasy hair.

'Yeah. So I guess if you're gonna come up and raid this place, I'll have my revenge. But I wouldn't want to get caught up in it. If it were to happen, you know?'

Foley nodded. 'You carrying a cell phone?'

'Yeah. They gave me one of those cheap things. Won't take pictures or play music, it's just a phone.'

'OK, you give me the number and if there's to be a raid, I'll do my damnedest to give you some warning. Probably be the best I can do. OK?'

'Yeah, man. I appreciate it.'

Chapter 32

Finished with what they'd set out to do, Steve pointed the van inland, stopping for a late lunch at Willow Creek and then going on to I-5, the interstate freeway bisecting the state north and south.

The two were quiet after leaving the coast behind, thinking about the past few days. At one point, Steve broke the silence by saying from what he'd seen, Freddie was spot on. The dope patch was a real work of art, he said, with evidence of lots of attention. He said he hadn't gotten close enough to the large tent on the other side of the creek but the odor was confirmation of what was going on inside.

'I didn't see anyone, but there are half a dozen or so large plastic drums lying around the place.'

'You think it will be enough to get Owens excited? Busting a major marijuana grow and a meth lab at the same time? Should count pretty high.'

'Yeah,' said Steve, then was quiet for a beat. 'You know, your friend, Freddie. You trust him not to warn Ralston? I'd hate like hell to get Owens all excited and then find the place abandoned when the law got there.'

'There's no question Freddie's a devious old fart. He's been skating on the edge of the law for a long time and so far been pretty successful at it. Not starving, as far as I could see. Yeah, I think we can trust him to do whatever comes along if he thinks it's best for him.'

Steve used his cell to call his boss. Foley listened, hoping he'd hear the senator's name. Steve merely identified himself and asked if the man was available. Quickly he brought the state legislator up to date on what they'd found, leaving out the little farm outside of Willow Creek and only briefly describing the other two large plantations but adding the news of the meth lab on Ralston's timber property. For the next few miles, he didn't say anything more, just drove on with the cell phone tight to his ear, listening.

'OK,' he said finally, 'I guess I can understand it, but I've got to say, I think politics stink. Very well. I'll be in touch.' Touching the red icon, he dropped the cell into his shirt pocket.

'The good senator was interested in what we'll be reporting to Mr. Owens. He didn't like hearing about the business going on with the Ralstons, though. It seems old man Ralston is a big contributor of Governor Vasconcellos's. The good senator warned us not to expect too much from Owens. He said he wouldn't be surprised if a raid on the Ralston property doesn't happen as soon as it should. He figures Vasconcellos will more than likely want some time to separate himself from the Ralston link. Damn fool politicians.'

When Steve called Owens to say they'd be getting into town late, probably close to four, he was told to meet Owens at the Posey's Club.

'You know Posey's?' Steve asked Brad after putting his cell in a pocket.

'No, I've never hobnobbed with the capitol's upper crust.'

Steve ignored the jibe. 'Posey's is a pretty popular restaurant. Used to be one of the favorite places for unofficial meetings between various members of the State Senate and State Assembly. My boss told me all about how, back in what he called the good old days, members of legislature would meet to discuss things and make deals. A lot like that restaurant up in Eureka, I'd say.

'Anyway, things have changed in the legislature but Posey's is still very popular. Now, though, it's mostly tourists wanting a peek at the scandalous past whose business supports the place. I guess it's only fitting Owens picked Posey's. Damn politicians,' he said.

Foley had to laugh.

Posey's was nearly empty when the two men arrived. They were a little late for the afternoon lunch trade and early for dinner so the restaurant was quiet.

'Might as well relax,' said Steve, heading toward the bar. 'Owens said he'd meet us here at four, so you can count on him being fifteen minutes late. Typical ploy to show us how important he is.'

Glancing back toward the restaurant proper Foley saw the place was mostly empty, only one of the half dozen tables had customers.

'Fine by me, as long as you're buying the beer.'

'Naw, we'll run a tab and let Mr. Important pay.'

Steve was off by ten minutes, it was closer to 4.30 before the Governor's right hand man came in.

'Let's take a table so we can talk,' Owens said by way of greeting. Leading the way to a table some distance from any of the other customers, he took a chair and smiled at Steve. 'Your other teams haven't got back yet. I hope you two were successful?'

Steve told him first about the plantation up in the Trinity National Forest, estimating how big it was and assured him he had the GPS coordinates. Owens smiled and all but clapped his hands.

'Wonderful, wonderful. This is what we were hoping for. Did you search out any of the others marked on the map?'

'Yeah. The one site east of the Redwood National Forest, right on the banks of Redwood Creek? Turns out to be a licensed medical marijuana farm. We talked to the man and he explained how he'd written to everybody who would be interested, explaining what he was doing and where he was located, hoping he'd be left alone. It's not much for size anyway, probably only a couple hundred plants.'

'Ah, yes, the medical marijuana law,' said Owens, glancing first at Steve then at Brad. 'Damn foolishness, I think. But the Governor was forced into signing it.'

The glance was the first indication of Owens acknowledging Foley's presence. It made Foley wonder.

'We found another major plantation closer to the coast,' Steve said. 'One big one not shown on the aerial map you gave us.'

Owens looked up, a slight frown furrowing his forehead. 'What led you to look beyond the map?'

'Well, both Brad and I were once with the sheriff's department up there and we'd heard reports of large dope fields. We thought, while we were in the area, it'd be a good idea to check it out.'

'And what did you find?'

'A major plantation, well maintained by a handful of men. Plus,' he hesitated to emphasize his report, 'there's a large tent on the other side of the grow. I'd say it's about twenty feet square. From the odor coming from it, I'd swear someone was cooking meth.'

'Marijuana and a meth lab? My God.'

'Yeah. Now the thing is, it's on private land. The forest it's hidden in belongs to the Scotia Lumber Company.'

'What? Hmm, aren't the owners the H. Fredrick Ralston family?' It was clear that Owens didn't like hearing of it. 'Private land, hmm.' He hesitated. 'It'll mean some research will have to be done. We'll have to determine exactly what methods are open to us to pursue it. Yes. Well,' he suddenly cheered up, 'at least you found one on public land which will serve our purpose. Good work. Now, Steve, can I expect a full written report in the next day or so?'

'Uh huh. I'll have it emailed to your office by tomorrow.'

'Good, good. Gentlemen, I think you've done a good job. Uh, by the way, Steve, I understand you are working with Senator Murkowski's office? Uh, Mr. Foley, have you ever given any thought to taking on such employment? I'd be glad to recommend you to someone if you'd like.'

Foley had to glance sideways at his partner. Senator Murkowski, indeed.

'No, thanks, but I like the life I've got right now.'

'I understand you're not permanently employed, though.'

'No need to be. I'm enjoying my semi-retired lifestyle. But thanks just the same.'

'Hmm, yes. Too bad. All right, gentlemen. I'd join you for dinner but I have another meeting to attend. Go ahead and enjoy yourselves. I'll tell the Maitre d' to put your bill on the Governor's account.'

The two men watched as the tall public servant left the restaurant.

'Well, if the Governor's buying,' Steve said, standing up, 'then let's have another beer.' Coming back with two tall frosty glasses, he sat one down in front of Foley. 'You know you just passed up a good job,' he said. 'Getting your nose in the public trough is everybody's dream. Little real work and always good money.'

'No. I don't think it's for me. Right now I don't want for anything and I don't have to kneel whenever some governmental flunky comes into the room. But his offer makes me wonder. A short time ago he was questioning whether your bringing me on board was a smart move, remember?'

'Well, yes, you're right. But maybe getting the result he wanted proved something.'

'Uh huh. And your Senator Froggybottom was right. Owens is going to sit on the Ralston grow as long as he can.'

On the drive home to Stinson Beach, Brad gave a lot of thought to the job offer the Governor's man had made him. He didn't say anything about his thoughts to his partner.

Chapter 33

Leonie Weems didn't smile when Brad Foley walked into the offices of Discreet Inquiries, Inc. The night before, he and Steve had had a nice dinner, at the expense of the Governor. After enjoying an eight ounce fillet, baked potato, green salad and coffee, topped off with an ounce of Grand Marnier and coffee, Steve had driven him home to Stinson Beach. Alone again, he opened up the house to let the air out, took a glass of red wine and went out to sit on the back deck. He savored the wine, a Zinfandel from one of the local wineries, as much as he had the orange liqueur.

Thinking about the offer Curtis Lee Owens had made him, he shook his head. Hard to say what drives someone who sits at the right hand of power. Brad slept in his own bed that night and didn't dream. At least he didn't think he did. He was awakened earlier than he'd planned the next morning by the phone. Mr. Gorman, Leonie Weems said, wanted to see him ASAP.

It was a typical summer morning for the City; San Francisco's famous fog hadn't burnt off yet and shrouded the hills like a thin damp cotton blanket. It didn't bother him when the guardian at the gate didn't smile. She never did, not for him anyway.

'Mr. Gorman said to send you in the moment you got here,' was all she said before going back to reading whatever file she was holding.

'One of the joys of my day is basking in your welcoming nature, Ms Weems. I want you to know, I missed you these past few days.'

'Don't dawdle, Mr. Gorman is waiting. He wants to see you.'

'Yes, ma'am. I'm on my way.'

'Took your time getting back,' barked Gorman with no sign of the pleasant nature he had been showing lately.

'According to my calendar, I was gone seven days, just what I had told you I would. So, what's happened that's caused you to get all pissy?'

'I'll tell you why I am, as you say, all pissy. This thing with the Steiner girl has almost cost me one of my best investigators. That's why.'

'What happened? I was under the assumption we'd reached a dead-end?'

'Well, someone didn't get the message.'

Suddenly he had a bad feeling. 'Where's Gretchen?'

'She's the one I'm talking about. I sent her home until you got back and we could discuss things.'

'What things? And what do you mean, you almost lost her?'

'You're yelling. Just settle down. She's all right, I just didn't want her out and about until you got back and until we had a chance to talk about it. I'll have Leonie call her and ask her to come in after lunch. Maybe by then you and I can come up with some answers.'

Foley frowned, more at his quick reaction than anything. What the hell caused him to respond without thinking? He didn't have an answer.

He took a deep breath, trying to calm down. 'OK. What happened? Why was she sent home? Is she safe?'

'Yes, she's safe. Unhappy, but safe. You know how it is, these young people think they are bulletproof. But, well, maybe it was nothing. I just didn't want to take any chances so I kept her out of the office and away from the Steiner thing.'

'I thought we were finished with that. What changed? Did you find something at the party you were going to?'

'No. However, I did have the opportunity to get Chief Sands aside and pump him a little about the police investigation into the deaths of the two girls his people are dealing with. Arnold wasn't too happy about my asking and wouldn't say much. It wasn't the right time or place, he said, so I let it go. The party itself was a dud, far I was concerned. The story in the *Chronicle* the next day reported how a lot of money had been raised to help pay for the renovation of City Hall. I wasn't impressed and made damn sure none of it was my money.'

'So,' asked Foley, trying to get back on track, 'from your non-talk with the chief, you have the feeling the investigative bureau reached the same dead-end we ran into? Was anything said about Cochrane's murder?'

'Not then, but Arnold called me early on Monday and invited me to lunch. He said he had a meeting out at the airport and would meet me at international terminal. At first he said the meeting was with a number of police administrators from overseas. When I asked what it was about, he kind of stammered. Gave a nonsensical answer. I got the idea he'd chosen the Japanese restaurant out at the airport so he'd be certain nobody would see us together. Ebisu is the name of the restaurant. Ever heard of it?'

Foley shook his head.

'I hadn't, either, not until then. Parking out there is damn difficult and then had to ask directions to find the place. Waste of time, far as I could see. There are plenty places here in the City where we could have met but what could I do? You ever eat sushi or sashimi?' Another head shake. 'Me, neither. I like my fish cooked.'

Foley wanted to cut to the chase. 'And he met you out there so he could tell you what?'

'Simply put, he wanted me to know the bureau wasn't doing much about the murders. About all three of the stabbings. He slipped in Cochrane's murder without my asking.'

'Did our names come up? Do the cops know we had been there before them?'

'No. Nothing was said to make me believe so. From what little he did say, I learned how the body was discovered. It appears someone in another office on the same floor as Cochrane's smelled something, thought it was a dead rat somewhere in the walls. He called the building manager who made the discovery and called the police. Really, all Arnold had to say about the murders was the investigation is going nowhere and for some reason, wasn't likely to go any farther.'

Foley nodded. 'Did he mean they've closed the book, do you think?'

'Yes, in so many words, he was saying exactly that. As far as the San Francisco Police Department is concerned, the case has joined those in the 'unsolved' file cabinet. Which, Chief Sands made a point of saying, was precisely what someone wanted. Someone from higher up in the food chain.'

Before Foley could ask, Gorman held up his hand. 'He didn't say who. Someone apparently talked to the Mayor. Someone with a lot of power. He doesn't know who and I believe him.'

'Damn it, someone knows.'

'Yes, I'm sure you're right. I don't know how we'd ever find out, though.

If Arnold isn't able to, what are our chances? I do wonder, though, this week you've just spent working on something. Could whatever it was have anything to do with this?'

'No. I don't see how it could. We were paid to locate a number of large illegal marijuana plantations up in the northern part of the state. It's all part of the Governor's plan to show the voters how strong his feelings are when it comes to doing battle against the bad guys. All political bullshit.'

Gorman frowned. 'Isn't that the most effective kind? Well, anyway, there's nothing more about the Steiner case, I can tell you.'

'OK, now tell me what happened that caused you to send Gretchen out of the line of fire.'

'Ah, now there is a new twist. Let's see, you were gone last Monday, weren't you? Yes. Well, young Gretchen moped around, looking lost. I sent her out with Andy Collier. He's been doing a background check on a company that had made the low bid on a project down in Silicon Valley. Apparently the bid was questionably close to the next bidder, one the contracting company was familiar with. These computer people can get a little paranoid at times, afraid someone is going to steal their software design before it's proven. I think they're all soft in the head, if you ask me.'

'But they pay their bill on time, don't they?'

'Oh, yes. Anyway, she worked with Andy until, hmm, Thursday. She helped him write up the report on their findings. Leonie said she took a phone call and signed out. Which, I'm told, is something you never do. But to get back to it, on Friday, Miss Bongiorno came in and told me she had met with a young woman named, hmm, Amy? Do you know who this person would be?'

'How about Emma?'

'Yes, Emma. How foolish of me not to remember. Apparently this Emma was frightened and wanted our Miss Bongiorno to tell her what she should do. Someone, this Emma person said, contacted her via an email to her website, requesting a three-day assignation. Apparently she didn't know anything about the man and wasn't able to find anything. She told Gretchen she didn't recognize the man's name. It wasn't one of her regular clients. What really bothered her was he gave Sophie as a reference and wanted to hire her for a weekend at Lake Tahoe. When he used Sophie's name, it alarmed her and she turned him down. When Gretchen told me about it, I suggested she not contact this young woman again and should go home until you got back. My thought was to keep her out of the picture. She just might be getting too close to danger.'

Foley didn't like the sound of any part of it. And once again was surprised at the protectiveness he suddenly felt toward the young woman. Careful, Bradford, he silently warned himself. It wouldn't do to get emotional about this.

'I still want to protect the company,' Gorman went on. 'My suggestion is for you to meet with Gretchen and find out if anything she learned could be helpful to us. Otherwise I'd say we should continue to step back. Use your own judgment on deciding where to go. If there is anything new, then we'll go back to my original plan of you two working on it as private citizens, leaving the company uninvolved.'

'So far it hasn't worked very well.'

'No, but we do have deniability in any case.'

'OK. I'll call Gretchen and have her meet me for lunch.'

'Keep me informed. And for heaven's sake, be careful.'

Chapter 34

GRETCHEN, HE DISCOVERED, lived in a studio apartment on the other side of the bay.

'Well, it's about time you got back,' was her greeting when he called.

'Good morning to you, too, Ms. Bongiorno.'

She didn't sound happy. 'Mr. Gorman wouldn't let me come into the office until you got back. What does he think? Somehow I need you to protect me from the bad guys?'

'From what I was told, I'd say he's trying to play Father Protector to his newest hire. How about not taking it out on me and letting me buy you lunch?'

'And you think buying me a hamburger at some fast food place will make me forget how mad I am?'

'Why should you be mad? Because the old man sent you home?'

'No, because he's treating me like a little girl. Damn it, I'm not. I'm an adult woman able to take care of myself.'

'Uh huh. And I'd guess that Ms. Sophie would have said the same thing. But I didn't call to argue. I was told to get together with you to talk about things. Try to find out what we should do from here, if anything. Now, you want have lunch and we can talk or wait until you get over your temper tantrum?'

Foley waited. Finally, after a long period of cold silence, she answered, sounding quietly calm.

'I live over across the bay. It'll take me a couple hours to get into the City. I don't have a car.'

'Oh, great. So how do you get around?'

'Did you ever hear of public transport? Not everyone sees the value of keeping a car, you know. I get around just right with either BART or a bus.'

He didn't groan. 'OK, then I'll come to you. Where do you live?'

'In Walnut Creek.'

'Name a restaurant and I'll meet you there in, say, forty-five minutes.'

'OK. There's a place I like, the 1515 Restaurant and Lounge. The address is 1515 North Main, right down town. Think you can find it?'

Foley nodded and said he could find it.

Brad Foley had grown up in Oregon and until he moved to Stinson Beach, his total experience with any part of what he called Southern California constituted of a single trip delivering a prisoner to the jail in San Jose. To him, Southern California started at San Francisco and from what he could see, there wasn't anything to like about anything there. The list of things he didn't like could be summed up in one word: too damn many people. Freeway driving was a big part of it. He was most comfortable with the highways and freeways and hiking trails up in the northern half of the state. Driving into the City to work for DII was hard to take at first, way too much traffic for him to feel at ease. Now he was heading deeper into freeway madness and even at this time of day, just about noon, traffic on the Oakland Bay Bridge was stressful.

The bridge, all eight miles of it, carried two levels of traffic, five going east on the lower level and five on the upper level heading west into the City. With the rumble of traffic and knowing of the tons of speeding cars and trucks above him, he wasn't feeling comfortable. The heavy robust steel barriers on either side of the five lanes seemed awfully narrow to him; he was ready to bolt. But there was nowhere to go except straight ahead. None of the other motorists covering all five lanes, packed in like sardines in a can, were paying any attention to it. Just to keep up with the traffic, he had to push the Chevy to almost twenty miles over the limit.

With both hands on the wheel, Foley had to consciously think about making his back muscles relax. Glancing out of the side window, he saw beyond the bridge railing, construction on a second bridge. Having another bridge should, he told himself, take some of the pressure off this one but he doubted it. Just as a bare desk top attracted heaps of paper, a new wider road seemed to create its own traffic glut. He wondered how long it would be after the other bridge was completed before traffic returned to this breakneck level. No more than a month, he figured.

There was, he discovered, coming off the bridge and back out into the early afternoon sunshine, one good thing. Eastbound was toll free. A small thing but it made him feel a little better thinking about it.

His feeling of relief didn't last long. All too soon the freeway he was on fed into another interstate. Almost immediately, another sign warned drivers the Walnut Creek exit was only a couple hundred yards from the junction. God, he cursed silently, who designed these cans-of-worms?

He almost didn't see the exit in time. Not wanting to think of where he would have ended up, he soon found himself driving in slower, stop-and-go city traffic on Broadway Street in beautiful downtown Walnut Creek. Spotting a Chevron gas station on the corner, he pulled in and filled the tank.

When he paid for the gas, he asked for directions. The man behind the bulletproof glass made change and wordlessly pointed to a rack of street maps.

'Next,' the man said, looking over Foley's shoulder at the next customer.

Foley frowned at the lack of service at the so-called service station and walked past the map rack without picking one up. A telephone booth on the other side of the pumps caught his eye. Rather than paying for an expensive map, he went over and picked up the thick, *Contra Costa County* phone book. The pages of street maps in the front section of the book were probably not as detailed as the maps the guy had pointed toward but then the price was right. Choosing the Walnut Creek page, Foley studied it a moment before returning to his car. Main Street was one block over from Broadway.

The front of the 1515 Restaurant and Lounge was a series of windows facing the street. Driving by slowly, Foley could see that the lunch business was brisk. Glancing at the dashboard clock, after finding a parking space around the corner on Lincoln Street, Foley saw he was nearly a half hour early. The trip had felt like it had taken hours. Maybe, he thought, his tension had messed with time. Oh, he said silently, how I'd hate to have to get used to big city life.

Taking his time, he walked back to Main Street and window shopped as he walked to the restaurant. Gretchen was already there, sitting at a small table over along the wall.

'I thought you'd get here quicker than you said. It really isn't far, coming across the bridge and traffic this time of day should have been fairly light,' she said in way of greeting. Foley didn't bother correcting her.

'Don't you ever simply say hello?' he asked as he took the chair across from her.

Pursing her lips, she tried not to smile. 'I think I'm trying to stay mad at you.'

'No reason to be. Have you ordered?'

'Yes. They have a delicious crab salad.'

'Sounds good.' He nodded to the waitress. 'Now then, how in hell do you get around, not having a car?'

'I told you, BART or the bus. And it's kind of cool, knowing to get across to the City the train is going deep under the bay. Plus the transit system is a lot less expensive than supporting a car. Remember, I'm a student. At least I was until Mr. Gorman hired me, and I will be again. '

'And you can get across to the City? Of course, you can,' he answered himself, 'BART under the bay or bus over the bridge.'

The Bay Area Rapid Transport trains linked up nearly every suburb of both San Francisco and Oakland. Tunnels under the bay linked the two major cities before spreading out both north and south. He'd never taken a BART train to get anywhere.

Gretchen must have gotten over her anger as she went on to explain about her choice of where to live. 'It costs a lot less to live here and use public transport, you know. And I do like it here in Walnut Creek. The weather over here is a lot milder than over in the City and there are trees and parks everywhere.'

'How far do you live from here?'

'On Lincoln, just around the corner. Fact is, there's a huge park just across the street from my building.'

'I live up the coast a little,' he said. 'In Stinson Beach. A helluva lot less crowded. More peaceful. Probably because you have to have a car to get there. No bus service and BART doesn't come close.'

She was right, the crab salad was good and the cold beer he'd asked for tasted even better.

'OK, tell me about your visit with Emma. What made her call you, anyhow?'

'I gave her my number the first time we talked. I told her to call me if she thought of anything about Sophie or the Steiner girl. When she got the call from the stranger asking about a trip to Lake Tahoe and using Sophie as a recommendation, she got scared and hung up on him then called me.'

'What name did he give her?'

'She said it sounded something like 'sister rio' or something.'

Foley sipped his beer, running the words over in his mind. 'Could it have been Cisterio?'

'That sounds good. Who is he?'

'Well, if it's Cisterio, then it is interesting. Remember? Cisterio was the guy who came over from the capitol to warn me about working as a PI without a license. Said he was from the state AG's office.'

'I thought it sounded familiar. But why would he … well, I guess big shot lawyers get horny, too.'

'Is that why you want to study law?'

'No, that isn't the reason,' she quickly responded petulantly.

Foley chuckled and motioned to the waitress for another bottle of beer. He hadn't known anything about local brews and had let the young waitress recommend one. She'd brought him Black Diamond pale ale which proved to be quite tasty. He thought one more wouldn't hurt.

'OK, so someone named Cisterio called her. As I remember the man we met, he didn't strike me as the type who would call halfway across the state for a prostitute. But I guess you never know.'

'There was something else Emma wanted to talk to me about. She has decided to stop working as an escort and wants out of the business. Whoever killed Cochrane had apparently messed up the computer links so her website had stopped getting responses. She hadn't known he'd been murdered and emailed him when she stopped getting calls. Not for almost a week. When she heard the news of Cochrane's murder, she decided to stop working and just be a full-time student.'

'Yeah, didn't she say something about getting out of the business the last time we talked to her?'

'Yes. But there's more. Late last week, the day before she got the call from Cisterio or whoever it was, she got an email telling her Cochrane's website, SF-eye-candy dot.com, was back up and running. She responded by saying she was dropping her web pages. Whoever took over the business tried to change her mind and she said no. When the emails got pushy, she started to simply delete them. Then she got a phone call warning her to rethink things. The warning really scared her.'

Foley frowned. 'Did she say who had taken over Cochrane's business?'

'No, but whoever it is certainly put the scare to her. Now she doesn't know what to do.'

'Hmm, maybe it'd be a good thing to find out who's taken King Cock's place. But what put the wind up Gorman's back enough he felt it necessary to protect you?'

'It was while I was on the bus going to work, some guy took the seat next to me. For the longest time he didn't say anything. Usually the buses are full at that time of morning and I didn't think anything about it until we were going over the bridge. It started when he looked at me and smiled. It would be a good thing, he said, if I didn't waste any more time trying to find out about the Steiner girl. That's what he said, the Steiner girl.'

Foley put his beer glass down and leaned forward. 'What did you say?'

'I was shocked. I mean, here we are, a whole bus load of people going to work and this guy starts talking to me, telling me things nobody else on the bus would know. Who was he, do you know?'

'No. How would I know? What did he look like?'

'Oh, I don't know. I was too scared to pay much attention. He was wearing a suit, some kind of black suit with a vest. He talked softly, just like as if we were talking about the weather. Only we weren't.'

'His warning, did he say anything else?'

'No. He said if I kept getting into things I shouldn't, I'd pay for it. Any time, on the bus in the morning or when I went home at night, there could be an accident. He even smiled when he said it. The man was staring right at me. I couldn't look away. He said you were out of the picture and for me to get smart and learn how to simply find lost cats or serve court documents. But I wasn't to go around asking any more questions about things that didn't concern me.'

Foley exhaled loudly; unaware he'd been holding his breath.

'And you didn't recognize the man? Hadn't seen him before, maybe?'

She shook her head. 'No. I don't know. He frightened me. I wasn't thinking about what he looked like, only what he said.'

'Did he say anything else?'

'No. When he said what he did, he got up and moved toward the back of the bus. A big fat woman sat down in his place. I tried to turn around to see where the man went but she was carrying a brief case and a shopping bag full of things and, well, by the time she got settled and I could look around, he was gone. I tried to get off at the next stop to see if I could see him but the woman took too long to get her things together.'

Foley waited.

'Brad, to tell the truth, I didn't want to see him again. He scared me. It's not very professional of me, is it.' She wasn't asking a question.

'Anyone threatened in such a cold manner would be a fool not to be scared. Don't think about it. Telling Gorman was the right thing to do. Now we have to think about what to do next.'

'Maybe we should let it go. Do what the man said and not ask any more questions.'

'I don't know. Let's see what …' He stopped and sat quietly for a long moment, thinking. When the waitress came by, nodding toward his beer glass, he shook his head and asked for the bill.

'No, Gretch, I think the old man was right. It'd be better if you worked with someone like Andy. He's been working in the City since before they made dirt and you can learn a lot from him.'

'Bullshit, Brad Foley,' she shot back, her face turning red, her lips thinning out and getting hard. 'You're full of it. You're just like Mr. Gorman. You don't think I can cut it. Well, I admit it, OK? The man scared me. But he can't chase me away from doing my job. If I'm going to let every stranger chase me away, I might as well stay home in bed.'

'Hoo whee. It doesn't take much to get your fires lit, does it? OK. Far as I'm concerned, you can't be frightened off the job. Only tell me, what do we do next?'

Slowly her face returned to its normal color and she quickly glanced around to see if anyone had heard her blow-up. Looking back at her partner, she frowned.

'I don't know. You're the one who is supposed to be teaching me, remember? So, teach me.'

'Well,' he said, standing up and reaching for his wallet, 'being a man, and we all know how exciting it is when a pretty woman says 'teach me', I can only shake my head. However, you're far too young. And I don't imagine it's what Gorman had in mind. So let's stick with the Steiner case.'

They stopped long enough to pay for their lunch. Holding open the door for her, Foley stood back to watch her step out onto the sidewalk.

Gretchen read his mind, and glancing up at him, she smiled. 'I don't know what you talk about, but it's obvious what you're thinking. Ms Weems warned me about you. She said there was something about your slick tongue made her think you have a dirty mind.' Taking his arm and walking down the street, she went on. 'She'll be glad to know she was right. Now, what are we going to do next ... about the Steiner case?'

'My car is down there,' he said as they turned the corner, 'let's go back to the City and see if we can catch up with Miss Emma. I'd like to hear more about who is pressuring her to stay in business.'

'What about the man who threatened me?'

'Didn't he tell you I wasn't around to protect you? Well, he was wrong, wasn't he?'

Chapter 35

'I DON'T WANT TO talk to you,' Emma said, staring angrily at Gretchen.

The trip back across the bay seemed to Brad Foley to be a lot quicker than going the other direction. He didn't want to consider it was because Gretchen was sitting in the passenger seat. They had gone up to her apartment, a studio on the second level with lots of wall to ceiling glass overlooking a greenway. Filled with warm afternoon sunshine and lots of pillows, framed photos, cute little knick-knacks and flowers both fresh and fake, her place was obviously home to a female. Standing at the window while Gretchen changed clothes, he thought about how bland her place made his appear. Looking down to the park where a man in shorts and t-shirt was tossing a Frisbee to a dog, he tried not to think about her getting undressed behind the bedroom door. Heaven, he mused, so near but yet so far away.

That is if heaven could be described as an attractive young female with long brown hair in a loose ponytail like she was wearing. Glancing around as she came out, he decided if she wasn't the vision of heaven, she was certainly nice to look at.

'Ready to go?' she asked, looping the strings of a colorful woven tote bag over a shoulder. 'Remember, you don't have to bring me back here when we're finished. I can get the bus, you know.'

'Yeah, I know. But it's my idea to go over to the City now and not wait until tomorrow.'

Walking down the wide stairway, he held the door for her. Earlier she had been wearing a pair of jeans so faded they were almost white and a multi-colored cotton shirt. The shirt, or probably more correctly the blouse, was tight enough the twin pockets high on the front only emphasized the shape of breasts. Not big, he had noticed, but more pointed than round. Foley was hoping she hadn't caught him staring.

Her outfit wasn't suitable for interviewing, she had said, and had changed into a tan khaki skirt ending just above her knees and her usual white business-style blouse. He liked the first outfit better.

Afternoon traffic over the bridge was only slightly better than what he'd battled earlier. Driving on the top tier, up in the sunshine, was a lot more pleasant than going in the other direction. The trip back into the City was far less stressful. Maybe, he thought, one should only travel in that direction. Or only with an attractive young woman in the passenger's side.

Emma Longenbough wasn't happy to see who it was when she opened her door.

'I don't want to talk to you,' she said, ignoring Foley and looking directly at Gretchen. 'I asked you to leave me alone and here you are again. What is there about "no, I don't want to talk to you" do you not understand? Why do you keep bothering me?'

'Look,' Foley said, forcing her to look at him, 'two of the women using the same source for their business as you have been murdered. The man who set the program up has also been killed. What makes you think you won't be next? We can guarantee you won't if we can finger the killer. Is it so difficult for you to understand? Now, how about we come in and talk?'

Shaking her head in disgust, the woman pushed her door open, turning away to settle on one end of a couch.

'I already have protection,' she said, not looking up. 'I was told not to talk to you or anyone and I'd be OK.'

'Who said that?'

Emma hesitated, then glancing sideways at Gretchen, shrugged. 'A man. When I stopped reading any emails from the Eye-Candy web site, I got a phone call. A man. He didn't bother saying who he was. He wanted to know why I hadn't responded to his email messages. I told him I was pulling my site and wasn't going to work anymore. That's when he got mean.'

Gretchen sat down next to her and took her hand. 'What did he say?'

'He said my site would stay up and running and I would continue working. Only from now on, I'd be paying him a bonus of $100 for every assignment I take. When I said no, I was finished with all that, he laughed. He had my phone number, he said, didn't I think he had my address too?

Remember what happened to Sophie, he said. I … I panicked and hung up the phone.'

After a pause, and pulling her hand from Gretchen's, she went on.

'He called right back. I didn't answer but the phone kept ringing and ringing and … well, I picked it up. He laughed and went on as if he hadn't heard a word I'd said. He warned me not to contact anyone, not to talk to anyone except customers. He'd be watching, he said, and expecting his money after every john paid up. Before I could say anything, he hung up.'

'Emma,' said Foley slowly, thinking, trying to figure out how this had happened, 'you say this guy told you he had access to your site?' Not looking up, she nodded. 'And is your phone number on your site?'

'No. All there is an email address. Addresses, I have four of them.'

'Did Cochrane have your telephone number?'

'Well, yes, on the form I had to fill out. Something about his having to prove all he was doing was providing internet access for our individual sites. You know, in case the police came calling.'

'And on his form, you gave him your address.'

'Yes.'

'OK, that helps. Do you really want to get out of accepting any more business? Are you serious about it?' He waited until she nodded. 'Then here's what you do. Don't respond to any email contacts. Write down your phone number for me. Tomorrow or possibly the next day I'll call you.'

'What are you going to do?' She was frightened.

Foley smiled and nodded to Gretchen. 'Go on about your classes and either Gretchen or I will call you and explain. If the man calls again, don't tell him anything. Don't argue. Don't panic. I doubt you'll hear from him for a few days anyway. If anything, he'll wait to see how this is going to work out. Trust us on this one. Just give us a couple days and let us see what we can do.'

Out on the sidewalk, Gretchen stopped Foley. 'And what exactly can we do?'

'Well, the first thing is find out if what I think happened did happen. Then, well, then I take you home.'

Parking the Chevy in the parking garage, Foley picked up a manila folder off the back seat, took Gretchen's arm and led her away from the elevators and up to the street.

'Aren't we going to see Mr. Gorman?' she asked. Foley only smiled and shook his head. 'Well then, where are we going?'

'It's only a couple blocks, we can walk it. The exercise will do us both good.'

Stopping, she grabbed his arm. 'I'm not going anywhere until you tell me where you're taking me.'

Chapter 36

FOLEY CHUCKLED AND taking her hand, he tucked it under his arm and started walking. 'All right, I'll tell you. First we're going to see what we can find is happening over in the Kroll Building. It's only a half dozen blocks or so. Think you can walk that far without getting too tired out?'

'The Kroll Building? Where Cochrane's office was?'

'Uh huh. I want to see what we can discover there. Then we'll come back to talk with the old man. Now, if you'd rather go back to DII and wait for me, I'll understand.'

'You are exasperating, do you know it?'

'Nope, never gave it a thought.'

From the outside, the Kroll Building looked the same as the last time they had visited. Inside, up on the fourth floor, there were a couple of changes.

'What are you going to do, Brad? Just walk in?'

'No. Watch and learn,' He smiled down at her and knocked on the wood door marked 412, turned the handle and walked in.

'What do you want?' said a young man, looking up from a pile of electronic parts scattered all over the top of the desk.

The last time they had seen the big desk, King Cock Cochrane had been sitting behind it. No, Foley corrected himself, the last time the webmaster had been lying in a pool of blood behind it. The man standing behind it now looked like he should still be in high school. Brad didn't know much about computers but enough to know what the bits and pieces on the desk belonged inside, not outside a computer.

'Oh,' Foley said, stopping to take a long look around the room before opening up the folder he'd been carrying and pretending to read something. Nothing had changed; three of the walls were still covered with

169

metal shelves, holding dozens and dozens of flat boxes. Cochrane's servers.

'Isn't this the law offices of Rockford and Rockford?' Glancing back at Gretchen, he frowned. 'Gosh, Miss Queen, you were right after all. I was sure we had the right address.' Turning back to the young man, he smiled. 'We're looking for room 412, Kroll Building, Union Street.'

'Well, you got the right address, but there are no lawyers in this office.'

'No, so I see. Why, there are enough computers on those shelves to, well, I'd say, to run Microsoft. What kind of business are you in, if I may ask?'

The young man straightened up and smiled. Here, Foley thought, was a good example of the word 'nerd'. Maybe it was all the computer innards lying on the table.

'Oh, this is a web service. The company hosts websites for people.'

'Hosts websites,' said Foley hesitantly, glancing at Gretchen then back to smile at the man. 'I've heard that phrase before but never knew exactly what it means. Are you a computer technician?'

The youngster's smile grew. 'No, I'm a programmer. And before you ask, no, I'm not tearing into this box to program something.' Looking around at the shelves, he frowned. 'I wish I were. My degrees are in pro-gramming and coding, the development of code, you know?'

'But you're not, uh, coding?'

'No,' he said wistfully, poking at a motherboard with a long slender screwdriver, 'they've got me troubleshooting and maintaining the servers. But I'm not complaining,' he quickly added, 'they're paying me good money. Damn good money. Money I can use to help pay off my student loans.'

'Oh, then this isn't your business?'

'No. I answered an ad in one of the student newspapers down at San Jose State. It's easy work, all I have to do is keep all these servers up and running.'

'It sounds way over my head. Who owns the company? Maybe they have a tie in with Rockford and Rockford.'

'I doubt it. A man named Mane signs my pay check. I don't think he's got a company name. If he does I've never seen it. All these servers are tied in with the local telephone company.'

'Well, obviously we got the wrong address. Thank you for your time and trying to explain these high tech things. Come on, Miss Queen, there's still time to get back to the office and sort this out.'

Turning quickly toward the door, he bumped into Gretchen, dropping the manila folder. Steadying her by touching her shoulder, he glanced sheepishly back at the young man and stooped to pick up his material.

'Clumsy of me. Again, thank you,' he said, following his partner out and gently closing the door behind him.

Back on the sidewalk, Gretchen couldn't miss the look of pride on her partner's face.

'OK, smarty pants,' she said as they walked back toward Fillmore Street, 'where did my name change to Queen?'

'Oh, didn't you see the humor? You're a PI, right? Well, one of the more famous fictional private investigators ever was Ellery Queen. I thought you'd be honored.'

'And I suppose the fictional lawyers, Rockford and Rockford, are a couple more television investigators?'

'You must have had a sheltered upbringing. Everybody knows Jim Rockford. The Rockford Files?' Seeing her lack of comprehension, he frowned and explained. 'One of television's best series. Going back, oh, I'd say, to the mid 1970s.'

'1970? I wasn't even born then.'

That made Foley's smile dissolve.

'Come on,' he said abruptly. 'We need to have to talk with the old man.'

Chapter 37

'You're taking a big chance, Brad,' Francis Gorman said, after hearing what Foley and Gretchen had been up to. 'Don't get me wrong, I applaud your originality in trying to find something to lead you to complete answers. However, involving Ms Bongiorno is unacceptable. I thought I'd made it clear she is to be kept out of the line of fire—'

'Wait just a moment, sir,' cut in Gretchen, putting emphasis on the sir. 'I was given the assignment to partner with Brad in order for him to mentor me. We, as partners, were given the job of finding out all we could about Anne Marie Steiner. Now you're chewing him out for doing his job. I am not a helpless woman who must be protected and I would appreciate it if you would let me learn what I have to in order to become a competent investigator.'

Foley worked hard to hold his poker face when he wanted to pat her on the back and say, 'Good job!'

Gorman turned his chair so he could look out of the big window. After a long pause, he nodded and he turned back to face the pair.

'I stand corrected. And I apologize. You are correct, which leaves me with one of two things to do. Either end your employment with this company and send you on your way, hoping you'll take up a more protected kind of employment, which I don't think you will, or let you use your own best judgment. I give up. Now, Mr. Foley, what are you planning to do with the information you two have turned up?'

'Well, I'd appreciate it if you'd contact your old friend, Tolliver Mane, and ask him about having taken over Cochrane's cyber-prostitution racket. My goal is to get Emma free to become nothing more than a student.'

'Hmm, and what will this do to help you with the Steiner case?'

'I'm not exactly sure it will. The questions I have are still there. I've been working on the premise that the answer to the deaths of both girls would be clear if we knew who the last man they had been with was known. From what Emma told us, someone hired the two girls to spend a weekend with him. She knew this because Sophie called her first to see if she was free to take the trip. Remember,' he glanced at Gretchen, 'Emma said she told Sophie she couldn't do it and suggested she ask Anne Marie. It was right after that that someone killed Anne Marie and a short time later, Sophie.'

Gorman slowly nodded. 'And how does this tie into Tolly having taken over Cochrane's business?'

'It doesn't. But what if I'm wrong? Instead of the girls being killed by a client and Cochrane being murdered because he might have known who the man was, what if it was all a way of simply taking over the computer prostitution business? According to Cochrane, there's a lot of money being made there and very little chance of it ever being in danger from the police. Don't you think those two reasons might be enough to interest your friend, Mane?'

'Hmm, well, I see your point. Yes, Tolly has a reputation of being in the prostitution business. Let's see what he has to say.'

As Gorman reached for the phone, Foley stood up and mumbled something about going to the bathroom.

Outside Gorman's office, he went to the reception desk. 'Ah, Ms Weems. I wonder if you'd know where I could find Andy Collier?'

'Why do you want to know? And what were you thinking, getting the young girl in danger?'

'Like what?' Foley said gruffly. 'She and I, and since he's heard the whole thing, old man Gorman all agree she wasn't in very much danger and she was just doing her job. Now are you going to do your job and give me the information I'm asking for or continue to act like mother hen to Ms Bongiorno, who by the way is a licensed investigator and a valued member of the team.'

'Nobody talks to me like that—' she started, only to be interrupted by Foley.

'Then it's about time someone did. You are not Gorman's conscience. From what I've heard, you are the receptionist and office manager. I'd leave running the investigators up to Gorman, if I were you. Now, where in the hell is Collier? Is he in the office or out on the street...?

For a moment Foley was afraid he'd gone too far and had made the older woman cry. Pursing her lips and visibly gritting her teeth, she looked down at her hands.

'You might try his office. Down the hall—'

'I know where it is. Thank you.'

'—and the first door on your left,' she finished, ignoring his interruption.

Collier was on the phone, sitting behind his desk, leaning back with his feet stretched out in front, heels resting on a bottom drawer. Waving a hand toward a chair, he went on talking.

'Now, Mrs. Anderson, let me be very clear with this. Yes, your attorney told you the truth, your husband did hire our firm to gather evidence which we did. The photos of you and a man not your husband, along with copies of the hotel register, were what we had been asked to gather up. I'm sorry but it wouldn't be ethical for us to accept an assignment from you to obtain the same type of evidence on your husband.' Pause. 'No, ma'am. But if you wish, I can recommend another company ...' Another longer pause. 'I understand fully. But I'm sure if you were to talk to your attorney about this, he would ... hello? Mrs. Anderson?'

Putting the phone on the cradle, Collier smiled at Brad. 'She hung up on me. She thought it'd help her case if the same investigator had to testify for her against her husband. Damn, I hate working divorce cases. But it pays the bills. Now then, what can I do for you?'

'A hypothetical question. Let's say there was a divorce case and the evidence you were collecting was all in an office. Let's say further you knew the office would be empty later in the evening. Who would you get to open the office door?'

'You mean break in? Hoo, that isn't all that easy. Hypothetically speaking, most office doors, especially in older buildings, usually have cylinder style locks. More modern office doors might have a pin-and-tumbler design or even both, two separate locks, one a sturdy deadbolt type. You can see how your question doesn't come with an easy answer, can't you?'

'Uh huh. I was able to look at the lock on the door I'd like to get open. The brand name was MBS. Does MBS engraved on the lock cover tell you anything?'

'Oh, yes, indeedy. How'd you go about getting the name? MBS is one of the better brands of cylinder locks. A very strong and well made locking system. Did you happen to see if it was an MBK 1 or MBK 2?'

'No, all I could see when I "accidentally" dropped a file as I went out the door were the letters, MBS.'

'Hmm. Well, it doesn't really matter. I wonder if what you want to find inside the office is really worth the effort. Working a good lock happens to be hard work. Delicate, you know?'

'There's nothing inside I want to find. All I want to do is get in and be able to spend a few minutes undisturbed.'

'This hypothetical endeavor isn't to look for papers or other documents?'

'Nope.'

'Hmm. Well, I do happen to know a fellow who has in his possession a practically new set of picks and rakes. There'd be a price to pay for his services, you understand.'

'Depending on whether I can afford it or not, let me get in touch with him and maybe we can reach an understanding. Who is this fellow?'

'Me. And the price is an explanation once it's done. An explanation given over at least one ounce of the best single malt Scotch in a nice uptown pub. No, better make it two ounces.'

Foley chuckled. 'You're on. But why are your picks and rakes practically new? Are you saying they're also slightly used? And what exactly are picks and rakes? I can picture the picks. Nearly every caper movie has at least one lock picking scene where the hero pulls out a hair pin and bends it a certain way in order to open a locked door.'

'Yes, the trusty hairpin taken from the pretty young girlfriend's perfect hairdo. Do you know some of the finest picks can also be made from bicycle spokes or even street cleaner bristles? It's true. My set are just your ordinary locksmith's tools. Illegal in the state of California to have if you're not a licensed locksmith. There's about a dozen little pieces, everything from a torsion wrench to offset diamond picks, short hooks, a saw rake and even one called a snake rake. It'd take me too long to explain what all those are and how they do the job.'

'But you don't use them very much?'

'Not at all. A set like the ones I'm talking about are almost only seen in museums today. Modern technology has come to the rescue. Nowadays we have such things as an electric pick gun. Very high end and quite expensive. It works by simply pressing a button which causes the pick to vibrate while at the same time the normal tension wrench is being used. I can't quite afford one of those. But I have something almost as good.'

'And you can open the lock and after I'm through, relock it?'

'Hardly ever fails. Just give me a minute or two and you're in and the door will lock itself when you leave.'

'How about later tonight? Say …' Foley hesitated, remembering he'd promised to drive Gretchen home. 'About ten?'

'OK. Pick me up here?'

'You got it. And thanks.'

'No thanks needed. Just a couple ounces of the good stuff in a nice heavy glass will be thanks enough. And an explanation.'

Back in Gorman's office, he learned Mane didn't deny taking over Cochrane's business.

'Damn Tolly,' Gorman said, shaking his head. 'Show him a way to make a dollar illegally and watch out. He's quite proud of it. He was happy to explain how, when he heard about Cochrane's death, he sent someone around to the building. By promising to pay for the clean up, new carpets and paint, as well as taking over the lease, he got Cochrane's office. And all his equipment. Then he hired one of those young, intellectually gifted programmers out of some high-tech school down the peninsula. Told the smart kid the equipment was the basis of the web hosting business and turned him loose. Only now Tolly has access to all the sites and all Cochrane's old clients. Gretchen described the banks of servers on the shelves of the office. From what you've said, Cochrane had a couple hundred sites he was hosting. Didn't the man brag about the thousands of dollars coming in every month? And then there's any income from creating new sites. Your programmer could do it in his sleep. Yes, trust Tolly Mane to get into the business over someone's dead body.'

'Brad,' said Gretchen, sounding depressed, 'Mane told Mr. Gorman he saw no reason to let Emma leave the business.'

'Yes,' said Gorman, 'he made it very clear. He doesn't see how he can afford to lose even one girl's business. With all the information he has on the girls, and the muscle boys to back him up, I don't see how things have changed. It's just like it was before, when the pimps operated by fear and intimidation. Again, it's sickening, especially with Tolly sounding so proud of himself.'

Gretchen nodded. 'And we promised Emma we'd do something to get her out of it. What can we do?'

Foley let a frown wrinkle his forehead. 'Well, I have to admit it doesn't look good right now. Let me think about all this. Maybe I can come up with something.'

Chapter 38

Taking Gretchen over to Walnut Creek was a quiet affair. After leaving the office, and before turning toward the bay bridge, Foley turned onto Turk Street, a one-way street heading away from the bridge.

'Now where are you taking me?' Gretchen asked suspiciously.

'Home, just as I promised. First, though, I want to stop over at University of San Francisco for a minute. Something I have to do there. Won't take long.'

'I don't entirely trust you, you know.'

He laughed. 'Yes, you've made it very clear. And I don't blame you. I'll wager your mother told you from a very early age not to trust men.'

'She did. And Sister Mary Margaret said the same thing; a girl's most prized possession must not be wasted. The love of the right man is God's answer, she told me.'

'Sister Mary Margaret. You went to Catholic schools?'

'You bet. My parents thought if they kept me out of public schools, they'd be saving me from the bad influences of drugs, sex and rock and roll.' It was her turn to giggle. 'Little did they know, little did they know.'

'And your Sister Mary Margaret, did she know?'

'Oh, she had to. She taught philosophy in high school. A very intelligent woman who understood a lot, I think. But she was a good friend to most of us girls.'

Stopping at USF, Foley parked in the War Memorial Gymnasium parking lot. Getting out of the Chevy, he turned back to look at Gretchen.

'Wait for me. I'll only be a second.'

Hurrying away before she could react, he headed across the street and pushed through the door marked KUSF, 90.3 FM.

True to his word, before Gretchen had time to get over being mad, he was back, carrying a shopping bag which he put on the floor behind the driver's seat.

'Now,' he said getting behind the wheel, 'next stop, your place over in the beautiful city of Walnut Creek.'

Once again, with the young woman sitting in the car with him, the half-hour drive went too quickly.

'What do you say we stop somewhere for a bit of dinner?' he asked coming off I-680 and onto Broadway. 'There must be some decent places here.'

'Ah, no. Thanks but I'll take a rain check. What are you planning to do next? With the Steiner case, I mean.'

'I'm not exactly sure what we can do. Once again, it seems we've hit a dead-end. Sure you don't want dinner?' he asked again, pulling to the curb in front of her apartment building.

'No,' she said, opening her door, 'but I do appreciate the invitation. See you in the morning.'

He watched as she walked through the big glass double doors. Ah, he sighed silently, so young, so round, so … so what.

Turning around in the street, he noticed there was a different man over on the grass, tossing a Frisbee to a different kind of dog.

With time to kill until picking up Andy, he decided to go down to the fisherman's wharf area for dinner. Since the Gold Rush days, San Francisco's wharf area has been home to a huge fishing fleet. A lot of Italian fishermen coming to California with dreams of getting their share of the gold reported to be in streams and rivers inland, discovered it was more profitable to sell their catch than hunt for the yellow metal. Then, a few generations later, the fishing industry fell on hard times. Although there was still a fishing fleet, owned and operated mostly by the grand-sons and great-grandsons of those earlier men, it is the tourist dollar most businesses on the wharf area chase.

Boat traffic still plays a big part of commerce on the bay. Pier 43 is home to the fleet of one of the big colorful ferry boats ferrying people home across the bay or tourists around the world famous prison, Alcatraz. In that same area, overlooking the remaining fleet of fishing boats was, in Brad Foley's view, one of the best of the City's eating establishments; Alioto's.

Most San Francisco residents turn their noses up at the idea of having a meal at one of the restaurants that brag about being "World Famous" but Alioto's was, for him anyway, the exception. If it wasn't famous world-wide, he thought it should be.

According to the tourist guides, a Sicilian immigrant named Nunzio Alioto Sr. started out with a fresh fish stall in the mid 1920s. Over the years the fish stew he made, using whatever of the day's catch that didn't sell, filled the bellies of men working on the docks and fishing boats. Based loosely on his Genoese grandmother's recipe for fish stew, which she called cioppino, Alioto's Restaurant gained in popularity. Add sour-dough bread and you have a meal fit for anyone, tourist or local.

Foley hunted until he found a parking spot and walked back for a meal of the stew, adding a bottle of Anchor Steam beer, a local brew, to the meal. With time to kill, he settled in to enjoy things. Things like the food, the beer and the people watching.

He had been watching people, tourists by their clothes, when two young girls caught his eye. He had to laugh. Both were wearing tight black pants that stopped halfway down their calves, thin soled sandals and bright colored tie-dyed T-shirts, the bottoms of which had been cut off to just below their nice, firm, uplifted breasts. Foley was sure of two things; one, neither wore a bra and secondly, they were very young and very proud of the attention their breasts were getting.

Watching them pass by, he thought of Gretchen. She was only a few years older than the two girls but somehow he doubted she had ever paraded down the street like that. Too bad, he reflected, her having missed out on ever enjoying the feeling. Frowning, he tried to explain to himself exactly why he had thoughts like that.

Shaking his head at his foolishness, he finished the second beer and was trying to talk himself into another when his cell phone vibrated.

'Yeah?' he almost snarled at the interruption. Carrying a cell had become a habit, but he rarely got any calls on it.

'Well, aren't we happy tonight or what?' said Steve.

Foley knew his partner was smiling. He always smiled when talking on a phone. Steve had read somewhere if he smiled into a telephone, the person he was talking to would know it and would smile back, putting everyone in a good mood. It became a habit of his to smile when making a phone call.

'It's nothing,' said Foley. 'I was just sitting here enjoying a few quiet minutes before doing something I'm not sure will work. What's up with you?'

'Well, I thought I'd let you know, Owens and his little army of drug cops made their raid this morning. Tomorrow's newspapers will be full of it. Lots of people in black jackets with POLICE in big letters on the back, all carrying the latest in assault rifles and looking serious. Great photos for the morning edition.'

'Make some arrests?'

'Yeah, I hear there were six men taken into custody. Owens said his men cut down tons of perfectly grown pot plants. I can just see the photo of the dope all piled up with someone setting it on fire. What a waste.'

'And the Governor gets a pat on the back and everybody's happy.'

'Yeah. And you and me, we got some extra money coming. The state's reward program, you know? I think I told you about it.'

'Uh huh. Well, money's always nice. By the way, in all your doings with the movers and shakers over in the capitol, have you ever run into a man named Cisterio?'

'Cisterio? Sure. He's a member of the State Assembly, Edward Cisterio. Why are you asking?'

'I'm not sure. That name came up in something I'm working on and I wanted to check it out.' Frowning he stopped. 'Edward Cisterio. You know, the name I was given was different. Uh, Robert Cisterio. Could Robert be your Edward's brother?'

'Nope. Neither of them are likely to be mine. So what's this Robert done? It doesn't have anything to do with the murder of those prostitutes we've been reading about in the papers, is it?'

'Uh huh.'

Steve chuckled. 'Well, that lets Edward out. From what I've heard, he's a strange duck. Ultra conservative and very religious. Not likely he'd have anything to do with prostitutes.'

'Interesting. Thanks. OK, so the big pot farm we found up in the Trinity National Forest is history. Any word on Ralston?'

'It's a funny thing. Apparently the Ralston family have been big contributors of the Governor and his party for years. Now all of a sudden, my senator is making noise about returning the campaign funds he took in from the family. But no, nothing's been said about if and when.'

'Be sure to let me know. I'd like to be in on a raid if possible.'

'Can do. OK, that's all the news from here. I'll get a check over your way in a few days and you can buy the beer.'

'You got it. Take care.' And hung up. Yep, life was looking good. Now if he was successful tonight he'd really have something to celebrate.

Chapter 39

THINKING ABOUT THINGS, mostly what Steve had just said about one of the state's lawmakers, took up the time it required to drink another beer. Another Anchor Steam. Studying the label on the bottle, he remembered someone explaining how steam beer had once been a popular beer making method. The two, steam and beer, didn't seem to go together but maybe, being in San Francisco, it did. Makes one wonder, doesn't it?

Foley frowned. Studying questions about beer while drinking beer might be a good indication he'd maybe had enough to drink. There was still a lot of work to get done before being able to relax and get a buzz on. This would have to be the last until time to go pick up Andy Collier.

After talking with Steve and finishing the bottle of beer, he still had a couple hours before he could pick up Collier. It'd be a good idea, he decided, to take a walk, clear his head for later.

Thinking about things going around, he aimed his time-killing stroll down the street ending up at the Powell-Hyde streetcar turntable. San Francisco's cable car system was an icon. Even he knew that. Loved and enjoyed by both tourists and locals, as with so many things purely San Francisco, the number of pictures taken of the unique cars were uncountable.

Foley didn't know much about the cable car system, except it was a hold-over from the earliest days and, he believed, had run continuously. Well, during the day, anyhow. He, and all the other touristy types, were just in time to watch the last turn-around for the day of one of the red and gold cars.

With the excitement over, he continued his stroll into the little park beyond the turntable. Sitting on a bench, he looked out at the bay. Not really seeing what was in front of him, he let his mind wander. Just

183

another tourist enjoying the early evening, contemplating world events or possibly his navel. Or the office he was about to break in. Or maybe not. Another pointless inquiry brought on by too much hops and malt, Foley decided, shaking his head. He looked at the time and decided he'd had enough lazing around. Almost time to go to work.

Andy Collier was standing on the sidewalk when Foley pulled up.

'Hey, I was afraid you'd forgotten me.'

'Why, I'm not late, am I?'

'Nope. A little early, actually. But I thought maybe you'd changed your mind about going where no man is supposed to be. You still say this isn't a snatch and grab?'

Foley smiled as he drove on, turning back toward the waterfront, taking Pine Street to Van Ness to get across town and Union Street. He waited to answer the question until pulling over to the curb in front of the Kroll Building.

'I'm not going to take a thing. You can stick around and watch if you'd like. Fact is, I'd appreciate it if you would. It shouldn't take me long and if possible, I'd like to have the door lock when we leave.'

'Oh, I'll watch. This little jaunt interests me.'

The outer door was unlocked but the elevator was not working. According to a small sign next to the control buttons, elevator service was turned off from 9 p.m. until 6 a.m. An arrow pointed toward the stairs.

'It's only four floors,' Foley said, leading the way, 'think you can make it?'

'Ha! Only four? I can run up that many and not even work up a sweat.'

Foley chuckled.

The lights along the fourth floor hallway were dim, the silence throughout the building almost felt thick and heavy. Standing in front of room 412, he watched as Andy studied the lock for a moment and then smiling over his shoulder, said, 'Watch and learn, my son. Watch and learn.'

From an inside pocket, he pulled out something Foley thought looked like a very thin, flat cigarette case. Only this one was 'L' shaped, with each side only a few inches long.

'This is old technology, perfect for lazy people,' said Collier softly. 'It's been around for ages and found in only the best B and E's pocket. It's the traditional manual pick gun. Old technology for this kind of thing. Does about the same thing as any of the new electronic picks I was telling you about. This one works,' he went on talking as he put the long end against the keyhole, 'by a metal spring inside. When I pull the trigger,' and he did, 'it causes the pick to slide inside the lock and vibrate.'

Foley wasn't sure but he thought he heard a faint series of clicks.

'See, what's happening is I'm putting tension on the cylinder and the spring is turning it one way, lining up the pins. When the pins are all in line, just what you'd do with a key, a little cam releases the bolt and the spring snaps it into place, and bingo!' he said proudly, turning the door knob and pushing the door open. 'You're in. There you go,' Andy said, smiling and putting the pick gun back in his pocket. 'Have fun, I'll watch.'

Foley took the shopping bag he'd brought from the car to the desk and removed what Andy thought was a faded yellow block of plastic.

'What the hell you got there?'

Holding it up by the bar handle on top, Foley let the attached electric cord hang down. 'An electromagnet. I borrowed it from one of the college radio stations. They use it to clean the cassette tapes they record their ads on. Plug it in and wipe it across the cassettes and – bingo! – you have a clean tape.'

'And what are you planning on doing with it here?'

Pointing around the room at the banks of shelving, Foley smiled. 'See those? They're computer servers, each one containing a huge hard drive. On those hard drives are hundreds of programmed websites.'

Next he pulled a long, heavy duty extension cord from the bag. Plugging it into a wall outlet, and the electromagnet to the extension cord, he glanced at his partner.

'Now, watch and learn, my friend.' Slowly moving the magnet over first one and then another of the metal cases, he moved from one shelf to the next.

'I don't see or hear anything,' said Collier. 'What's happening?'

'If you got close, you might be able to hear the magnetic coil inside this box vibrate. What I'm doing is wiping all the hard drives. All the information stored in them will either be gone or so jumbled as to be unreadable.'

'But why? Seems like a lot of work for nothing.'

'It's something I told a young woman I'd do for her. Wait until I'm through and we go have a drink and I'll tell you all about it while I pay your bill.'

185

Chapter 40

GORMAN WAS OUT of the office and would be until after lunch, Leonie Weems told Foley the next morning. She actually smiled when she gave out the news, which he thought was a sign of her mellowing until he realized she hoped it would mean no work for him. 'Sorry to disappoint you,' he said under his breath, returned her smile and went back down to the sidewalk to wait for Gretchen.

'Good morning, favorite partner,' he said, giving her an honest and actually friendly 100-watt smile. 'The big boss is out of the office this morning so there's no reason to go up. But I do have one thing we can do. Let's go have a little discussion with your new friend, Emma what's-her-name. What I have to tell her will be news she'll appreciate.'

'What is it? You know she's been really upset over being forced into working her website.'

'Yeah, I know. C'mon, this is worth getting my car out of the garage.'

He hadn't counted on what it'd take to find a place to park at that time of morning. When he did, they had to walk back four or five blocks to Emma's apartment building.

'You know,' he said, holding the outer door for his partner, 'I didn't think about it, but she might have left for class already.'

'She'll be home. The threats she's been getting are making her scared to leave the apartment. Brad, we've just got to do something about it, somehow.'

'Gretchen, old girl, never fear. It's all been taken care of.'

There was no answer when Gretchen pushed the door bell. Foley put his ear against the door and knocked.

'Hey, Emma, open the door. It's Gretchen and Brad. We've got something to talk to you about.'

For a long pause there was no sound, then quietly and very cautiously, the door opened as far as the security chain would let it.

'Oh, God, I was afraid...' Emma's face was pale and drawn looking. It was obvious she'd been crying. 'Wait a minute, let me ...' she said, closing the door and dropping the chain. Opening the door again, she opened it, looking past Gretchen and Foley, making sure the hallway was empty.

'Come in, please. I'm sorry about the way things look,' she closed the door and quickly replaced the chain before rushing around, picking up sections of the morning newspaper and pieces of clothing. 'I just haven't been able to get motivated to do any cleaning up this morning. To tell the truth, I was trying to figure out whether to start packing things up to move first or go look for another apartment and then pack.'

Gretchen took the handful of things she'd been holding and nodded toward the couch. 'Sit down, Emma, and relax a little. Brad says he's got something to tell you.'

Foley couldn't keep from smiling. 'This is a nice apartment, Emma. You don't really want to move, do you?'

'No, but those men had my phone number and told me they know where I live. It's either try to get away or do as they say and I don't want to do it anymore.'

He nodded. 'Well, they don't have your phone number anymore. Or your address, either. Fact is, right now I'd bet the guy who took over for Cochrane is yelling at the computer whiz-kid he hired to run the Eye-Candy dot.com website. For some unexplained reason, all the information Cochrane had collected on his computers is gone. Not only all the information on your personal website stored in Cochrane's computers but everything to do with all the other sites including his own.'

'What do you mean?'

'Think of it as a virus getting into the Eye-Candy computer and eating up all the little bits and bytes. I have it on good authority the business is no longer able to operate. The computers are coming up empty. What this means is no one has any information about you or any of the other girls. Each of them will have to start over if they want to continue making contact with their clients. Or not.'

'You mean I can relax? I'm safe?'

'Yep. Unless you want to find another website to host your site, which you would have to build all over again, you're out of business.'

'How did you do it?'

'Now that's something you don't want to know about,' he said, standing up. 'And as much as I enjoy being in the company of a lovely young woman, there is no reason for us to bother you again. So go study hard and prosper. Come on, Gretch, you can buy the coffee.'

He waited outside the apartment while the two women talked, saying their goodbyes. Out on the sidewalk, Foley only smiled when Gretchen started asking questions.

Shaking his head, he lifted his chin toward the espresso bar on the corner where they'd had coffee once before. Inhaling the rich smell of roast coffee as they went in, he tried to remember what he'd ordered back then. He recalled really enjoying it and quickly studied the list of specialties on the chalkboard on the wall behind the barista's work station. Yes, the cute little name for drip coffee with a shot of espresso. Gretchen, just like the time before, had chamomile tea.

'Now, Mr. Mysterious, what did you do to put the computer pimp website out of business? And don't think you can just shine me off. I told Emma I'd get it out of you. Right now, neither of us really believe what you told her.'

'OK. It's like this, without confessing to anything, let's say someone got into old Cochrane's office and screwed with all those servers he had hanging on the walls. It really happened and there is no way anything can be brought back. Think of it as making scrambled eggs. Not only can the eggs not be put back in their shells but in this case, you couldn't even tell it was eggs you had in the pan. Now that's all I'm saying. When you've dealt with lawbreakers as long as I have, you'll discover there are times when the law just isn't able to do its job. That's when someone starts looking for another solution.'

Gretchen sipped her tea and thought about it. 'And you're sure? One hundred per cent sure?'

'Even more than sure. It's not likely there's any way to prove it, but your friend Emma won't be getting any more threatening phone calls.'

Chapter 41

Returning the Chevy to his parking spot, they went up to the office, not expecting to find Gorman back from wherever he had spent his morning.

'Well,' Ms Weems said, frowning at Foley but smiling in Gretchen's direction, 'Mr. Gorman just came in and has asked where you two were. He said for you to go right in when you finally came to work this morning.'

Foley was about to respond but changed his mind, simply casting what he hoped was his friendliest smile toward the older woman.

'Ah, good, good,' Gorman said, smiling and pointing toward two chairs. 'Now tell me, Mr. Foley, what have you been up to?'

'We just had a brief discussion with one of the girls...' was as far as he got before the older man stopped him.

'No, I don't mean this morning. I'm talking about last night.'

'Oh, well. Nothing. I mean, after taking Gretchen home, I had dinner down on the wharf and, well, went home. Why?' he said, glancing briefly toward his partner, hoping she'd get the message not to say anything.

'Why? Why do I think you're leaving something out? Because I got a phone call from a very angry, very dangerous man. Tolly Mane called, wanting to know what we'd done. I didn't know what he was talking about. It seems someone has damaged the computers he was using to run one of his businesses. He really wasn't making a lot of sense, but in my experience, getting on the bad side of Tolly isn't a good thing. Now, what can you tell me about whatever it was that upset him?'

Foley hesitated, trying to think how to explain without putting his foot in a trap.

'Uh, Mr. Gorman,' said Gretchen slowly, almost shyly, 'maybe I can help. Remember one of the girls we had talked with about the murder of those two prostitutes? Emma? Well, the man who hosted the websites the girls were using was taken over by your friend, Mr. Mane, after the man who'd set it up was killed. Rex Cochrane. You see, Emma wanted to get out of the business but, as you know, Mr. Mane, or one of his men, told her she was going to continue. He said he had too much information on her for her not to do as she was told. I don't know what Brad did, he won't tell me. But this morning, he told Emma that she had nothing to worry about.'

Gorman leaned back in his chair, folding his hands over his stomach and studying the man sitting on the other side of his desk. Looking first at one then the other, he pursed his lips, thinking. Then smiling, nodded.

Brad relaxed. He wouldn't have to lie to his boss.

'Wonderful,' Gorman was suddenly all smiles. 'Good for you, Mr. Foley. Whatever you did, and as long as it can't come back to this office, I don't want to know. Good job. Now,' he said, getting serious and leaning forward, 'do we have anything new on the Steiner case? I'm going to have to make a report to Henry pretty quick. He called yesterday but I neglected to tell you.'

'I had an interesting conversation yesterday with my buddy, Steve,' said Foley. 'Steve and I were partners when we worked up in the northern part of the state, before I came down here. He ended up over in Sacramento working for one of the state senators. He called to let me know the outcome of some of the work we did last week, while I was out of the office.'

'You never did say too much about your week long holiday,' said Gorman, not asking but wanting to know.

'That doesn't matter. But I asked him if he knew of anyone over there named Cisterio. Remember, that was the name of the man who told us he was representing the state attorney general's office? Warned us to stop getting in the way of the police or someone would lose their license?' Glancing at his partner, Foley nodded. 'Yeah, well, the same name was used by the guy who contacted Emma about hiring her for a weekend at Lake Tahoe. She said it scared her when this Cisterio mentioned Sophie. He gave her Sophie's name as a recommendation and it upset her. I can understand that. It would bother me, too.'

'Yeah,' continued Foley. 'I asked Steve about it and learned there actually is a Cisterio. He's a member of the State Assembly. Edward Cisterio, according to Steve. As I recall, the man from the AG's office was a Robert Cisterio. '

Gorman settled back in his chair. 'Could he be the one who called about taking Emma to Lake Tahoe? Are you suggesting this might be the last contact that either of the two murdered girls had?'

'No, I don't think so,' said Foley, smiling.

'Why not?'

'Steve says the state legislator named Cisterio is an overly straight arrow kind of guy. In that case, I can't see him calling an escort girl asking for a weekend situation in some lakeside resort. I'd say it was someone using Cisterio's name. Maybe as a joke but most likely just as a cover.'

Francis Gorman nodded. 'But,' he said after a moment's thought, 'the same question comes up once again; where does all this leave us on the Steiner situation?'

Foley shook his head. 'I'd have to say, the answer is about the same: nowhere. I thought for a while Mane had to have something to do with it. He's the only one who appeared to benefit from the death of Cochrane. But it doesn't look like that holds water any longer. You know, I wonder… Gretch, didn't you say that the man who talked to you on the bus said something about your not being able to count on me?'

'Yes, he made me feel all creepy. I can remember exactly what he said. I was to stop asking questions concerning the Steiner girl. Not woman, but girl. If I didn't, I would pay for it. And he could get to me any time he wanted. If I didn't get smart and simply work as a process server or look for lost cats, I'd have an accident. You couldn't help me, either. He said you were out of the picture. He laughed and said you were out of the picture. What'd he mean?'

'I'm not sure,' Foley said slowly, trying to make all the bits and pieces fit. 'However,' looking back toward Gorman, 'it seems we've run out of alleys to search. Unless you know something?'

The older man pursed his lips and slowly shook his head. 'I do wish I could think of something. Telling Henry his daughter was killed for being in the wrong place at the wrong time won't be enough. I think what he really wants to hear is his daughter was working for some charitable organization and was mugged. Remember? He wanted us to prove that she wasn't part of a prostitution ring.'

'But do you think he really knew what she was doing?' Foley asked.

'Oh, yes. He had to know. It doesn't mean he had to accept it, though. This just couldn't happen. Not to one of the San Francisco Steiners anyway. People with a famous name are just too perfect to break any laws.'

'Or,' Foley said quietly, 'get stabbed south of Market Street.'

Chapter 42

GRETCHEN DECIDED AGAINST a late lunch, wanting to stay in the office and talk to Gorman about another assignment. On the other hand, Foley opted to go home early. Unless there was something pressing, he told the boss, he felt the need for a walk on the beach.

The sun had just set when he got back to his place. Looking at what food there was, he decided going out someplace for dinner might be best. A trip to the grocery store would have to wait until tomorrow.

Pouring himself a glass of wine from the open bottle he hadn't finished the night before, he was leaning back against the counter, relaxed and feeling content when he noticed the red light on his telephone recorder was flashing.

'Hey, damn it, Bradford,' Steve's voice came booming out of the speaker. 'Why in hell don't you carry your cell? I've been trying to get … oh, never mind. Listen. Call me when you get in. No matter what time tonight, call me. And charge up the battery of your cell phone, you idiot.'

Foley smiled and did as his old partner said. Cell phones, he mused. A blight on the world second, in his opinion, only to television. Using the phone in the living room, he dialed Steve's number.

When he was a kid, the family home didn't have a telephone. The nearest one was in a booth down at the corner market. Back then, people only used a phone to call for an ambulance or the cops. Now it was the cell phone. Carry one of those damn little things and you were at everybody's beck and call. Ah, he nodded, listening to the ring, the good old days.

'Hello,' Steve said, sounding like he had something to smile about.

'I was taking a walk up the beach, trying to clear my mind and work through a couple of things. The kind of contemplation only works when

193

it's not interrupted by someone with nothing better to do than call my cell phone.'

'Feeling a bit peckish, are we? OK then, old buddy, if you don't want in, then I'll go up to the big beautiful forest by myself. Oh, wait a minute. No, I can't leave you out. Your new benefactor, C. L. Owens, personally requested the benefit of your company. Now I wonder why?'

'Just to let you know, I am, as we speak, charging my cell. What do you mean, Owens wants me to go up north with you? What's up?'

'I don't know what he's thinking about, but the invitation is to a pot raid. This, believe it or not, is to be raided on a specific section of wooded area presently owned by the Scotia Lumber Company.'

'So the governor's campaign advisers are overlooking the Ralston family financial support for another dope raid? Good for them. But what are you saying about Owens asking for me to be there? I thought he wasn't all that sure of my value.'

'Now where did you get that idea? He did offer to get you a job with one of his party's legislators, didn't he?'

'Uh huh.'

'Which, by the way, is something you ought to consider. I mean really think about. There's a lot of easy money to be had.'

'What does your tame state senator think of Owens, has he ever said?'

'Not really. Senator Murkowski supports most of the Governor's plans but I get the feeling he's only playing party politics. Not long ago, I overheard a conversation touching on something Governor Vasconcellos was rumored to be involved in. I couldn't make out what it was, but I heard Murkowski say Vasconcellos was going to have to clean up his act. The Gov is, according to Murkowski, too much into drugs, sex and rock and roll. Those were his words. I don't know what he was talking about but maybe it's why his advisers are telling him to go after the big marijuana plantations.'

'Which brings us back to the Ralston grow. When is it scheduled for?'

'Late tomorrow afternoon. I figure I'll pick you up about ten in the morning and we'll have lunch on the way. We're all supposed to meet up at the Humboldt County Fair Grounds at three.'

'OK. Maybe this will have to be enough revenge for the beating Anton and his buddy, Cully, gave me. OK, I'll be ready.'

The fairgrounds were on the north side of Eureka, which, according to Steve, was about 270 miles up Highway 101, more popularly known as the Redwood Highway.

Foley wanted to get to Eureka in time for lunch. There was a little Mom and Pop restaurant on the south side of town he remembered. Pop did the cooking and Mom took care of the customers. Foley could almost taste the lunch special. With Mom and Pop, it didn't matter what day of the week it was or, even what time of day. The special was always the same: meatloaf, mashed potatoes and gravy, peas, freshly made bread and coffee – $2.75 plus tax. He smiled, remembering it.

Steve broke up the daydream. 'I'm hungry,' he said. 'There's a little place a few blocks from the river I stopped at once. Uh, it's in Rio Dell. I can't remember the name of the restaurant but there isn't much chance we can miss it. Great Mexican food and cold beer. I don't figure one beer with lunch will cause any harm.'

Foley wanted meatloaf but not enough to argue about it. After all, he was only part of this raid business because the Governor's right hand man invited him.

'I don't think I've ever been in Rio Dell.'

'It's just like a lot of little towns up here. You and I spent all our time on the north side of the county but they all went through the same thing, losing people as jobs in the mills and forests died. Only about half the population once there is there now but it's still a nice little town. I suppose it's the river that keeps things alive, salmon and trout fishermen. And probably deer hunters in the fall.'

'Uh huh,' Foley muttered, giving up on the meatloaf when Steve took the Wildwood exit. Then it came to him. 'I got it. You're keeping us out of downtown Eureka, aren't you? You're afraid someone will see us and wonder what we're up to, being back in town. Well, I guess it makes sense.'

'Yeah. I wouldn't want to have to explain anything to anyone. Would you?'

'And,' Foley went on, not directly answering his old partner, 'it couldn't mean the local law dogs are being kept out of the Governor's raid, could it?'

'Sorta. I'm told Sheriff Millard was informed of the coming raid a week or so ago. Owens said he mentioned you and me were in on it, being part of the deal. Owens said he told Millard how we had found it in the first place. According to Owens, when our names were mentioned, the good sheriff said he didn't want anything to do with it. I'm not sure Millard holds something against us or just doesn't like helping the Governor get re-elected.'

'I can see how it'd be. Millard would want to run the show and him in the driver's seat wouldn't help Owens or his boss at all.'

'Yeah. It's the most important part for Mr. Kingmaker Owens. He can get quite ruthless when it comes to advancing old Vasconcellos's career.'

Foley's little smile was missed by Steve. Lots of little pieces of the puzzle had been rattling around Brad's head. Slowly he was starting to see some kind of pattern emerging. Like any good jigsaw puzzle, all he needed was the corner pieces to make things start to fit.

Chapter 43

THE BIG SURPRISE came at the fairgrounds.

'Well, I gotta tell you, boys,' said Sheriff Millard called as Steve parked next to a stretch limousine, 'I never expected to see the two of you up in this neck of the woods again, and certainly not in such high ranking company.'

Sticking out his hand, there was nothing for the two to do but take it. Ah, yes, Foley said silently, all good friends once again. Bull dust.

'Someone said you'd opted out of this little party,' Steve said, dropping the sheriff's handshake.

Sheriff Con Millard had held the office for almost the last twenty years. Con, short for Constantine, Millard was born to be a small town sheriff. From his $400 Tony Lama cowboy boots, alligator skin with a two-inch heel, of course, to his tailored tan uniform all topped off with a brushed dove colored Stetson, he looked the part.

California's Constitution called for each county to elect a person to the office of sheriff. In most places, the sheriff was simply paid to transport convicts, serve legal documents and issue dog and gun licenses. Many elected to the office also acted as the county coroner. Humboldt County's sheriff was one of the other sort, law enforcement officers who took the job of crime detection and investigation in the unincorporated areas seriously. Millard liked to think of himself as a carry-over from the old west. He didn't like to think of himself as a politician but every four years, he was forced to admit that he had to face the voters.

'Yeah,' he said, smiling his politician smile, 'I have to admit it. My first reaction anyway. Just between us and the fence post, I don't think too much of Vasconcellos's brand of politics. Too damn liberal, for my taste. However, while I'm fortunate not to be up for re-election this year, I figured it wouldn't look good if the county's leading lawman wasn't part of a major drug bust in his own county. Anyway, when Graham called to say you two were on your way north, well, what could I do? I mean, hell's bells, boys, the department hasn't been the same since you guys left.'

Foley frowned. 'Who's this Graham fellow?'

'Oh, I guess you never met him. Graham Marks, Chief of Police down in Rio Dell. He recognized you, Tichenor. Not knowing the whole story, only that you two had left the department under a cloud, he figured I should know you were coming this way. C'mon over and meet the rest of the crew.'

'So much for not being recognized, Steve,' Foley snarled under his breath as they followed the uniformed official. 'We could have come into town and had a good meal and it wouldn't have mattered.'

'Hey, boys,' Millard called out to the half dozen men standing around in a group, 'look who we got here. These two boys are just the ones to take us up to where we want to go.'

Looking around the group, Foley saw only a couple of faces he recognized. Curtis Lee Owens was front and center.

Glancing at the newcomers and flashing a thin smile, Owens lifted his chin to the sheriff. 'Sheriff Millard, can I have a word with you?' Not waiting, he turned and walked a few yards away.

'Hey there, Cletus.' Steve nodded to one of the men. Belatedly Foley saw it was one of the county deputies. 'What the hell is going on? I was told Millard wasn't interested in this event.'

'Yeah, he wasn't. Not until he heard the Governor himself is dropping in to give us a pep talk. Hey, Brad. How the hell are ya?'

Steve chuckled. 'The Gov himself, huh? Now that really makes this a party.'

'Yep, and I'd bet a dollar to a bag of donuts old Millard is getting an earful right now. You watch, he'll come back meek as a lamb once he learns this is not his show.'

Cletus's prediction was spot on. Owens and the sheriff rejoined the bunch with Millard following a step or two behind.

'OK, men,' Owens raised a hand to catch everyone's attention. 'Here's the plan. We've got half a dozen officers from CAMP coming. For you who haven't heard of this unit, it's a special task force federally funded to help stamp out illegal drugs. They'll be arriving in a few minutes,' he went on, glancing at his wristwatch, 'along with Governor Vasconcellos.

The Governor is very interested in this raid. He wants everyone to know he won't tolerate flaunting of the law, no matter who you are. The person listed as owner of the land we are raiding is and has been a large campaign contributor. Well, the Governor wants people to know you can't buy your way out if you allow such things as this to happen.

'Now then, with those six men, we have two from the Humboldt County Sheriff's Department, including Sheriff Millard himself. We in the Governor's office thank you, Sheriff, for taking part in this. Four of you are State Troopers working out of uniform and you've met the two special investigators responsible for discovering this major marijuana plantation. Mr. Tichenor, is there anything you wish to say about the country we're going into?'

Caught off guard, Steve hesitated, then shook his head. 'Not really. It's not far from the Fern Canyon trail head, like Mr. Owens said, on privately owned land right next to the Redwood National Forest boundary. When Brad here and I scouted it out a short time back, we found a pretty big operation. It looked to be well maintained and there were four or five men on the site. Oh, and up at the far end of the grow, I spotted a huge tent back in the trees. It's alongside a pretty good sized creek. I didn't get too close to it, but from the odor, I think someone was cooking meth—'

Owens cut in. 'And that means we'll have to be very careful. If there is a meth lab then we can count on it being protected. I've laid out a plan which will, I think, keep most of the danger at a minimum.'

Foley wanted to laugh. How in hell does he get off making plans without ever having seen the grow or knowing how many men might be up there? Shooting a glance at Steve, he saw the man had the same thought and was fighting to keep his poker face.

Glancing once again at his watch, Owens went on to explain. 'Our target time is fifteen hundred hours. We'll drive up in the vans we've leased with Mr. Tichenor and Mr. Foley in the lead rig. According to the latest topographic map, there is a large parking lot near where the plantation is located. It's the trailhead for a half dozen hiking trails into the National Forest. This is where we will break up into two squads. One, with Mr. Tichenor leading, will range ahead, keeping to the high ground a little west of the plantation. How long do you estimate it'll take you to get above the site, Mr. Tichenor?'

Once again, Steve was caught off guard. This time because he was trying hard not to snicker over this desk jockey's use of military time ... fifteen hundred hours, for Gawd's sake. Quickly he brought his attention back to the question.

'Uh, well, I guess half a dozen men working our way up on the high side of the ridge, say, half to three-quarters of a mile, then coming back down, we'd be damn close to the tent.'

'How long would it take you?' Owens said impatiently, keeping an eye on the time.

'Hmm, oh, no more than half an hour.'

'OK, the rest of us will wait that half hour and move directly toward the nearest edge of the plantation. From the report filed by Tichenor and Foley, there is a trail of sorts leading to it. OK.' He stopped and hearing the drone of a helicopter, looked up before going on, speaking quickly. 'I'll be leading that part of the group. It'll be a pincer movement. The goal is to arrest the growers and then destroy the plants and the lab. Everybody got it?' Not waiting for answers, he pointed up.

'That'll be the Governor's chopper. He wants to say a few words and then we're off.'

Foley thought this would be his best chance. 'Hey, Sheriff,' he asked, keeping his voice low, 'any idea where I can take a leak before this fiasco gets off the ground?'

Millard smiled and pointed to a group of Porta-Potties off to one side.

'Oh, didn't see them. Thanks. Steve, if the Governor or his honor, Mr Owens misses me, tell them I just couldn't wait.'

'Hurry back. You don't want to miss out on all the fun.'

Getting to the first of the blue fiberglass outhouses, Foley glanced back to see if anyone was watching. Owens was front and center, watching the CHP's Bell Long Ranger helicopter touching gently down. His small army of drug raiders stood in a semi-circle behind him, all ducking their heads in the cloud of dust kicked up by the big man's arrival. Feeling safe, and wanting to be able to keep an eye on the group, he ducked around behind one of the Porta-Potties.

Quickly punching in the numbers Freddie had given him, he made his call.

'C'mon, damn it,' he said impatiently as the phone rang on the other end, 'pick it up, Freddie. I haven't got all—' Freddie's growl interrupted him.

'Yeah.'

'Freddie, you know who this is?'

'Huh? Oh, yeah, I recognize your voice. What's up?'

'Here it is. Today, this afternoon at three you're going to have company. I'd suggest you take a hike well before then. Before any strangers come waltzing in. Got it?'

'This afternoon. Hey, you know what? It couldn't be any better. You'll never guess who went up the trail an hour or so ago. Probably wanted to make sure there ain't no fuck ups at the lab. There's been a lot of problems getting things working or so I hear tell.'

'C'mon, man. I gotta get back before someone comes wondering who I'm calling.'

'OK. But hear this, the big man himself is here. Hubert and his side-kick, Anton, went up the trail. Didn't even say by your leave, hiya or nothing. Just walked by as if they owned the world. Serves 'em right if they're still up there when you and all the cops in the world drops in.'

'I like the way that sounds. But I gotta go. Get your buns outa there.'

'Thanks, man. I owe you.'

Dropping his cell in a pocket and making a show of zipping up his fly, Foley walked away from the blue toilets, a big smile on his face. Maybe Lady Luck was finally going to make his day.

Chapter 44

NOT MUCH WAS said on the trip up to the trailhead at Fern Canyon. Given a choice, Foley thought he'd like to someday come back to this part of the state. Huge forests of tall stately trees, some had to be more than a couple hundred years old, stretching out for miles. Lots of people had come to retire in the small towns and villages and were living a quiet life, taking advantage of the hunting and fishing. There was, he knew, some quality trout fishing in dozens of small creeks through those mountain canyons. And right off the coast was some of the Pacific Ocean's best sport fishing. Yeah, this part of the world would be hard to beat. Too damn bad they'd been fired and had to leave under a cloud.

Riding in the back of the nine passenger van, neither he nor Steve had an opportunity to talk privately. Owens had taken the front passenger's seat next to the driver who Foley figured to be a State Trooper. He wasn't in uniform but was wearing a holstered Glock 9mm around his waist. Cops, both state and local, seemed to like the Glock. Of course, Sheriff Millard, sitting right behind the driver, had his long barreled Colt revolver strapped to his thigh.

Foley had seen Owens belt a holstered pistol around his waist as soon as the Governor's helicopter was airborne but he couldn't see what kind of weapon it was. Making his phone call, he'd hadn't heard what the big man had had to say, but didn't think he'd missed much. From the snort Steve responded with when he asked about it, Foley understood it'd all been typical political BS.

'How damn far is it up there, Tichenor?' Owens called back, sounding irritated.

'Another ten miles or so before we turn off the highway, then it's a dozen miles or so on gravel to the trailhead.'

Steve shot a glance at Foley but didn't say anything. He didn't have to; the same thought crossed both men's mind. Hadn't Owens said something about researching this raid using the latest topo maps? Then what the hell was he asking how far it was? Just like a spoiled child, Foley thought, asking the age-old question: 'Are we there yet?'

None of the other passengers said anything.

'Is there a sign or anything to let us know where the turn-off is?' Owens asked.

'Uh huh. It's one of the Forest Service's signs. Can't miss it.'

'God, then a dozen miles on gravel you say. Means it'll be dusty. We'll keep the windows rolled up and turn the air conditioner on.'

Yeah, miles through some of the most beautiful forests you could ever want to see, Foley thought. Damn fool desk jockey. It'd serve the idiot right if the county road department hadn't been over the road yet this year. Let it be filled with chuckholes, he silently asked the gods who ruled such things.

A few miles into the Sequoia and pine tree forest, Owens had the driver slow down. 'We don't want to get there too early,' he explained. 'I've set this raid up for three, thinking anyone working up there might be taking an afternoon break. I'd like to arrive at the trailhead right at three. We might have to stop a couple miles short and wait to make sure of our timing.'

Possibly in response to Foley's plea, large sections of the dirt road was washboarded in places and potholed in others. It didn't matter, though, slowing down the heavy SUV smoothed out the road.

The large clearing was empty of vehicles when the two vans pulled in. The early summer weather had turned nasty with the forecast for a spring rain storm expected to come in from the coast. That would be enough to keep hikers, backpackers and horse people out of the woods, a situation suiting Owens and his gang of lawmen just fine.

'OK,' he said, keeping his voice low as if the dope growers were just behind the large sign with the hiking trail maps on it, 'here's where it all starts. Tichenor will take six of you with him up and around, coming down from on top. The rest of us will wait thirty minutes before coming up from this end. Now …' He stopped as another dusty 4WD Toyota pulled in.

'What the hell is this?' Sheriff Millard snarled and started walking over just as a young man and woman got out of the front seat and another man out of the back.

'It's all right, Sheriff,' called Owens. 'These people are here at my invitation.'

Looking the trio over, it was easy to see what they were about. The stocky man who had been riding in back had four cameras hanging by black leather straps from his neck. Both the man and the woman were dressed in pressed Levis and matching brown canvas bush jackets. Probably called safari jackets and found only in stores like Abercrombie and Fitch. Foley wasn't sure there was even a one of those stores anywhere in California. These were journalists bringing their own cameraman along for the story.

'Let's get this straight,' said Owens, raising his voice a little. 'The Governor wants this raid to get wide coverage. His reasoning is two-fold, first to show his government will not allow anyone to think they are above the law. Secondly, as a warning to anyone believing they can operate a meth lab or major marijuana plantation and get away with it. To that end, he has invited these members of the media. They will follow my group, staying well behind and out of any danger. You understand?' he asked the reporters who nodded their agreement.

'Sure,' Steve muttered under his breath. 'The camera guy is going to hold back and not get the one photo that'll win him an award. Of course he is.'

'OK,' Owens turned back to the group of armed men, 'it's close enough to three. Let's get this show on the road. Tichenor, get your men and take off. The rest of you, uh, take a break.'

Foley didn't laugh. Stepping close to Steve's shoulder, he kept his voice down. 'I got inside information. Hubert and his buddy, Anton, are up there somewhere. Keep your eye out. I got a bone to pick with that pair.'

'OK, but be careful. Having those damn journalists along could make things dicey.'

'Yeah. Good luck and see you for beer later.'

Watching the men, each carrying a mean looking military style automatic rifle, scramble up the slope, disappearing into the brush, those in Owens's crew relaxed, leaning against the gate or standing around studying the big directional sign. They were all armed with the same type of weapon, one Foley didn't recognize. Dressed in black jumpsuits, made bulky by bullet-proof vests and web belts holding packets containing who knew what.

With Owens watching the clock, Foley knew he had thirty minutes to wait. Opening the door to one of the vans, he pulled himself up to get comfortable in the leather seat. Nobody had offered him a weapon. This gave him a good reason to hold back when things got hairy. He had to smile to himself when he saw Owens go over to one side to speak to the reporters. Yeah, anything to get his buddy, the Governor, re-elected.

'How far up the trail did you say their camp was?' He hadn't seen Owens come over to the van.

'A couple hundred yards.'

'And the path there on the other side of the gate goes right to it?'

'Uh huh. Right along the top of the ridge.'

Owens leaned against the open van door, looking up at Foley. 'You know, you threw away a good opportunity when you didn't take me up on the offer I made you. You recall? I could have got you a place with someone in the Legislature. Something similar to what your pal there, Tichenor has.'

'Not my kind of work, but thanks anyhow.'

'No, your kind of work is putting your nose in places it doesn't belong. You and what's her name, the girl you got working with you. Nosey busybodies, that's all you are.'

Foley frowned. 'What are you talking about?' he started to say, then stopped. Ah, yes. One of the corners on the jigsaw puzzle. 'Wait a minute. Yeah, now it makes sense. It had to be a big shot with pull over in the capitol to set someone from the attorney general's office on me. You fit the picture. Now why would you do that? Because I was asking questions,' he answered himself, 'that's why. Gretchen and I were talking to people about the murdered Steiner girl. OK.' He nodded, noticing Owens was simply standing there, smiling up at him. 'And what was it about? Oh, because Anne Marie was working as an escort, a high class prostitute. Uh huh, and so was her friend Sophie, who was also murdered. But I'm not telling you anything you didn't already know, am I? Now it makes me wonder what threat they were to you.'

'It wasn't me they were planning to cause trouble for. No, all I did, all I've ever done, was work to protect Hugo.'

Another puzzle piece. Another, bigger corner now in place.

'The Governor,' said Foley softly, glancing back toward the reporters.

'Don't worry about them. They'll stay over there until we go up the trail. Yes, the Governor. He and I have been together since high school. Even back then he knew where he was going. First get elected to the Legislature and then to the Governor's mansion. He thinks it's just the beginning. And all the time I was there to smooth over his mistakes.'

'And what mistakes were those two girls causing?'

'Oh, well, if there is one weakness Hugo has, it's young women,' he said, shaking his head sadly. 'It's been the way for him. Ever since, well, since he discovered what to do with that thing hanging between his legs. He just can't seem to control himself. Usually I just arrange things for him. Pay off the girl afterwards and everything is sweet. But lately it hasn't been enough. Meeting a girl in a hotel in Seattle or over at Lake Tahoe wasn't sufficient. He suggested getting two girls. Well, in today's world, anything is doable. Just expensive.' He chuckled. 'But when you've got your finger on the state budget, it isn't hard to squeeze a little here or there. Who's to know? The bean counters can't manage every fund to the penny.'

Foley wanted to keep the man talking. 'So what went wrong?' he asked.

'One of those damn cell phones with a camera was where it went wrong. I don't know whose idea it was but Hugo thought it'd be brilliant to have photos of him fucking a beautiful young woman. Something, he said when he told me about it, something he could look at when he got too old to get it up any more. So there it was, his being up for re-election, sure, he was on his way to the White House and these two stupid girls with a camera full of photos.'

Foley remembered Emma saying something about the opportunity for blackmail. 'Did either of them try to sell the photos?'

'No. But it didn't mean they wouldn't. Especially when it got close to election day. The ever worrisome 'October Surprise', you understand?'

'Yeah. An issue coming up at the last minute, just before the election, too late to go into damage control. What happened?'

'Well, nothing really. I mean, I had to do something, didn't I?'

'So you did.'

'Yes. I contacted the Steiner girl and had her meet me. I told her there was going to be another weekend party. I asked her to give me her cell phone but she wouldn't. What could I do? I mean, really?'

'And the other one? Sophie?'

'I was afraid she would know what happened. I had to close her mouth, too. I did the same thing, had her meet me up at the park. She thought it was for a quickie.' He laughed softly.

'And you stabbed her. Was that when you learned about Cochrane?'

'The knife was perfect. Until I used it on the Steiner girl, I had always thought a pistol was the perfect weapon, but it isn't. The knife was a gift from the Governor of Texas, you know. It's a custom handmade replica of the famous Bowie knife, a real beauty. Actually, it's known as the Fowler Bowie; with its black ebony handle, it's identical to the one on display at the Alamo. Oh, you asked about Cochrane. No, I knew of him before. It was his website I used to find the young girls for Hugo. A brilliant idea, don't you think?'

'Why did you kill him?'

'I couldn't be sure what he knew. Maybe the girls weren't behind it. I was afraid they had shared their plan to embarrass Hugo so he had to go.'

'From what I learned, there never was a plan to blackmail anyone. Did you ever think of that?'

'Oh, come on. You know better. Anyone with information on someone in a high political office? Or photos like those girls would have? Of course, it's the first thing they'd do. And once it started it would never end. Hugo would have been bled to death. I couldn't allow it, now could I?'

'And now you're telling me. Aren't you afraid of what I can do? Gretchen and I, with the resources we have on hand? We'll dig until we get the proof we need.'

Owens chuckled. 'Your sad little shadow? What good will she be? I frightened her once and can do it again. And what can you do? Tell those foolish journalists over there? Would they believe you without any proof? I don't think so.'

'But now knowing what I know, you can't afford to let me get back to San Francisco, can you.' It wasn't a question.

'I told you back at the fairgrounds I had planned it all out. In a few minutes, we'll go up the trail to the camp where we'll find the dope growers, and don't forget the meth lab. Everyone knows how dangerous those kinds of people can be. I wouldn't be surprised if, once we come busting over the hill with everybody yelling and screaming, there wasn't some gun fire. It'll be hard to say what will happen.'

'As long as you keep me in front of you.'

'Oh, I don't think so. See my pet cameraman over there? I've told him to stay close to me. To get the best shots, you know.' He smiled at the thought. 'That's almost a pun, isn't it, get the best shots. No, you'll be between the cameraman and the reporters. There won't be much you can do. By the time we all get into the camp, well, I expect it to be a real comedy of errors for a few minutes. And when it's all over, well, for you it'll be all over. Who'll be able to say whether it was enemy fire or not? It'll be a real disaster, but it'll only add pathos to the Governor's press conference. You can be proud for having helped him win the election.'

Foley smiled. 'You're starting to lose it, aren't you; a comedy of errors. It's the first sign of your losing control.'

'Don't kid yourself. This is my forte, always being in complete control. It's why I'm so valuable to Hugo. And nothing is going to change. Now,' he said, pushing himself away from the van, 'I think it's about time we got this show on the road, as they say.'

Foley watched as he rounded up his team, trying to see a way out of this and coming up dry. It was reasonable to expect Owens was right on the money. Once all the heavily armed law officers started pushing, there were sure to be guns going off. Even if he kept his eye on Owens to make sure he never let the man get in a position to use the pistol he was carrying, he couldn't count on it. He'd just have to be careful and alert and wait his chance. Sooner or later, Owens would have to make a mistake. Or Mrs. Foley's only son was in big trouble.

Chapter 45

'LET'S GO, PEOPLE,' called Owens, waving to Foley, a big smile showing lots of white teeth. 'Mr. Foley, you've been here before so you had better come up with me,' he said and waited.

Not seeing any way around it, Foley nodded and stepped out. Owens didn't miss a beat, dropping right behind him as he went past the single bar gate with the PRIVATE sign hanging from it.

Coming to the place in the trail where Freddie had stopped them before, Foley remembered the noise-making booby traps. There was no sign of the lookout.

'Hey,' he called out quietly, 'better wait up a minute.'

'What?' Owens stepped up closer, 'What's the problem?'

'I just remembered something. Up ahead in the trail,' he stopped, trying to recall exactly what Freddie had said, 'there are, hmm, two booby traps. Trip wires set up to topple a pile of tin cans down in the camp. Noise-makers to give warning, you know?'

'Are you certain?' asked Owens, stepping close.

'Look, Owens,' Foley said quietly, 'you and I may have some unfinished business but spoiling this raid isn't on that list. Somewhere coming from the other end of this little valley is my partner. I may not care what happens to you, but I don't want any of these men you brought out here getting killed.'

'OK, OK. So there are warning traps. How are they set up?'

'Trip wires across the trail.'

'How far until this so-called trail reaches the camp?'

'Another fifty or sixty yards, I'd say. The trail drops down off this ridge, directly into the camp. Lots of garbage lying around, down there, boxes and empty fertilizer sacks. Junk mainly.'

'All right. Lazlo,' he turned to the man holding the camera, ready to begin taking photos, 'you'd better drop back a few yards behind. Watch where I step when I get to the trip wires and don't make any mistakes. Got it?'

'Uh huh,' the guy muttered.

Foley saw he was holding the camera up in his left hand, peering through the viewfinder and wondered if he hadn't already been taking photos. It would be just like Owens to want full color prints of his back, making like Daniel Boone, hiking through the forest primeval.

Nodding, Owens took off, studying the ground in front very carefully. Foley waited until he saw the leader step high and gingerly over an unseen object then watched the cameraman do the same.

Looking back at the men following him, he asked if they heard about the trip wires. 'Pass the warning back. Make sure everyone knows it. I'll stick a branch in the dirt when I get to it.'

'Right on, man. Let's get this shit over with, what d'ya say?' came the response.

Tough men, he thought. Just the kind the Governor's right hand man would bring.

Spotting the first trip wire, he looked around and found a broken tree limb. Jamming it into the ground, he looked back to see the man behind him nod.

Owens and the camera carrying journalist had gotten a little ahead and was out of sight when Foley saw the second trip wire. He had to step off the trail a few yards to find a suitable branch and was just about to poke it into the ground to mark the wire when a shotgun blast went off up ahead.

'What the...?' he said, waving to the men following him and ignoring the wire, took off running down the trail.

'I got it,' Lazlo yammered, standing in the middle of the trail, still holding his camera. 'I got it. Perfect. Mr. Owens was smiling and looking back, pointing down the path at something when someone blew his freaking head off. I got the shot. Wow. I've never seen anything like it before. Wow.' He was still talking about it when the last of the team had rushed past him.

'Coming through,' one of the team members growled and ran past, not bothering to stop. The rest of them, each holding their automatic weapons ready to fire, rushed down and into the camp.

Not waiting for the two reporters, Foley took off running down the trail behind the armed men. He didn't even pause when he passed where Owens's body was lying off to the side, all crumpled and twisted. He didn't stop to investigate, he didn't need to. Nobody could look like that and be alive.

From somewhere up ahead he heard scattered gunfire and yelling. Then silence.

Chapter 46

IT WAS EARLY evening before Foley and Tichenor got free from the hassles and were able to head back down Highway 101. Once the dope farm had been secured, the growers arrested and the destruction of the nearly full grown marijuana plants started, Sheriff Millard had called in extra transportation. At the same time, he also notified the Governor's office of Owens's death.

Thinking back on the day caused Foley to smile.

'Boy, for a moment, Millard was in sheriff's heaven, wasn't he?'

Steve chuckled. 'Yeah, when he got the word Owens was dead and gone, he didn't waste any time taking over the show. As my daddy would have said, he was in tall cotton. Until the State Troopers arrived.'

'Uh huh. He should have known once the Governor found out his best friend and Chief of Staff had been killed, it would become a high level matter.'

'A damn good thing that newspaper photographer had been taking so many shots. For a still camera he ended up with the whole thing, almost like a stop-action video.'

The cameraman's digital camera had caught it all, a fact he was sure would earn him some kind of award. The photos made it very clear, saving Foley a lot of explaining.

'There's one thing I've been thinking about, though,' Steve said slowly.

'And what's that?'

'According to what those reporters said, you warned Owens about the noise-making booby trip wires. How come you knew about them and not about the wire set up with the shotgun?'

Foley didn't answer, but sat silently, thinking.

'This senator you work for, how powerful is he in the state government?'

'Senator Murkowski? Well, he's in line to be the next Majority Leader in the Senate. Why?'

'If he contacted the AG's office, would he have enough pull to get some action?'

'What the hell are you talking about?'

'How about if you talked to your senator and warned him to start putting some distance between his office and the Governor.' Holding up a hand, he stopped Steve from interrupting. 'Look, Owens was dirty and the proof is there. If your senator directed the Attorney General's office to come up with a warrant to have Owens's office searched, and they went looking for a certain item, they would have what they needed.'

'OK, and what would that certain item be?'

'A knife. A replica of the famous Bowie knife. If they found such a weapon and did some DNA testing on it, they should be able to find material matching at least one of three people murdered recently over in the City.'

For the next thirty miles, Steve drove while Foley explained.

They stopped for a late dinner at Chad's Fish and Chips in the little town of Willits. While waiting for their order, Steve went outside to make a call on his cell phone. Foley was about finished with his meal when his partner came back in.

'Afraid your fish is cold.'

'Yeah, I had a hell of a time convincing Claude he had to act right now. It wasn't something that could be put off until the Senator got back to town from wherever he is. Damn fool.'

'Who's Claude?'

'Oh, some toad brain works the office evenings and weekends. Thinks he's running the show.'

'But you got him moving?'

'Yeah. I had to threaten to call Mrs. Murkowski at home. Nobody's supposed to have her number and it scared Claude when he thought I had it.'

'Do you?'

'Hell, no. But Claude doesn't know that. Anyway, he finally called the Senator himself and patched me through. I had to explain it all again. Then Shit-for-brains got the message and things are happening down there.' He took a bite of the cold fish and grimaced. 'You're right, it is cold.'

*

Steve dropped Foley off at his house, promising to call the next day.

After a long shower, Foley poured a glass from the bottle of wine he'd left in the refrigerator and went to sit on the back deck for a while. Sipping the chilled chardonnay and relaxing, he thought over the raid. Not a bad day, all in all.

Thinking back to when the drug cops had rounded up the crew at the Ralstons' dope farm, Foley had to smile. Once he learned of Owens's death, Sheriff Millard had stepped right up, taking control of things. Quickly, before anyone could head him off, he had started barking orders, getting the prisoners secured with white plastic restraining ties and starting the destruction of the illegal dope farm. Foley was pleased to see Hubert Ralston standing a little apart from the others. He wanted to go over and laugh at the young dope dealer but held back. Let's see your father get you out of this, punk.

Ralston hadn't appeared worried. Looking almost stylish in a pair of khaki Dockers, a pressed Pendleton shirt open at the throat and leather lace up boots, his thin smile, Foley thought, had been typical of someone believing himself to be above it all. To make it even better, standing next to Ralston had been a broad shouldered man wearing plain garden-variety Levis, Anton. Unlike his boss, Foley saw, the big man was worried.

And the icing on the cake, as far as Foley was concerned, was when he had recognized another of the men with his wrists bound by thin plastic ties. This was the one who'd helped Anton give him the beating over some missing drug money. Sipping the wine and staring out over the Pacific Ocean toward Japan, he was smiling like he'd won the lottery. Oh, happy days.

Chapter 47

'DISCREET INQUIRIES, HOW may I help you?' Ms Weems chanted into the phone sounding, Foley thought, like she was happy and smiling. Maybe she had been, but when she saw him push through the office door, she shot the usual frown his way.

'I'm sorry, wait a minute, he just walked in. One moment, please.' She punched a button on the phone and glared. 'It's for you, Mr. Foley. And let me remind you of the company policy about personal phone calls. You can take it in that office,' she pointed with her chin to an open door, 'Andy is on a special assignment at the moment.'

Foley smiled. 'Why, thank you, Ms Weems. But I hardly think, as I do work here occasionally, the call could be classified as personal. It just might be a client, but then again, rather than upset any rules you may have, maybe you should just tell them to forget it.' And headed the other direction, toward Gorman's office.

That brought her to her feet. 'Wait a minute. You can't just go barging into Mr. Gorman's office. He may have a client in there.'

'Well, does he or doesn't he?' Foley asked, his hand on the door knob.

'But you can't just walk in unannounced.'

'Oh?' He opened the door before she could move, closing it behind him.

'Good morning,' he called out, then smiled, seeing Gretchen sitting in one of the client chairs. 'Just the people I want to see.'

Gorman smiled and nodded. 'And a good morning to you. Have you had a chance to see the morning newspaper?'

'Nope. Something interesting in it?'

'Didn't you mention being involved with investigating illegal marijuana plantations for the Governor's office?' Not waiting for an answer, he went on. 'Then you probably already know more than what the media is reporting.'

When his desk phone buzzed, he handed the paper to Foley and picked up the receiver.

'Good morning,' Brad smiled at Gretchen. 'Are you getting on OK without me?'

'Uh huh. But if what the newspaper says is true, it sounds as if you've been having all the fun.'

'It's for you, Bradford,' Gorman said, handing the phone across.

'Hello, Brad Foley here.'

It was Steve. 'I thought she put me on hold and forgot all about me. Look, are you able to get over here tomorrow morning? Senator Murkowski would like to meet with you.'

'I don't know. Just got into the office and haven't had a chance to talk with the big boss yet. Why? What's the man want to do, pat me on the back?'

'No. This is serious. He wants to offer you a job.'

'We've already been down that road, remember? With Owens.'

'Yeah, but this is too good to pass up. C'mon, give it a listen, anyhow. What'll it hurt? If you time it right, we can probably get the Senator to pay for lunch. For both of us.'

Foley hesitated, glancing at Gretchen. Damn, if only she were a couple years older, or if his ethical standards weren't so strict. Sighing, he nodded. 'OK. I can be there about lunchtime.'

'Good. Remember how to get to the Posey's? Let's make it for one o'clock. And for Gawd's sake, don't be a smart ass. Just give him a chance to explain what he's thinking of, all right?'

'Yeah, I'll be on my best behavior. See ya.'

'Yeah,' Steve mumbled.

'Thanks,' said Foley, handing the phone back.

'So, tell us all about it. The raid.'

'Well, there are a couple things not in the paper. Things you two should know. Gretchen, you don't have to worry about the guy who threatened you on the bus. He's, well, let's just say he's history.'

'History?' asked Gorman. 'Are you saying he's no longer a threat?'

'Not to anyone. And we can wrap up the Steiner case, too. Fact is, if the state investigators do their job, we should soon be reading about how they solved the murders of those two women and old King Cock.'

'Wait a minute, are you telling us those people getting killed are all connected to the dope raid?'

'There was a connection. Not direct, just the fool who threatened Gretch is the same fool who did the stabbing. All three of them.'

'And he's no longer a threat.' It wasn't a question. 'Bradford, you didn't, I mean, the newspaper story does say there was one of the state officials killed. You didn't have anything to do with it, did you?'

'Well, not directly. I didn't pull any trigger, if that's what you're asking. If anything, I can honestly say I did nothing. Or maybe just all that needed to be done.'

Gorman snorted. 'Now you're sounding like that fat German guard on the old TV show, *Hogan's Heroes* ... "I know nothing!" You ever watch it? One of my favorite shows.'

'Your German accent is terrible,' laughed Foley. 'Anyway, you can tell old man Steiner his daughter's murderer has been punished. And, I suppose, the end of the Steiner mess means I won't get to work with you anymore, Gretchen.'

Gorman chuckled. 'We were just talking about that. Our Ms Bongiorno was trying to explain why she was late coming in this morning.'

'Please, Mr. Gorman, there's no reason to bring Mr. Foley into it, is there?'

'Oh, but there is. It was while working with Bradford as your partner you made contact. Don't you think he deserves to know?'

'You're laughing at me. All right, but Brad, you have to promise not to laugh. I was late because I missed my bus this morning and had to wait until the next one. That's all.'

Gorman held up a hand, laughing. 'No, no, that won't do. Tell him why you missed the bus.'

'I overslept, that's why. I was on a date last night and we went dancing and, well, we got in late and I missed the alarm going off. Now, are you satisfied?' she demanded.

Foley waited. There had to be more, Gorman was still chuckling. 'Who was the date with, missy?'

Disgusted at being pressured, she quickly glanced sideways at Foley before looking away. 'Dan Pan asked me out and ... he just wouldn't give up and so to get him to stop, I, well, I accepted. He took me to dinner and then dancing. Now,' she glared at Gorman, who couldn't stop smiling, 'are you satisfied?'

'Danny Pan?' said Foley questioningly. 'You went out with San Francisco Officer Daniel Pan? Well, good for you. He struck me as being a nice young man. I'm sure Father Gorman, here, would approve if he got to meet him. But you have my blessing, for what it's worth.'

'Oh, hell, Bradford,' Gorman said, 'you take all the fun out of it.'

'And on that note, I'll leave you two private investigators to take care of business. Oh, and I won't be in tomorrow, either. Got a lunch date with a state senator. There was a promise, at one point, something about if our work was successful, some strings could be pulled which would see me able to apply for a state PI license. You never know.'

Gorman smiled. 'That's good news. Be sure to keep us informed.'

'I will. And Gretch, good luck with your Danny Pan.'

'It was just one date,' she said. 'It's not like I'll go out with him again or anything.'

'Uh huh. Sure.'

Chapter 48

Wᴵᵀʜ ɴᴏᴛʜɪɴɢ ᴏɴ his list of things to do, Foley decided on lunch in Sausalito. Enjoying one of the special hamburgers at Henry's Bar and Grill, he relaxed with a second bottle of beer.

Thinking maybe he'd take a walk down the beach to the spit, he drove on home, only to find someone had called and left a message on his answering machine.

It took a moment for him to figure out it was Freddie Isham.

'Hey, Mr. Foley,' Freddie's hard voice came blasting out of the machine, 'this is Freddie. Remember me? Did you see this morning's *Eureka Clarion*? Probably not. Seems those drug police that raided Ralston's marijuana garden up in the Fern Canyon area have made a big arrest. That's what the paper called it, a garden. Here, I'll read it to you.

"'Local timber baron's grandson arrested,"' Freddie's voice came out of the speaker sounding educated and with authority. 'That's the headline. Don't you love it?

"'Hubert F. Ralston",' he read on sonorously, "'was among those arrested in a raid on a suspected marijuana garden in the pristine old-growth forests north-east of Eureka Friday afternoon. State and local law enforcement officials, following an anonymous tip, conducted the raid resulting in the death of one man and the arrest of four unidentified men, two members of the Apache Motorcycle gang and three local residents. Charged with the cultivation of marijuana and possession of marijuana for sale and manufacture of methamphetamine was Ralston, son of H. Fredrick Ralston, owner of the Scotia Development Corporation, Anton Dash and Cully Haines, reportedly employees of SDC. The arrests were made after law enforcement officers from the California Drug Enforcement Task Force, California State Police and Humboldt County

Sheriff's Department entered into the marijuana garden on Friday afternoon and found Ralston and the others in the garden which contained 5,165 marijuana plants. An incomplete methamphetamine laboratory was also reportedly discovered in the area. Also found within the marijuana garden were two loaded pistols and a loaded rifle.

'*The dead man, whose identity has not been released pending notification of next of kin, was reportedly the victim of a deadly booby trap set to protect the garden area.*'

'That's all the paper said,' said Freddie, once again sounding like the bearded man. 'Don't know what they'll do to the members of the motorcycle gang. But I heard a couple things that didn't get in the papers. Remember your friend, Anton? Seems someone, probably his good buddy, Cully, told the state boys something 'cause I hear they made a raid on Anton's little apartment there at old man Ralston's place, Scotia House, and found more pot all packaged and ready to go. Ain't that a hoot? From the rumors floating around, Anton claimed it was Hubert Ralston who was the brains behind the deal. I guess it won't matter much, though, 'cause I also hear murder charges are gonna be filed against those three based on the shooting of the unnamed state official. That's the rumor, anyways.

'Well, Mr. Foley, there you go. I thought this might be something you'd like to know about. Oh, and I heard about this plastic surgeon down south who can maybe fix my ear. It'll be expensive but I came into some money a while back and can probably afford it. Well, that's all. You take care now and maybe we'll run into each other someday. I figure I still owe you, and I ain't about to forget that debt. Bye.'

Foley sat back, chuckling, thinking things couldn't get much better.